P9-CFM-907

SHEILA ROBERTS

the summer retreat

mira

mira

ISBN-13: 978-0-7783-6940-0

The Summer Retreat

Recycling programs
for this product may
not exist in your area.

For Liz

Dear Reader,

I'm so happy you could join me for another visit to Moonlight Harbor, our third. This time around we'll be going there with Jenna's sister, Celeste, who really needs to figure out her love life.

Have you ever thought you were with the right one only to find out you were wrong? Ever thought you were making the perfect choice when, good as that person was, it was still the wrong choice for you? I certainly have been there. I went through a lot of Mr. Wrongs, even got engaged to one, only to realize that he was the perfect man...for someone else. But I do believe when it comes to love that if we take a step back and a deep breath, things have a way of working out and eventually we can get it right. I did!

Fingers crossed that it works out that way for Celeste. (And some of the other new characters you'll meet.) There are certainly some great guys in Moonlight Harbor. I fell in love with a couple of them myself while I was writing this story. I hope you will, too.

So come on down. There's no better place to be than the beach. Give yourself permission to take a break and enjoy a summer retreat.

Sheila

the summer retreat

Chapter One

Celeste Jones had kissed so many frogs looking for her prince, she should have turned green and grown warts on her lips. But she'd finally gotten it right in the man department. Emerson Willis was strong and smart. And sexy. Masculine and excitingly alpha. And a spectacular dancer. And sexy. And a cop. Did it get any sexier than that? They'd been together a year, and what a great year it had been. He'd spent so much time at her place, he might as well have moved in, but he felt it wouldn't look good, with her being a teacher and all. As if first-graders knew anything about the birds and the bees or cared what their teacher did in her off hours. As if anyone cared what anyone did with anyone else these days. It had been sweet of him to think of that, though, and she loved him all the more for it.

Still, why not make what they had official since it was so great? "We're having a good time," he was always saying. "Relax and enjoy the ride."

She could do that. Spring had come, and she was looking ahead to a summer of off-roading, trips to

Eastern Washington to visit the wineries, hitting the shooting range—you had to do that when you were with a cop—and meeting each other's families.

Nothing wrong with taking your family along on the ride. But whenever she tried to get him over to her mother's or suggested a trip to the beach to meet her sister, Jenna, and her great-aunt Edie, something came up to prevent it. Same with meeting his family. There was always an excuse. His parents were busy. He was busy. He had to work an extra shift. That seemed to happen a lot lately. Was it normal for a police officer to have to pull so many extra shifts?

If it wasn't for his reluctance to take things to the next level, Emerson Willis would be perfect. No, no, he *was* perfect. He just didn't want to rush into anything. And really, there was nothing wrong with that. Celeste had done her share of rushing and it hadn't led to anything good. But after all this time, it was hardly rushing to meet the parents.

They needed to have a talk, she thought as she left school late on a Friday afternoon. She and Emerson were planning to hit the gym together; then he was coming over to her place for pizza and to watch a movie. Before they got lost in movie land, she was determined they'd talk about what was going on in the real world. She stopped by Papa Murphy's and picked up a take-and-bake pizza, then popped into the grocery store for a six-pack of Hale's Ales, his favorite microbrew, to go with it, along with some salad makings.

She was getting into her car when he called on

her cell. "Can't hang out tonight, babe," he said. "I feel like shit."

"Oh, no. What's wrong?"

"I think I've got a fever. Maybe it's the flu."

Flu in late May? She thought people got that during the winter. "I'm sorry," she said. "And here I just picked up pizza for tonight."

"Freeze it."

"It's Papa Murphy's." Okay, did that sound like she was trying to guilt him or bribe him into coming over? Yes, she wanted to see him, but she didn't want him to get worse. And while she wanted to see *him*, she didn't want to see his germs. "I guess I'll bake it and then freeze it. We can have it when you're well."

"Whatever," he said.

Whatever was right. As if he cared what she was going to do with their pizza when he was sick. "Well, feel better," she said. "Love you, Law and Order."

"Back atcha," he said and ended the call.

Back atcha. That was about as close as he ever came to getting mushy. Oh, he had no problem saying he wanted her, was crazy about her, was into her, but the *L*-word seemed to get stuck in his mouth.

A couple of times she'd tried to teasingly pull it out of him, offering to give him speech therapy. "Repeat after me, looooove." He would smile and shake his head and say, "You know how I feel about you."

She did. Of course she did. Didn't she?

"I'm not sure about this," Celeste's sister, Jenna, had said when she'd checked in after Valentine's Day and learned there was still no ring, no proposal, no mention of meeting the family.

"Remember, he was married once before," Celeste had reminded her. "He's just cautious. You should understand that."

"There's cautious and then there's taking advantage of a woman," Jenna had said.

That was when Celeste had to go…do something, anything. Bye. Her sister's words had sounded like what their mother would say—if her mother knew that Celeste and Emerson had hooked up. Months ago. Fortunately, Mom never asked, and Celeste never volunteered the information.

But Mom did ask when she was going to meet the "amazing" man in Celeste's life.

Soon, Celeste decided. As soon as he got well, she was hauling him over to her mother's house. Even if she had to use his handcuffs on him.

Meanwhile, though, the poor guy. What could she do to help him feel better? Chicken soup! She wasn't the most talented cook around, but she did make a mean chicken soup. And even though the weather was warm, when you were sick you needed soup. She went back into the store and bought a rotisserie chicken, then drove to her apartment and got to work.

Within an hour she was pulling a fragrant chicken rice soup off the burner to cool. That would make him feel better. While it cooled she redid her makeup, checked out Instagram and Facebook and texted her friend Vanita. Then she put her soup in a container, hopped in her Prius and drove over to Emerson's apartment on her mission of mercy.

He rented a slick unit in a building that had a pool and a party room. Two bedrooms. Plenty of room to spread out. Okay, once they moved in together, someone would have to sacrifice some stuff because his place was pretty full and her apartment, also two bedrooms, was packed to the gills with furniture and cute garage-sale finds. Her second bedroom served as an office and craft room. They could always buy a house.

She wanted a house. And a yard. And kids. And a dog. Emerson needed to get with the program. She was enjoying the ride, but she'd enjoy it a lot more if she knew they were going to get serious. She was thirty-six, for crying out loud. Thirty-six and a half, to be exact. The alarm on her biological clock was going off. Yes, once he was well, they were definitely going to have that talk, she decided as she went up the stairs to his second-floor unit.

She was sure she heard music coming from inside as she knocked on the door. And voices. Did he have the TV on?

She was about to knock again when the door opened. There stood Emerson in swimming trunks, chest bare, muscles on display. Why?… What?… Was he taking a swim to cool his fevered brow?

"Is that the pizza delivery?" called a female voice.

Pizza delivery! Emerson had a fever going, all right, but it wasn't from the flu. "I thought you were sick." *You big, rotten lizard.*

He blinked as if trying to bring her into focus. "Uh, I'm feeling better."

"I just bet you are," she snapped and pushed past him.

"Celeste," he protested.

There, coming out of his second bedroom, was a woman showing off long hair with an expensive rainbow tint job. Her hair wasn't all she was showing off. That bikini barely covered anything. Not that she had much to cover.

Really? Emerson was cheating on her with that? Celeste looked so much better in her bikini.

"Not pizza delivery," she snarled as she marched to the kitchen. "Chicken soup. For the sickie." She slammed the container on the counter.

Emerson was in the living room now, looking back and forth between the women, his Adam's apple bobbing.

"Aren't you going to introduce us?" Celeste demanded.

He swallowed. "This is Becky."

"Becky," Celeste said sweetly. "I'm Celeste. The girlfriend. Emerson and I have been seeing each other for a year now. You know, hanging out, taking trips, going to the shooting range. Having sex," she added, throwing him the look of death. "How about you, Becky? How long have you and Emerson been seeing each other?" *Having sex.*

Becky's eyes were slits, and she turned them on Emerson. "You…bastard." She wheeled around and marched back to the bedroom.

"Becky, wait," he called. Then he frowned at Celeste. "What are you doing here?"

"I made you chicken soup because I thought you were sick. You're sick, all right, you rotten, cheating douchebag." She grabbed her offering. "You don't deserve this." And he sure didn't deserve her.

Emerson trailed after her. "She doesn't mean anything to me."

Yeah, that was why he'd lowered his voice.

But Becky had heard. She'd gathered her clothes and was steaming toward the door. "Thanks a lot," she yelled.

"Obviously, I don't mean anything, either," Celeste said and followed her.

"Beck, I mean, Celeste, wait!" he called.

Celeste stopped long enough to glare at him. "I wasted so many kisses on you. And a year of my life I'll never get back." She pointed a finger at him. "I thought you were so noble. A cop, for heaven's sake. There oughta be a law against cheating and you oughta be sent to love jail. For life."

With that parting shot, she banged the door shut and stamped down the stairs behind Becky, almost as fast as the tears racing down her cheeks.

"I'm sorry," Becky said as the two women walked to the parking lot, fuming side by side. "I had no idea. He said he was divorced."

"Oh, he is. His wife was a bitch."

"Wouldn't have sex with him," Becky added. "Didn't really care about him."

Celeste wiped away a tear. What a pair of fools they were. "How long...?"

"Three months."

Three months! For three months he'd been playing her, seeing another woman on the side. "So you were those extra shifts he's been pulling." Enjoy the ride, he'd kept saying. Some ride.

"He told me he had to work extra shifts, too," Becky said. She stopped at the jazzy little convertible next to Celeste's Prius. "I really am sorry."

"It's not your fault," Celeste assured her. "I just hope someday he gets what's coming to him."

The smile blooming on Becky's face looked positively evil. "He will. My dad's his chief. And Daddy feels strongly about his men living up to the badge they wear."

Celeste gave her a smile in return. "Good. I'm sorry we met like this. I hope next time you find someone who's not a...Emerson."

"I will," Becky said with confidence. "You, too."

Celeste thanked her and got in her car. With her chicken soup. Then she cried her way home. Emerson had seemed so perfect. She'd wanted him so much, given so much of herself to the relationship, and all she'd gotten in return was a broken heart.

"Girl, I don't know how you do it," her friend Vanita said later that night as they sat on Celeste's little balcony. She'd called Vanita, who had come over to be with her in her time of sorrow, bringing a listening ear and ice cream.

"What is wrong with me that I didn't figure out

what was going on?" Celeste gave her chocolate cherry ice cream a stir. Her second bowl, but who was counting? At least she wasn't eating out of the carton. She hadn't stooped to that.

"Other than the fact that you're too trusting and figure everyone has principles? Nothing."

"I shouldn't have gotten serious so fast," Celeste said with a frown. "Jenna's right. I'm always rushing into relationships."

"Well, I gotta say, he did seem like a keeper." She shook her head. "What a pile of poop that man is."

"Now I know why he never said he loved me. He didn't." Oh, boy, here came the tears again. Celeste dabbed at her eyes and took a big spoonful of ice cream.

"Be glad you found out now. What if he'd finally asked you to marry him? If he'd cheat on you now, you know he'd do it when you were married."

"I am so through with men."

"Your sister said the same thing and look at her now, with *two fabulous* men after her. Guys aren't all bad. Your perfect man will come along."

"There is no such thing."

Vanita pointed her spoon at Celeste. "Don't you go talking like that. You're gonna find someone who appreciates you. Meanwhile, don't be such a pushover for a great bod and a nice smile."

"I'm not *that* shallow!"

"No, but you're just too… I don't know. Eager."

Yes, she supposed she was. But darn it all, she only wanted a good man and that TV sitcom happy life she'd yearned for as a kid. Not that her mother and grandparents hadn't given her and her sister a good life. But there'd been a key part missing. A dad. Her father had died when she was a baby.

So was that her problem? Was she always looking for the father she'd never had? Did she need therapy?

No, darn it. She needed a man who wouldn't cheat.

"You gotta start protecting your heart, girl. And don't be givin' it away to every man who comes along with a smooth line."

"Hey, no shaming," Celeste said irritably.

"I'm not shaming. I'm lecturing. Get tough."

Get tough. Yeah. She could do that. Next time she went to the gym and saw Emerson… Eew. She didn't want to go to the gym anymore. She was bound to see him there.

What if she did run into him? What if he told her he realized he'd been a fool and he wanted her back?

Heaven help her, she'd probably take him with open arms. She had to get out of town.

"Why don't you go spend some time with your sister this summer," her mom suggested when Celeste told her that she and Emerson were no more. "Life is always good at the beach."

"Life isn't good anywhere right now," Celeste grumbled.

"It'll get better," her mom promised. And if anyone should know, it would be Melody Jones. Widowed young and left with two little girls to raise, she'd carved out a happy life for herself. And all without a man. "Meanwhile," she added.

"I know. Look for the rainbow in the storm."

"Exactly."

Her mom was right. What was the sense in moping? When the going got tough, the tough…went to the beach.

So as soon as school was out, Celeste packed her bikini and flip-flops and drove to Moonlight Harbor, a small beach town on the Washington Coast, to stay with her sister and niece and great-aunt. Jenna had been more than happy at the idea of her sister coming for a long stay. Between running the Driftwood Inn, keeping her massage business going, and being mother of the year, Jenna was always busy. She'd insisted she could use the help as much as Celeste could use a change of scenery.

And there was no better place for that than Moonlight Harbor. Mom had brought Jenna and Celeste there for many happy visits when they were kids, so it felt like coming home as she drove through the white stone gateway at the town's entrance.

There was Nora Singleton's ice cream parlor, where their great-uncle Ralph took them for sundaes back when he was alive. There were the cute cabana shops she'd enjoyed visiting her last time down. There were the deer, grazing on the grass in the median. They drove the town's gardeners nuts, eating up flowers before they could bloom and strolling across lawns like they owned the place, which they did, but Celeste thought they were sweet. She loved their big, trusting brown eyes. They all had brains the size of a peanut and often trotted out in front of oncoming cars, but luckily for the deer, people always stopped for them. Yes, here people cared for the clueless and trusting. Moonlight Harbor was the perfect place to mend a broken heart.

Or get stopped by a cop. She could feel her sunny smile slipping away as she pulled over. She was scowling by the time one of Moonlight Harbor's finest came up to her car window. He was cute, with sandy hair and hazel eyes. He, too, probably had a six-pack just like Emerson.

"What?" she demanded, making him blink.

"Uh, you've got a taillight out," he stammered, his cheeks turning pink.

"Oh." Okay, she needed to holster her guns. "Um, thank you, Officer. That was really nice of you. I'll get it fixed right away."

He nodded and told her to have a good day, then returned to his car.

"Everyone is not an Emerson," she told herself. But she was so over cops.

The very thought of Emerson put that frown back on her face, until she pulled into the parking lot of the Driftwood Inn. A one-story building with only twenty rooms, it was a relic from the sixties. But it was a refurbished relic with lots of charm, painted blue with white trim. The office had driftwood outside it and a fisherman's net hanging on the front exterior. And the pool, that was the best. It had a mermaid swimming under a full moon painted on the bottom. The whole place called, "Come on back to when life was simple. Stay and have a good time." She intended to.

Her sister was working the front desk when she walked in, and Jenna's face lit up at the sight of her. "You're here!" she cried and rushed to hug Celeste.

"I am so ready to turn into a sand crab," Celeste said.

"And we're all ready to have you. Perfect timing, too, since my latest maid quit."

"You're going to work me to death in housekeeping on my summer break?"

"Only mornings," Jenna said with a grin. "Come on, let's go over to the house."

"Don't you have to stay in the office?"

"No one's due to check in," Jenna said. "Besides, my cell number is posted in the rooms. If anyone has an emergency they can call me."

Only the week before Jenna had been summoned to a room to deal with an overflowing toilet. Her sister was a saint.

Their great-aunt's house where Jenna and her daughter, Sabrina, lived was an old, two-story charmer complete with gables and a big front porch. Jenna had focused her first summer on getting the motel up and running. This summer the house was getting a facelift with blue paint and white trim to match the motel. Work had begun, and the second story was already half-painted.

They went inside to find Aunt Edie settled on the couch, crocheting granny squares for an afghan. Jolly Roger, her parrot, was perched behind her, supervising. She was wearing her favorite elastic-waist slacks and a pink sweatshirt that clashed with her cherry-red, tightly permed hair and her coral lipstick.

"Look what I found," Jenna announced.

"Oh, Celeste darling!" Aunt Edie cried, pushing herself up from the couch and coming to greet her great-niece. In her early eighties and still active and happy, she was an inspiration.

"Thanks for letting me come," Celeste said, bending over to hug her. What there was of her. Father Time had stuck Aunt Edie in a compactor, shrinking her.

"You know you're always welcome here," she told Celeste. "Isn't she, Roger?"

"Always welcome," Roger repeated, walking along the top of the couch back. "Call the cops."

"No more cops," Celeste cracked.

This made her aunt look at her in concern. "How are you doing?"

"I'm fine," Celeste said. "I had a lucky escape."

"Not all police are like that. We have some good ones here. And several of them are single."

"Oh, yeah." Jenna grinned. "Frank Stubbs would be more than happy to help you heal your heartache."

"I was thinking of that nice Victor King," said Aunt Edie.

"I might have met him on my way in," Celeste said. "Kind of tall. Blushes easily?"

"That would be the one," Jenna said. "He's a sweetie."

"There is no such thing. Not when you're talking about cops."

"Oh, my," said Aunt Edie, sounding worried.

"Call the cops," advised Roger.

"We have to teach him some new words," Celeste said. "Emerson's a rat. Can you say that, Roger? Emerson's a rat."

Roger shook out his feathers and shut his beak.

"You men all stick together," Celeste muttered.

"Well," Aunt Edie said briskly. "You know where to put your things. I'll get some lemonade and cookies."

"And I'll call Sabrina," Jenna told Celeste. "She and Tristan are at the tennis courts with Jennifer and Hudson, trying to play tennis."

"Don't drag her away. I'll see her soon enough."

"No, she's going to want to see you. Anyway, she'll just bring the whole gang here. They're all addicted to Aunt Edie's cookies."

Lemonade, cookies and her family. What more did a girl need?

Sex.

Sigh.

Chapter Two

Celeste's first evening with the family was a happy one. The kids returned from the tennis court sweaty, happy and hungry, and devoured Aunt Edie's beach sandies, one of her cookie specialties. Of course, everyone decided to hang out for dinner and Pete, Aunt Edie's not-so-handy handyman, was sent across the parking lot to fetch goodies from the Seafood Shack. After eating more than his share of the popcorn shrimp, he announced his intention to go to The Drunken Sailor for a beer.

"Too damn noisy here," he complained.

"Gee, we hate to see you go," Jenna murmured as he slumped out the back door, Aunt Edie seeing him on his way. "Why she keeps him around, I'll never know."

Pete, with his laziness and mooching, was a constant irritation for Celeste's hardworking sister, so of course she couldn't help teasing, "He's her boy toy."

Who knew what was going on between Aunt Edie and grizzled, old Pete? Probably nothing, since she had to be a good ten years older. But it was fun to yank her big sister's chain.

Jenna looked as if she'd eaten raw seaweed. "Eew. Just, eew."

"Love is blind," Celeste quipped. Boy, was it ever. She suddenly didn't feel in such a party mood.

But there had to be partying when you had a teenager. And partying was the best medicine, so Celeste was soon engrossed in the fun and games. Aunt Edie hung around for the milder ones like Apples to Apples. After she went to bed, the kids all wanted to play Spoons, a more rambunctious game that required cards, some spoons and a very competitive spirit.

"Nobody beats me at Spoons," Celeste bragged, and she proved her superiority when she almost broke poor Tristan's wrist wrenching one from his hand and making him yelp.

"You gotta be tough," she informed him with a smirk.

That was true on so many levels.

The kids finally went home, and Sabrina went to bed to read the new novel she'd started about a blind female superhero who was busy saving her fellow teens in a post-apocalyptic world where all the parents had been killed.

"I'm glad you're here," she said before she left, hugging Celeste.

"Me, too," Celeste said.

"Me, three," Jenna said.

With everyone else gone, the two sisters poured themselves some lavender lemonade and moved to the living room. "Was it cheesy of me to invite myself down for the whole summer?" Celeste asked as they settled on the couch. "I mean, you're stuck sharing a bed with me."

"Just like every time you visit. You know that's not a problem. I'm glad you're here. That way I can keep an eye on you."

Celeste frowned. "Obviously, I need someone to keep an eye on me."

"Don't beat yourself up over the cheater. That's all on him, not you."

"I shouldn't have rushed into the relationship. You tried to warn me, but I didn't listen."

Jenna shrugged. "Women in love do stupid things."

"I'm done being stupid. And I'm done falling for a handsome face and a hot bod. Maybe I'll find me a rich, old geezer who needs a trophy wife."

"Yeah, I can see *that* happening."

"Or maybe I'll stay single and adopt a child." It wouldn't be the traditional family Celeste had always dreamed about but, oh, well. "And get a dog," she added with a smile. "Dogs are loyal."

"Which is more than you can say for some men," Jenna said, and Celeste knew she was talking about her ex, Damien the *artiste*, who'd left her for another woman.

"Well, then," Celeste said, raising her glass, "here's to dogs."

"To dogs," Jenna said and they clinked glasses and finished their lemonade. "And now I need to go to bed. I've got a ton of paperwork waiting for me tomorrow and clients lined up for massages as soon as Courtney comes in to relieve me."

"And I have to start my first day as a maid," Celeste said.

"It should be a light day. We're only half full at the moment, and all you need to do is make the beds and clean the bathrooms."

"I can help work the check-in desk, too, you know."

"I might take you up on that."

"Anyone interesting staying here?" Celeste asked as they went upstairs to the bedroom.

"Two couples, a family with two little kids, a group of girlfriends who are taking three of our rooms, a pair of newlyweds—make sure you call 'housekeeping' loudly before going in—and we've got more people checking in on Friday and one on Sunday. That should be enough to keep you busy."

"I'd say so." But Celeste wanted to be busy, too busy to think about her lame love life. Doomed to be a love loser.

Oh, yeah, that was positive thinking. Look for the rainbow in the storm, she reminded herself. That wasn't hard. She was with the people she loved best and she was at the beach. She'd do a beach walk first thing in the morning before starting maid patrol. Maybe she'd get lucky and find an agate.

She didn't find an agate the next morning, but she did find some inspiration. The steadiness of the waves, the vastness of the ocean, the cry of the seagulls—it reminded her that there was a big, beautiful world out there and more to life than one disappointment. The waves swooshed in, washed away the writing in the sand and provided a clean slate, so to speak. That was what she was getting down here. Now, if she could just forget what had been written...

When she returned to the house Aunt Edie was already at the stove, making breakfast. Jenna was giving Pete his to-do list for the day and Pete was complaining about his sore back. Yes, some things never changed.

The aroma of coffee drew Celeste over to her aunt's vintage coffeemaker. She pulled a mug from the cupboard, filled it and took a sip. Oh, yes, a great way to start the day.

There was something so cozy about hanging out in her aunt's kitchen. Maybe it was because the kitchen was packed with happy memories—baking cookies with Aunt Edie, working on crafts at the kitchen table or playing anagrams, drinking hot chocolate in the morning and eating...

"Pancakes," she said happily, looking over her aunt's shoulder. "Do you need help?"

"No, you sit down and enjoy."

"That won't be hard. Pancakes are the best."

"Pancakes are the best," Roger echoed from his kitchen perch.

Jenna was getting up as Celeste sat down. "Where are you going?" Celeste asked.

"That paperwork is calling. Come on over to the office when you're done and I'll give you the key to the supply room."

"She's gonna work you to death," Pete predicted.

Jenna frowned at him. "A motel is like a farm, Pete. We all work. It's what keeps us in pancakes."

He grunted. "You're gonna kill me."

"You're too tough to die," Jenna said, obviously unconcerned with Pete's precarious future. She kissed Aunt Edie on the cheek, said, "See you later," to Celeste and left.

"That woman's a slave driver," Pete said and forked more pancake into his mouth.

Celeste didn't mind working. She much preferred staying busy to sitting around moping over the sad ending to her latest love story.

She was happy to find no plugged toilets on her first day as a maid, and only nice guests who all told her how much they were enjoying their stay.

"I love it here," said one of the women who were having girl time at the beach. "Good stress relief." Her name was Shari and, chatting with her, Celeste learned that she was a nurse.

"Good to know in case I hurt my back or something," Celeste joked.

"Be careful how you lift things," Shari cautioned.

Hopefully, Celeste wouldn't have to do much heavy lifting.

An older couple asked about the best places to eat in town, and Celeste was happy to tell them. "And don't forget Good Times Ice Cream Parlor," she added. "Their huckleberry ice cream is to die for."

The newlyweds had the Do Not Disturb sign hung on their door. No visiting with them. Celeste figured she'd have to come back later with clean towels. Maybe days later.

She was wheeling her cart of cleaning supplies and dirty towels to the supply room to start a load of wash when Jenna's other Driftwood Inn resident and part-time handyman, Seth Waters, appeared. Unlike Pete, he actually paid rent on his room. He had a mold removal business that kept him busy most days, but he helped around the place when he could.

He was gorgeous and sexy and crazy about Jenna— and as commitment-shy as she was. The looks they sneaked in each other's direction were hot enough to set the dune grass on fire, but so far they were resisting becoming a couple. Talk about willpower.

Then there was Brody Green, the other man in her sister's life. He was always taking her out to eat. With a man like Brody you'd never need dessert. Two great guys. At some point Jenna was going to cave and give love a second chance, but it was still anyone's guess which one she'd cave with.

Right now Seth looked pretty yummy in his paint-spattered T-shirt and jeans. It wasn't hard to figure out what he was dressed for.

"Welcome back," he greeted her. "Your sister sure didn't waste any time drafting you."

She held up her scrub brush. "You can call me Your Majesty. I'm now queen of the toilets."

"That's some kingdom. So your life's gone to shit?"

She suddenly found it difficult to hold her lips up in a smile. Did he know? "You could say that."

He sobered. "It really has, huh?"

Okay, he *hadn't* known, and she was paranoid. And looked like a loser. "Let's just say I needed a change of scenery for the summer." It had been easy enough to arrange. She'd sublet her apartment for the summer to a new hire at school who'd moved up from Oregon. She was staying at the Driftwood free. She would come out ahead financially.

"Can't find a better place to forget your troubles. See you around."

She stood for a moment, watching him walk away. With that dark hair, swarthy skin and gorgeous muscled bod, he was a walking work of art. Why was Seth Waters here, in Moonlight Harbor? Alone, no less. Why wasn't he married and making house payments? She'd asked her sister on more than one occasion, but Jenna was evasive.

Seth Waters was a mystery. What woman would let him out of her sight?

Speaking of double lives, what was Emerson doing right now?

Who knew? Who cared? She hoped he'd gotten demoted and was giving out parking tickets. Even that was too good for him.

He'd taught her a valuable lesson, though. From now on, she was going to guard her heart like Fort Knox. No more sexy alpha males. No more jumping into anything.

When Jenna and Aunt Edie's friends came over for their usual Friday-night gathering, she was reminded that she wasn't the only woman ever to have man problems. Annie Albright, who was a waitress at Sandy's, one of the town's favorite restaurants, was on the verge of leaving her alcoholic husband.

"I hate to do it," she told the others, "but he's out of control and I don't think it's good for Emma."

"I'm glad you're finally realizing that," said Courtney Moore, who was her best friend. "He's a mean drunk."

"He hasn't hit me," Annie said, defending her husband.

"Yet," Courtney said. "I've heard him yelling at you. It's only a matter of time."

"You don't want your daughter exposed to that," put in Nora Singleton, who had brought dessert from her ice cream parlor for everyone. "And if you move out, maybe it'll be a wake-up call for him."

"Sometimes we all need a wake-up call," said Taylor Marsh. She'd gotten one when she stayed at the Driftwood in December, and now she and her family were living in Moonlight Harbor and she was working for Brody, selling houses.

Annie wiped at the corners of her eyes where the tears were gathering. "I hope so. I still love him."

"Oh, sweetie." Tyrella Lamb gave her a hug. Tyrella owned Beach Hardware. She'd had her share of trouble, her husband dying only a few years earlier. "We're just going to have to pray that boy out of his alcohol addiction."

"Good luck with that," said Courtney, the cynic. "Men," she added in disgust.

Celeste's feelings exactly.

"Not all men are evil," Tyrella lectured. "And what's with this attitude when *you've* found someone online?"

"Found him and lost him ASAP," Courtney said with a frown. "You know how he said he had such a great job, VP in charge of marketing? Well, that great job actually vanished six months ago. The guy's out trolling for a sugar mama."

Patricia Whitehead, who owned the Oyster Inn, shook her head sadly. "What is wrong with men these days?"

"There've always been no-good ones," Aunt Edie said as she passed around a plate of cookies. "Don't give up," she said to Courtney. "I didn't start out well, either, but then I wound up with Ralph and he was worth the wait. I think if you're patient, a good man eventually comes along."

Patience. Was that all there was to it? Celeste sighed and spooned the last of the ice cream from her bowl.

Patience was certainly paying off for Jenna. Brody was crazy about her, and it was nice to see a man showing her the appreciation her ex had deprived her of. She was keeping him in the friends corner, but it was obvious he was determined to turn their relationship into something more serious.

Celeste could see her sister being happy with either him or Seth, she thought as he escorted the sisters into the Porthole for dinner on Saturday night. It was the town's nicest restaurant, and it offered a killer view. He'd secured a window seat so they could watch the waves curling onto the beach in a lacy froth.

"How much did Jenna pay you to bring me along?" Celeste asked, only half teasing.

"Since when does someone have to pay me to take out two beautiful women?" he replied. Oh, yeah.

Brody Green was a charmer. And as good to look at as the view out the window.

Drool-worthy, charming, well-off. Yeah, not a bad choice. "Could we clone you?"

Jenna groaned. "One of him is enough."

"More than enough," he said, winking at her.

"Well, it's very inconsiderate of you not to have a younger brother," Celeste told him.

"I don't think you need any help from me," he said. "The men are going to be lining up from here to Moclips."

"I'm not holding my breath."

"Just because one man blew it?" Brody looked suddenly self-conscious and Celeste realized her sister had been talking about her. Who else knew she was a love loser? She gave Jenna a scowl that promised an inquisition when they got home.

He cleared his throat. "So what would you ladies like to drink? I'm guessing white wine?"

"Poison for my sister," Celeste muttered.

"Check out that view," Jenna said. "What a gorgeous night."

The rest of the evening went smoothly with talk of how things were going at the Driftwood, the listing Brody had just gotten—"Let me know when you're ready to buy a house, Celeste. I'll find you a deal"—some Chamber of Commerce gossip. And of course, Brody asked Celeste how it felt to be back in Moonlight Harbor.

"Guess you two spent time here when you were kids," he said.

"We always loved coming down," she told him. "I'm glad Jenna's settled here."

"I'd love it if Celeste and Mom would move down, too, and we'd all be together," said Jenna.

"If my mom and sister moved here, I'd relocate," Brody said. "That would be two interfering women too many."

Jenna was not going to interfere in her sister's life. It wasn't interfering to help her find her feet socially and introduce her to some of the decent men in town. Starting with Pastor Paul Welch. A minister could be exactly what Celeste needed, and this one was good-looking, sweet, had his act together. Oh, yes. Celeste could do a lot worse. Victor King would be a good choice, too. He was tough on crime but soft on women, so easily embarrassed it was adorable. Celeste had options, and there was nothing wrong with introducing her to them.

Okay, she shouldn't have told Brody why Celeste had come to town for the summer. That had been...

"None of his business," Celeste said later, as soon as Brody had dropped them off. "I suppose the whole Friday-night group knows about me, too."

Only Nora and Tyrella, and thank God they hadn't opened their big mouths and stuck in their feet like Brody had. "I'm sorry. It sort of came out when he asked me to dinner."

Celeste glared at her. "Don't tell me, let me guess. You said, 'I'm not going out with you unless you take my sister, too.'"

"Something like that."

"I'm a big girl. I can treat my wounds on my own."

Jenna cocked an eyebrow. "And that's why you came down here, to treat your wounds on your own?"

"I needed a change of scenery and some sister time. So sue me." Celeste plopped on the bed and kicked off her shoes. "What I don't need is everyone in Moonlight Harbor knowing every frickin' detail of my life."

Jenna sat down next to her. "I'm sorry. Really, really sorry. I shouldn't have blabbed. But remember, everybody has breakups."

"And you had to explain why you wanted to bring your sister along on a date."

"That wasn't how it went."

"Close enough."

"I didn't want to abandon you the minute you got here," Jenna said in her own defense.

Celeste sighed. "I hate being a love loser."

"You know that old saying—you have to kiss a lot of frogs before you find your prince."

Celeste had done a lot of frog-kissing. She hoped her prince was waiting for her in Moonlight Harbor. If he was, Jenna was determined to find him.

Chapter Three

Celeste had never been an early riser and on weekends made a habit of sleeping in. Which she was doing Sunday morning, splayed out on her stomach, one pedicured foot sticking out from under the covers, when Jenna shook her by the shoulder and announced it was time for breakfast.

"I'll get something later," she mumbled and turned her head away.

Oh, no. Nice try. "There is no later. We have to get out the door to church in forty minutes."

Celeste turned back and gaped at her. "Church?"

"Yeah, you know, that place Mom always took us to when we were growing up."

"I'm done growing up." Celeste settled back onto the pillow.

Jenna pulled it out from under her.

"Hey!" she protested.

"Now that you're here for the summer, you have to come with us and set an example for Sabrina."

"Is Aunt Edie going?"

"No, she's old and she doesn't like the loud music."

Celeste grabbed her pillow back. "Tell Sabrina I felt it was my duty to stay home and keep Aunt Edie company."

"Come on, don't give me grief. It's only an hour out of your day."

"An hour of lost sleep."

"Come on," Jenna repeated. "Please?"

"Oh, all right. But I'll probably sleep through the sermon."

Not once she saw Pastor Paul she wouldn't.

Forty minutes later they were walking into the church foyer. Sabrina's two best friends, Jennifer and Hudson, had been waiting for her and instantly swept her off to hang with the other kids, the three of them talking and giggling.

What a difference from when they'd first come to town and Sabrina had resented not only being at church but also being in Moonlight Harbor. Jenna had been relieved when she'd finally found some friends.

She'd also found a boyfriend. Tristan was a nice kid, but four years older than Sabrina. Due to their age difference, and rampaging hormones, Jenna had limited boyfriend time to parties and hanging out at the house. He'd just graduated from high school and would be going off to college in the fall, and she suspected her daughter's year-long romance would come to a painful end once he met some cute college girl.

Sometimes it seemed that all the women in her family were love-challenged. Sabrina had fallen for a senior when she was only a freshman. Celeste fell for users and losers. Their mom had never found another man to take their father's place. And there was Jenna herself. After her disastrous marriage she was standing at the edge of the love pool with just one toe in the water, even though Brody was ready to catch her and urging her to jump in. Would she jump if Seth was in the pool? In spite of the chemistry between them, he wasn't holding out open arms.

She'd figure that all out once she helped Celeste get her love life right.

Maybe it wouldn't be so hard, considering the way Celeste was looking at Pastor Paul, who was approaching them. She could almost see the thoughts swirling in her sister's head. *Prince or frog?*

"Yes, he's single," Jenna said.

"Just because he's in a church doesn't mean he's got it together," Celeste whispered.

"This man does," Jenna assured her. "Hi, Paul," she greeted him. "I don't think you've met my sister yet. Celeste, this is Paul Welch, our pastor."

Celeste's eyes got big. "P-pastor?" she stuttered.

Paul Welch was the polar opposite of balding, potbellied Pastor Munsen, the minister at the church they'd attended growing up.

"Welcome to Moonlight Harbor," he said to Celeste.

"Thanks. You're a pastor?"

He raised his eyebrows curiously. "Is that a bad thing?"

"No, it's just that you don't look like a pastor."

"What does a pastor look like?" he asked, an easy smile on his face.

"Old. I mean…not like you."

"Give me time, I'll get there," he said. "I hope you enjoy your visit with us today."

"I will if you're not boring," Celeste teased, recovering from her shock.

"I'll try not to be," he said, still smiling. Someone called to him and he moved on, but not before saying, "I'm glad you could join us today, Celeste."

Jenna elbowed her. "See what you missed when you didn't come to church with me last summer?"

"Old." Celeste rolled her eyes. "You could've warned me."

"About what? That I have a cute pastor?"

"And an ulterior motive for getting me here."

"You needed to get to church," Jenna said as her friend Tyrella walked in. She waved and Tyrella joined them.

"You look too cute," she said, giving Celeste a hug. "I swear, God overblessed you two when it came to looks," she continued, hugging Jenna, also. "Have you been introducing her around?" she asked Jenna.

"Only to Pastor Paul so far."

"I bet he'll have trouble concentrating on his sermon now," Tyrella joked. She waved at Hyacinth Brown, who was standing nearby, talking to two other women while simultaneously assessing Celeste. "Hyacinth, come on over and meet Jenna's sister."

Jenna didn't know Hyacinth very well. She was a skinny little thing with big brown eyes who dressed in drab colors. She'd pretty much kept her distance since Jenna had been attending the church. Jenna had put it down to her being shy.

But now she felt the chill as Hyacinth said a polite hello to Celeste. Okay, so Hyacinth wasn't simply shy. She was also insecure and not open to welcoming single women into the church family, especially curvy ones with platinum hair, green eyes and plenty of personality. Considering who their pastor was, that shouldn't have been surprising. Half the women in church crushed on Pastor Paul, and Jenna supposed Hyacinth was a member of his fan club. Maybe all that volunteer work she did around church had a hidden agenda.

"Is this your first time here at Moonlight Harbor Evangelical?" she asked Celeste.

Celeste nodded. "I came with my sister."

"Oh." Hyacinth took a moment to digest that. "Are you visiting?"

"I'm here for the summer. I'm going to help out at the Driftwood Inn. How about you? Have you been in Moonlight Harbor long?"

"Two years," Hyacinth said, and didn't volunteer any more information about herself. *There will be no effort made to become friends.*

"She owns the fabric store," said Tyrella. "And you're offering quilting classes right now, aren't you?"

Hyacinth nodded but didn't share any information about her classes, either.

"She made all the banners in the sanctuary," Tyrella went on, "and she and Susan Frank are on the decorating committee. Actually, they *are* the decorating committee. They do the flowers for church every week."

"That's appropriate," Celeste quipped.

Hyacinth managed a wilted smile. "So you're here with your…husband?"

Talk about the third degree. Was it because she'd seen Paul talking with Celeste?

Celeste's smile suddenly looked a little wilted, too. "No husband. Not even a boyfriend."

"Oh." Hyacinth sounded surprised.

"I'm in between men," Celeste said lightly, hiding her heartbreak.

Apparently, Hyacinth didn't approve of being in between men. "I hope you enjoy your visit," she said briskly, then excused herself and went back to the group of people she'd been talking with before Tyrella called her over.

"Yeah, I'll bet you do," Celeste said.

"A pretty woman in between men, just what the other single women want to see," Tyrella cracked. "Come on, let's go get a seat."

Jenna enjoyed the service. She didn't play an instrument and could never manage to sing in the same key as everyone else, but she loved music and she loved the morning's selection of songs, which were all positive and encouraging.

Pastor Paul's sermon was encouraging, too, although a couple of times he seemed to lose his place. Funny how those times coincided with when he happened to glance over at Celeste. "I know some of you have been going through hard times," he said.

That was for sure. One of their members was battling melanoma. An older man had recently lost his wife. Annie, who'd slipped in late, was struggling with her alcoholic husband, and Jenna saw she was dabbing her eyes. And then, suddenly, right next to her, her sister was taking a shaky breath.

Pastor Paul looked Celeste's way at that moment, and Jenna could have sworn that if he hadn't been in the middle of a sermon, he'd have hurried over to offer comfort. "But," he began. "Uh. But…" He cleared his throat and stared at his notes. "We can't lose hope."

Celeste sniffed, and Jenna took her hand and squeezed it.

"Let's remember to embrace those difficult times in our lives," he concluded, "knowing that they're building perseverance and helping us mature in our faith. All things work together for good for those who love God."

"Even those who haven't been in church for a while," Jenna whispered to her sister.

"He's so right," Tyrella said as they walked out of the sanctuary to an upbeat song the musicians were playing. "I have no idea why it is, but the times we seem to grow the most are when we're under pressure. Like diamonds," she added.

Celeste sighed. "I think I'd rather stay a lump of coal."

"Too late for that," Jenna said, linking arms with her. "You're already a diamond in the rough."

"Okay, then, let's settle for that. I don't want to be under pressure anymore."

"As if you have a choice," Tyrella scoffed. "Life's gonna squeeze you whether you want it to or not. May as well work on learning to sparkle."

Celeste had plenty of sparkle. She just needed to find a man who appreciated it.

Paul was at the door, shaking hands and visiting with people as they left. "A very good sermon, Pastor," Susan Frank was telling him as they approached. She saw Jenna and managed her usual sour smile. "Good morning, Jenna. Say hi to your aunt for me."

"I will," Jenna said.

Not that it would make any difference. Aunt Edie hadn't been in Susan's clothing shop since Susan had dissed Jenna and her brain baby, the Seaside with Santa festival. That had been the end of a beautiful retail relationship.

"Thanks for coming," Paul said and smiled at Celeste.

Oh, yeah. He'd be stopping by the house for a visit before the week was out.

"Can I drive home?" Sabrina asked as they crossed the parking lot.

Her baby was now fifteen and going to driving school every afternoon. Jenna didn't know which was scarier—seeing her daughter growing up so fast or having to ride with her behind the wheel. But Sabrina had to log in a certain number of hours, and it was a short drive from church to home, so she handed over the keys.

And then turned into Nag Mom. "Don't forget to adjust your mirrors," she said as Sabrina buckled her seat belt.

"I know, Mom."

"Are we gonna die?" Celeste joked from the backseat.

"Mom will probably have a heart attack," said Sabrina.

It was a possibility. Jenna had sprouted two new gray hairs since Sabrina started driver's ed. Of course, she'd pulled them. She hoped she didn't wind up bald by the time Sabrina got her license. At least sixteen was still several months away.

"Make sure there's nobody behind you," Jenna cautioned. "Look out for Willie Jorgenson."

"I see him, Mom," Sabrina said, her tone of voice adding, "Stop already."

"Okay, good," Jenna said.

Just then the boyfriend walked past and Sabrina had to wave at him as she backed up. A yelp behind them made her slam on the brakes, pitching Jenna forward. Thank God for seat belts!

Susan Frank walked past with a scowl. "Watch where you're going, young lady," she called, and Sabrina's cheeks flamed. Jenna's cheeks were feeling a little hot, too. That would've been all they needed, to clobber her nemesis with the Toyota.

"You have to watch where you're going," she scolded.

"I am," Sabrina said, her voice filled with teen umbrage.

Yes, how dare Susan Frank have the nerve to try and get them to hit her?

They made it out of the church parking lot without taking anyone down, and Jenna released the breath she'd been holding. No toddlers had been squashed and Susan had been allowed to live another day.

Sabrina drove down the street, then turned the corner. "Well done," Celeste said from the backseat, and Jenna echoed the praise. *Yes, positive reinforcement. Don't forget that.*

"Hey, Hudson's driving, too," Sabrina said, looking in the rearview mirror and waving.

"Never mind her," said Jenna. "Watch the road."

"I *am.*"

"The part of the road that's in front of us."

They turned onto Sand Dune Drive. "Watch out for the deer," Jenna warned, praying the doe and fawn she'd just seen wouldn't decide to cross the street until they'd driven by. Deer could be unpredictable.

"I see them, Mom."

"She sees them, Mom," Celeste teased from the backseat.

"Good." Deep breath. A quick stop at the grocery store, where they survived getting in and out of the parking lot, and they made it safely onto Harbor Boulevard. Sabrina was doing fine and the Driftwood Inn was in sight. "Don't forget to turn on your—" Jenna began, then shut up as her daughter flipped on the turn signal. "All right. Good," she said again as they pulled into the motel parking lot.

"You did great," Celeste complimented Sabrina and she smiled.

"See, Mom? I did great."

Jenna nodded, her heart rate coming back down to normal. "Yes, you did." *Do I have any new gray hairs?*

"I'm going to have a nervous breakdown before she gets her license," she predicted as she and Celeste followed Sabrina, who was already running up the steps of the half-painted house.

"I don't know why you're so nervous," Celeste said. "She did fine."

"She's improving. But before you got here, she backed into the front of Tristan's car and took out one of Nora's rhododendrons."

"Oh, well, that's part of the process, and rhodies are replaceable."

"Yes, but Sabrina's not. I worry about her getting hurt."

"You just plain worry."

"I do," Jenna admitted. Parenthood was the most stressful job in the world.

"If you want, I can go out with her," Celeste offered. "I can probably stay a little more mellow."

"I don't know," Jenna said. The thought of her daughter driving was nerve-racking. Her daughter off driving with Celeste or anyone else for that matter, with her nowhere around, was terrifying.

"I've never even had a speeding ticket," Celeste reminded her. Which, considering how her sister drove, was a miracle.

"We'll see," she said, making no commitments.

Courtney worked the office on Sunday mornings and Jenna had an hour before she was scheduled to relieve her, so the sisters grabbed sandwiches and hit the beach, Sabrina joining them to demonstrate her kite-flying abilities. Celeste found a small agate and proclaimed it a sign that sunny skies were around the corner.

"Actually, they're already here," she said as they walked back to the house. "This is the best place in the world to be."

"It sure is," Jenna agreed, looking to where Seth stood on a ladder, turning Aunt Edie's house back to the pretty shade of blue it had once been.

"Does Brody know he still has competition?" Celeste asked.

Jenna's gaze zipped away from the hottie on the ladder. "He doesn't have any."

"Right. And my eyes have been pecked out by buzzards."

"He doesn't want to get involved with anyone," Jenna said. No need to specify which *he*. Her sister knew.

"Except you. Don't forget I caught you together on New Year's Eve."

"He was wishing me a happy New Year."

"Right," scoffed Celeste.

But she left it at that, and Jenna was glad she did. There was no point in talking about Seth. The two of them had stalled out and that was that.

"A smooth morning," Courtney informed her as

she walked into the motel's office later. "Everyone checked out on time and our one check-in is safely installed in room twelve. And now I'm off to go home and play with fabric for a couple of hours. I've got some dresses to deliver to Patricia's boutique tomorrow."

And Jenna had some new pictures to post on the Driftwood's Facebook page and paperwork to do, which kept her busy for the afternoon. As she walked back to the house later, she caught sight of a Jeep parked outside room twelve and couldn't help wondering about the person occupying the room. A Henry Gilbert had made the reservation, and he'd taken the room clear until the end of August.

Guests usually booked for a weekend or at most a week. What was his story? Did he have a wife with him? Maybe he was a teacher and had summers off; that would explain why he was staying so long. It was about the only explanation Jenna could come up with, except for the guy being a dot-com millionaire. But that wasn't likely. Cute as the Driftwood Inn was, no millionaire would bother renting a room there.

Oh, well. She was sure she'd meet him eventually. Who knew? Maybe she'd even make a new friend to add to the growing list of previous guests who were fast becoming regulars.

By evening it was time to close the office and have a life. Tristan swept Sabrina off to hang out with their friends, and Aunt Edie and Pete settled in with cheese and crackers to watch reruns of *Murder, She Wrote*.

Jenna decided to expose her sister to more Moonlight Harbor men. "The Drunken Sailor has line dancing on Sunday nights," she said to Celeste.

"Don't they have normal dancing anywhere?"

"Not on Sunday night. Come on," Jenna coaxed. "You'll love this. I promise. Anyway, it's either that or TV with Aunt Edie and Pete."

"When do we leave?"

Half an hour later the sisters entered the popular pub. The place was busy and Jenna saw plenty of people she knew, including Seth. He was playing pool with a couple of guys, leaning on his cue stick, waiting for his turn to clear the table. He looked gorgeous as usual in jeans and a fitted shirt that showed off his pecs and broad shoulders. He sent her a casual wave. She waved back, ignoring the flash of heat in her chest as she and Celeste walked to the bar.

The bar was a long one that offered plenty of seating and gave drinkers a ringside seat to watch the dancers on the large, wooden dance floor. Several male patrons were already parked there for the night, including Brody.

"You made it," he said, flashing his gorgeous Brody smile. "Want your usual?" Jenna nodded and he turned to Celeste. "How about you, Celeste?"

"Beer," she said, and he ordered one for her and a giant Coke for Jenna.

Victor King, who was one of the Sunday-night regulars, had seen them come in and he hurried over to say hi. "I think you two might have met," Jenna said when she introduced him to Celeste.

His face flushed and he nodded. "Did you get your taillight fixed?" he asked.

"Not yet, but I'm going to. So don't even think about giving me a ticket," she said with a frown.

The flush got redder but he tried for suave anyway. "Don't worry, I'm off duty. Are you here for the dancing?"

"Looks like it."

Celeste wasn't exactly being her usual cute, flirty self. What was her problem? Jenna wanted to kick her.

"Well, uh, guess I'll see you on the dance floor," he said, and boot-scooted away.

"What is wrong with you?" she demanded after they'd gotten their drinks and were making their way to the dance floor where the dancers were gathering.

"What do you mean?"

"You know what I mean. Victor's a nice guy."

"He's a cop. I am so done with cops."

"They aren't all like Emerson. In fact, I bet hardly any are like Emerson. Victor certainly isn't."

"I don't care. Not interested, so he can keep his nightstick to himself."

Jenna shook her head. This was why her sister had man trouble. She couldn't tell the good ones from the bad. "You know what your problem is?"

"Right now? You."

Jenna gave up.

The rest of the dancers drifted in. Jenna waved to two of her favorite dance-floor buddies, Patricia Cho and her friend Barb, two pretty fifty-something dancers who were new to town. They had the moves and could out-dance all the younger women.

Many of the dancers wore boots and almost all of them wore jeans with T-shirts or sleeveless tops. Celeste in her ballet slippers and short black-and-white polka-dot skirt stood out like the diamond in the rough that she was, and Jenna caught more than one man checking her out.

Courtney made it, looking stylish in jeans and a frayed top that looked like a Courtney creation. "Got everything done and now I can play," she announced.

Victor joined them on the dance floor, offering to help Celeste with her steps, to which she replied, "You just watch yours, Mr. CSI Moonlight Harbor."

If that was meant to discourage him, it had the opposite effect. He did his usual Victor King blush but he also smiled. "You're pretty funny."

Celeste just rolled her eyes.

"You can help me anytime," Courtney said, and it seemed that between her and Celeste they were going to keep poor Victor's face looking sunburned all night long.

Tyrella arrived next. "Good, I made it. I got talking on the phone and lost track of time. Thought I was gonna be late."

"You cut it close," Jenna said as Austin Banks, their fearless leader, greeted everyone.

Austin was a transplanted Texan, and tonight she was dressed in tight jeans and a Western shirt, with gold hoop earrings dangling from her ears. Her husband, Roy, sat by a computer and speaker setup, happy to run the music and watch the others work up a sweat.

"Are y'all ready to shake your booty?" she asked.

"Ready," called Tyrella, who had plenty of booty to shake, and several other dancers gave Austin an enthusiastic *yes*, as well.

"Good," she drawled. "I see we got a couple of newcomers tonight. We're glad to have y'all with us. We're gonna start out with 'Deep South,' which we learned last week. It's a four-wall dance, and you newcomers don't worry. You'll catch on. We start with a rolling grapevine."

"A what?" Celeste whispered.

"You'll pick it up," Jenna said.

Austin demonstrated the steps, then they all did them together.

"Now with count," she said, and they started in again.

Celeste kept up fine.

Until about three-quarters of the way through. Then she began to get lost. And once the music began and they started the dance in earnest, she looked exactly the same as Jenna had on her first night, losing track of the steps and turning in the wrong direction.

But Victor was on hand to help her and she was embarrassed enough to let him.

"Your sister seems to be finding her feet," Brody observed as Jenna joined him at the bar when the dancers took a drink break.

She looked to where Celeste and Victor stood talking. Celeste wasn't exactly in flirt mode, but she wasn't frowning anymore. "I hope she gives him a chance."

"I feel sorry for the poor guy if she's anything like her sister."

"Now, what's that supposed to mean?"

"You Jones women are hard to win over."

"We Jones women haven't always made the best choices. That's why we're cautious."

"When are you going to stop being so cautious?" he asked softly.

"Do we have a deadline?" Brody was everything a woman could want. He was fun to be with and handsome and honest. A loyal friend. A great kisser. What was her problem?

Seth Waters.

But Seth was never going to commit. He'd said as much. In some ways he was even more bound by his past than Jenna. Even though he'd gone to prison for something he hadn't done, she suspected he still carried the stigma.

She cared about Brody. A lot. But it was hardly fair to commit to him when she still felt the crazy pull of attraction to Seth. He, too, was handsome and honest and loyal.

And she was…a mess. It had been a year since she'd come to Moonlight Harbor. Surely, it was time to start getting un-messed.

Well, her sister first. Then she'd worry about her own love life.

Still, poor Brody. "Are you getting tired of waiting for me to get myself together?"

He smiled his killer smile. "What do *you* think?"

She felt guilty about not being able to make up her mind. "I think maybe you should give up." It wasn't fair to keep him in limbo.

"Give up on the prettiest woman in Moonlight Harbor? How stupid do I look?" He turned serious. "I know you're waiting for that wound to heal, Jenna. And I know there are lots of men who'd like to help you with that. I happen to think I'm the best man for the job."

He was working on proving it as he ran a finger along her bare arm, making her nerve endings do a little line dance of their own.

"You are more tempting than chocolate cake," she informed him.

It was true. Brody was practically irresistible.

"That's what I like to hear. So how about it? Give in to temptation." He leaned in close to her, their shoulders touching. She could feel his breath warm on her neck and that started a line dance in a whole new region.

She *should* give in to temptation, as he'd said. Make the logical choice. Have her chocolate cake and eat it, too.

"Here's your Coke," said Misty, the bartender. "Hope I'm not interrupting anything," she added with a smirk.

"You are. Go away," Brody told her.

Austin was starting to teach a new dance. "Speaking of going away," Jenna said and stood up to leave.

He caught her hand. "As long as you come back."

Good Lord, Brody Green really was something
else. Only an idiot wouldn't grab him by his besot-
ted heart and hold on for dear love.

Obviously, she was an idiot. How was she ever
going to be able to help her sister with her love life
when she couldn't even sort out her own?

Celeste hadn't realized how much fun line dancing could be. "That was great," she said later as Jenna
drove them home. "And the best thing about it is you
don't need a partner."

"Although it looks like you could have one if you
want," said Jenna.

Celeste heaved a sigh. "I have to admit, Victor
is nice. But I don't know if I can get over the fact
that he's a cop." Anyway, he was almost *too* nice.
He didn't give her that same live-wire sizzle Emerson had.

He also didn't have a black heart, she reminded
herself. But if there wasn't any chemistry, what was
the point?

And yet... Chemistry. What use was it if things
always blew up in your face? Celeste heaved a sigh.

"He's a good cop," Jenna pointed out. "And a good
man. That doesn't mean he's the right man," she hurried to add. "But you shouldn't rule him out."

"I'm not really looking," Celeste reminded both
her sister and herself. "Not rushing into anything.
Remember?"

"Dating isn't rushing."

"The way I date, it is." Deep inside, that burning

desire to find someone to fill the empty spot a dead father had left behind always seemed to push her into some man's arms. But in the end they were never the right arms. There'd been Billy Harris in high school. Captain of the football team—how clichéd!—and so in love with himself there hadn't been room for her in that relationship. He was followed by Richard, who wasn't as smart as she was. That wouldn't have worked. And in college it had been all about Kenny Norris. "This is it," she'd told her sister. Kenny was perfect—gorgeous and smart. Too smart. He'd excelled at making Celeste feel inferior, sneering at the romance novels she read, wondering about her inability to balance her checkbook, looking down on her career choice. "Not much challenge in teaching little kids," he'd said on their last date ever, to which she'd responded, "Little kids are our future." Then she'd added, "I don't think we're really a match." So much for yet another "this is it" relationship. She hadn't been a match with Theo, either, who'd been so charming and fabulous when they first began dating that she was sure she'd struck gold. But he turned out to be fool's gold. Theo was abusive. At least she'd seen the signs of that early on and got out before he started smacking her around. Then there'd been Josh, the musician, a very short-lived romance, followed by Edward. She was so sure *he* was The One that she'd gotten herself a subscription to *Bride* magazine. He'd seen a copy on her nightstand and had broken up with her the next morning. "Nothing personal, Celeste. I'm just not ready for that kind of commitment." She'd made the mistake of asking when he thought he might be ready and that was all it took to send him screaming into the night. Or rather broad daylight. Finally, there'd been Emerson, the cheating lizard. Good grief. Talk about a pack of losers.

She couldn't afford to keep betting her heart on men like that. From now on she was going to guard it, even against nice, line-dancing cops.

Who had time for romance anyway? She was busy enjoying her family and helping out around the Driftwood.

Monday found her with the maid's cart, making her rounds and cleaning up after the guests who'd departed the day before. Happily, there hadn't been so many check-outs that she'd had to work all afternoon on Sunday, and she'd enjoyed spending time on the beach with her sister and niece and then later playing cards with Aunt Edie. Line dancing that evening had turned out to be fun, too. And today, after she was done working, she was going to grab a thermos of lemonade, a book and a beach towel, and find a spot on a sand dune to soak up some sun. Yep, life was good at the beach.

She knocked on the door of room twelve. "Housekeeping."

There was no answer, so she used her key and went inside with her towels. Hearing the shower running in the bathroom, she decided she'd better leave the towels on the bed and scram.

As she set them down, she noticed a steno tablet

lying on the bedspread. Some sort of list was written on the top page.

None of her business, of course.

She craned her neck to see.

Kind of an odd list, with things written under columns. Odd column headings, too. *Where. How.*

The water was still running. She picked up the tablet. As she began to read what was listed under *Where* the hairs on her neck stood up. This was no grocery list. *Alley in back of the club, apartment parking lot, side of road—need to slash a tire for this to work.* She moved to the other column, *How.* The word at the top of that list made her heart stop. *Hunting knife.*

Knife? She gulped. What kind of sicko was staying in room twelve?

"What are you doing?" demanded a male voice.

Chapter Four

Celeste dropped the tablet as if her fingers were on fire. There in the bathroom doorway stood a man wearing nothing but a towel. He was lean, somewhere in his thirties and had reddish hair, which was still damp from his shower. Chest hair, too. You didn't see that very much anymore. It was so…manly. But his face, and that expression in his eyes—this was what a psychopath looked like.

"Sorry," she stammered, backing toward the door. "I just brought you some clean towels."

He cocked an eyebrow. Evilly.

She fumbled for the doorknob. Her heart was pounding so loudly she could hardly hear herself say, "Bye." She yanked open the door and rushed out, slamming it behind her. If he didn't have a room key, she'd have used her master and locked him in.

Abandoning her supply cart, she raced for the office where Jenna was studying an Excel spreadsheet on her computer. "We've got to call the cops!"

Jenna looked up, her eyes big. "*What?* What's wrong?"

"There's a murderer staying in room twelve."

Jenna stared at her as if she was nuts. "What are you talking about?"

"The man in room twelve is planning to bump someone off."

Jenna frowned. "And you know this how?"

"I know this because I saw his list of where and how to do it."

Jenna rubbed her forehead. "Okay, you'd better start from the beginning."

Celeste recounted what she'd seen, then pulled her cell phone out of her jeans back pocket.

"You can't go calling the police just because you saw a list," Jenna told her.

"Yeah, I can." What was wrong with her sister anyway? Celeste started punching in 911. "Are you forgetting what happened to Rachel Mills?"

Celeste sure hadn't. The woman had lived in their Seattle neighborhood, a few houses down from them. She was a newlywed and had enjoyed decorating her new home and collecting gardening tips from her neighbors. One summer night she'd gone to the mall and was spotted by a sicko. While she was shopping, he'd managed to slash one of her tires unseen. He'd followed her out of the mall and when she'd pulled over with a flat, he'd stopped and offered to help, luring her out of her car. Then he'd threatened her with a knife and tried to kidnap her. She'd gotten away, but the experience had changed her from a happy, outgoing woman to a shy, frightened shadow who rarely left her house.

"This is nothing like that." Jenna jumped up and

snatched away the phone before Celeste could hit the final digit. "Remember the last time you called the police for me?"

"You heard a noise and thought it was a burglar."

"No, *you* thought it was a burglar," Jenna corrected her.

"So did you," Celeste insisted.

"And it turned out to be Pete. Trust me. There's a logical explanation for the list in that guy's room."

"Yeah? What?"

"I don't know," Jenna said, sounding exasperated. "All I know is Henry Gilbert isn't partying and keeping people up all night, he doesn't smoke and his credit card didn't get declined. He's the ideal guest."

"Until he croaks someone. Some poor woman's going to have her tires slashed and her throat cut. We need to do something before someone gets hurt."

"I'm not calling 911 on a paying guest, especially one who's booked for the whole summer," Jenna said stubbornly.

"All right. We won't call 911," Celeste said.

"Good."

"But we can at least ask your buddy Victor what he thinks."

Jenna let out a sigh.

"Come on. What if this guy's planning to bump someone off?"

Her sister still hesitated. "I saw the list," Celeste said. "You don't write down possible places to kill a person and the weapon you want to use for no reason. At least, let's call the station and see if Victor's on duty."

Jenna sighed again. "Okay, I'll call." Then she went back to her spreadsheet.

With a scowl, Celeste snatched her phone from the desk. "Now. If you don't, I will."

"Okay, okay. But this is stupid."

Celeste stood by as her sister talked to the front-desk person at the station. "He's on patrol? Oh, well, then..."

Celeste grabbed the phone and said, "Ask him if he'll come by the Driftwood Inn. We may have a situation." Then she pushed End.

"Oh, great. That's going to be good for business," Jenna said. "He'll probably come in with lights flashing."

"It won't be so good for business if people find out we've got a crazed murderer staying here. You have heard of the Bates Motel, haven't you?"

Sure enough, a few minutes later Victor King rolled in. Right behind him came his partner, Jenna's admirer, Frank Stubbs, a short, squat middle-aged man who lived up to his name. Victor had been subtle but Frank had his car's top hat spinning.

He swaggered into the office, Victor behind him. "What's the problem, Jenna?"

Jenna gave Celeste the disgusted older sister look she'd perfected back when she was thirteen. "Nothing, I'm sure. My sister thinks we have a crazed murderer staying with us."

Frank's eyebrows shot up toward his receding hair-line. "Whoa."

"It'll probably turn out to be like the time I thought we had a burglar," Jenna continued.

"Better safe than sorry," Frank told her. Then, to Celeste, "What makes you think you've got a killer staying here?"

Celeste repeated her story. Neither policeman laughed at her, which she considered vindication.

"Planning to commit a crime can be a crime," Victor said.

"See?" Celeste turned to Jenna. "I told you."

"But," he went on, "you've got to have more evidence than just some ideas on paper before it's a crime, though."

"What does that mean?" Celeste demanded.

"It means we leave our guest alone," Jenna said firmly.

To go and murder some poor, unsuspecting person? "You guys can't do anything?"

"Not at the moment," Victor said.

"Well, great," Celeste snapped, throwing up her hands. "So we have to wait until he slashes our tires for you to come to life."

Victor feared no man, but women seemed to be another story. His cheeks took on that familiar rosy hue.

Frank, however, wasn't intimidated by female scorn. "The law's the law. But you keep your eyes peeled. If he puts down any more details, let us know."

Honestly, what more did they need? "Like what?"

"A name would be helpful," Victor said. "We really can't move on something as vague as what you've told us."

Jenna stepped in before Celeste could say any more. "We understand. We'll keep an eye on him."

"*You* keep an eye on him," Celeste said to her. "I'm not getting my throat cut."

"You're not going to get your throat cut," Jenna assured her.

Easy for her to say. She hadn't been in the room with Hannibal Lecter, Jr.

He watched her walk into the club with another woman dressed as slutty as she was. Her laugh echoed to the alley where he stood, and her red heels glinted under the neon light of the club's sign. There was a line of people waiting to get in, but he knew she'd have no trouble getting past the muscled idiot at the door. She'd toss that long, dark hair, bat her false eyelashes at him and be in, just like that. He watched the swing of her hips. The hem of her dress barely covered her ass. The thong underneath wouldn't cover it at all. Yeah, she was dressed to kill.

Except tonight she was dressed to be killed. Yeah, the bitch must die.

Henry Gilbert read the comforting, violent words on his laptop screen with a smile. It was going to be so satisfying to kill Nikki. Over and over again. He loved being a serial killer.

On paper. In real life the only thing he'd ever killed were spiders. And a rattler when he was camping in Eastern Washington with some of his writing buddies. He suspected if he had to hunt his own food, he'd turn vegetarian. In real life he didn't have the stomach for blood.

Fiction was a different story. As a kid he'd been a Marvel comic addict. As a teenager he'd devoured books by James Patterson, Dean Koontz and Stephen King the way some kids wolfed down cookies.

His life wasn't as action-packed as his writing. No fights, no murders, no mysteries to solve. No drugs or drunken orgies. He'd partied some in high school, but never to the extent of getting into trouble. Too goal-focused for that. He'd lettered in track—cross country specifically—partly because he liked to run, partly because he liked to think, and the solitude on those long runs gave him plenty of time for that. He'd been president of the honor society and graduated from college summa cum laude. Now, as an adult, the partying consisted of meeting with his writing critique group, playing pool once in a while with a couple of old college buddies and the occasional on-line gaming binge.

How had he wound up with a woman who hadn't cracked a book since high school? Nikki's favorite pastimes had been reality TV and shopping.

He'd met her when he and his friends had tried out a new sports bar in Seattle. They were playing pool and drinking a beer when she and a girlfriend sashayed up to the table next to theirs. He'd seen her bend over the table, lining up a shot, and that had been that. Nikki had the cutest butt in all of Seattle. And yes, she favored thongs. So beer, pool and hot underwear—just what every lasting relationship should be built on.

What a fool. It had served him right when it all caved in. Thank God he could escape into his world of murder and mayhem. Writing was good therapy, better than a shrink.

And obviously, what he was working on was convincing, if that goofy maid he'd caught snooping through his stuff was any indication. He'd seen the flashing blue lights meant to convey a police presence a few minutes after she'd fled the room and he had enjoyed a chuckle. Oh, yeah, the killer in room twelve. Hey, there was a title for a future book.

Meanwhile, though, he had to finish *She Must Die*, which was due at the end of August. First book in a two-book contract. Ha!

How many times had Nikki taunted him about never selling anything? "Give up and get your job back, Henry," she kept saying. "You're not going to make it as a writer. You should know that by now." Yeah, behind every great man was a woman who dissed him and made him all the more determined to prove her wrong.

What a different tune from when they'd first met. She'd thought it was sexy that he was so smart and writing a book. But then, she'd also thought it was sexy that he was making a buttload of money working for a big dot-com company. She'd also thought his houseboat on Lake Union was sexy. She'd liked how creatively romantic Henry was. That was especially sexy. She'd moved in a month after they'd hooked up.

Then he'd decided to quit his job, live off his savings and work on his book. That hadn't been so sexy.

"What were you thinking?" she'd demanded. "You don't even know if you're going to sell the thing."

"I'll sell it," he'd said. He'd been writing off and on since middle school; he'd already sold a couple of short stories to literary magazines when he was in college. Payment had been in free copies, but still... He had faith in himself even if she didn't.

Sad to think how everything had unraveled. She'd gone from "You're so smart" to "You're such a loser." And in between had been the complaints. Those had actually started before he'd quit his job. She'd hated it that he spent chunks of his Saturdays working on his book when she wanted to go to the mall or get away for the weekend. "We don't do anything anymore," she'd complain. "You're becoming boring." Translation: *You're not entertaining me every minute of every day.*

Yes, moving in together had been a big mistake. Even dance lessons—effing dance lessons, for crying out loud!—couldn't save them, and he'd been a star pupil if he did say so himself. She'd gotten tired of his "little project" as she began to call it. "You're never gonna make any money at this," she'd predicted.

"You're wrong. I'm gonna make it as a writer," he kept insisting.

Nikki hadn't been willing to stick around to find out. She'd finally given him an ultimatum, right after Valentine's Day—had to stick around for the chocolate and flowers. It was either her or his stupid book. He'd chosen his stupid book.

If only, on the evening of their last fight, she hadn't backed out in a huff and run over his dog.

Who shouldn't have been out. Henry always had Gus on a leash when they went for a walk or to the dog park, not just because there was a leash law, but also because cities with their traffic and crazy drivers weren't safe places for animals. But Nikki had been so preoccupied with hauling her crap out to her car she'd left the door half-open. Gus had slipped out and she hadn't even noticed. How could she not have noticed?

Henry had his excuse. He'd been in the tiny back bedroom that served as his office, pouting and pretending to write. Too late, he'd realized Gus was missing. He'd gotten to the door in time to see her screeching away in her car like she was at the Indy 500. And slamming into his dog. Poor old Gus hadn't stood a chance.

To her credit, Nikki had been beside herself. She might not have loved Henry, but she'd loved Gus. Not enough to go with Henry when he rushed the poor old guy to the animal hospital, though.

He'd lost both his dog and his girl on the same night. The dog had been the bigger loss.

Shortly after she split he found an agent. Come spring, that agent had found an editor who liked his writing, and before he knew it, he had a two-book contract and an extensive rewrite to do. And with that Dirk Slade was born. Goodbye, Henry. Hello, Dirk.

People said you should never quit your day job until you had several books under your belt, but *people*, whoever that was, hadn't been saving up for the day when a book contract would arrive. Henry could afford to take the summer off.

Before everything blew up he'd planned on surprising Nikki with a two-week vacation in Cabo. Now he was glad she'd split before he could tell her. He switched from Cabo to the funky little motel on the Washington coast and went from two weeks to all summer, letting one of the guys in his critique group crash in his houseboat.

Why not? Jenna Jones, the manager, had been delighted when he booked with her. And now here he was.

The funky old place suited him perfectly. He could do early-morning runs on the beach, write during the day and eat take-out, then duck into one of the local dives for a drink at night.

Nikki wouldn't have liked this old-fashioned motel stuck in a time warp. She'd have wanted to know where the spa was and the gift shop. And she'd have wanted to know when he was going to get done with his stupid book so they could have a life.

Ha! He had a life now and it suited him fine. He liked being by himself. No woman to drive him nuts and make demands. No woman to chide him and make him feel like a loser.

And no dog.

He scowled and went back to his list of possible ways to kill his victims. Funny how every woman the serial killer in his book went after was cute and bubbly. Like the ex. And shallow. Like the ex. And great in bed. Like the ex.

Eventually, his detective would catch his killer, but until then—lots of vengeance to come.

Henry frowned. He was so over Nikki. He was so over women, period. Even cute, nosy ones with platinum curls, big green eyes and a nice pair of coconuts. Yes, even over women like that. And if he'd given the maid a scare, well, it served her right. Looking through a guy's stuff was just plain wrong.

Maybe when she came to clean the room again she'd find him sharpening his hunting knife. Yeah.

Except he didn't own one, and only a sick bastard would do something like that.

The next day when she appeared with her towels and her little scrub brush, she found him in jeans and a T-shirt, barefoot and sitting on the bed, typing on his laptop.

"Um, room service?" she squeaked.

"Thanks. Left my dirty towels in the bathroom. You don't have to make the bed since I'm on it."

She nodded and scuttled off to the bathroom, casting a quick glance over her shoulder—probably to make sure he wasn't following with his trusty hunting knife. Then she scuttled back, carrying his dirty towels. Towel patrol finished, she raced for the bathroom again, this time with her cleaning supplies.

He could hear her in there, running the water. He was tempted to sneak up on her and say, "Boo," but he didn't. That, too, would be sick, and sick was re-served for fictional villains.

Still, when she came back out, he couldn't resist saying, "I see you called the cops on me yesterday."

The color disappeared from her face. "The police were here yesterday," she admitted, hurrying for the door, all the while trying to look as though she wasn't hurrying. "They keep a close eye on things."

"Do they, now? A lot of crime here in Moonlight Harbor?"

"No," she said, injecting bravado into her voice, "and we like to keep it that way."

"Always on the watch for bad guys, huh? Is that why you were snooping in my things?"

Now her color came back, painting her cheeks red. "I wasn't snooping."

"Oh? What would you call it? I came out here to find you reading my notes."

She licked her lips. "I was just straightening up."

"You're a lousy liar."

"I'd rather be a lousy liar than a lousy person," she retorted and grabbed the door handle.

"Well, good thing I'm neither," he said. She was halfway out the door when he added, "I'm a writer."

She turned and gaped at him. "You're a…what?"

"You know. One of those people who sit around and make up shit."

"Like…?"

"Murder shit."

For a moment she looked shocked. Then her eyes narrowed and her lips pressed into an angry line.

"Surprise," he muttered.

"You should've said something."

"You shouldn't have been snooping."

She stood there in the doorway for a moment, wearing a pouty frown. She had the kind of lips a man dreamed of having on him. But he'd settle for putting her and her lips in a book.

"Okay," she said with a nod. "You're right. I shouldn't have."

A woman who could admit when she was wrong?

"I'm sorry."

And one who said she was sorry? He'd figured that model had died out with his mom's generation.

"No harm done," he said. But he made sure to say it grudgingly to show her what he thought of nosy women.

"I did call the police," she admitted. "Did you know you can be arrested for planning to commit a crime?"

"Do tell."

"But it takes more evidence than I found. When I was snooping," she added with a smile. And what a smile it was.

He supposed the incident would make a great anecdote to share when promoting his book. *There was this nosy maid who saw my notes and thought I was a killer.*

"You're a writer. That's cool," she said, stepping back into the room.

That was what Nikki had said when he first met her. The walls went up.

"I've thought about writing a book."

Who hadn't?

"A children's book."

Next thing she'd be asking him if he knew a publisher who'd be interested in making her rich and famous. It was always that or, "Hey, why don't you write my life story?"

"I thought of a great title the other day when I was on the beach," she continued. *"The Happy Clam."*

"The Happy Clam?" he repeated. *Good Lord.*

"I think it's a cute title," she said defensively.

"I wouldn't know. I don't write kid stuff." Okay, that had sounded condescending.

"No, obviously, you're into murdering people," she shot at him before he could apologize.

Sticks and stones, baby. "Who doesn't like a good serial killer?" he quipped.

Her features scrunched up as if he'd just offered to let her watch an autopsy. "You're writing about a serial killer? Don't you think that's kind of sick?"

Now the clam girl was judging him? "No sicker than looking through people's stuff."

Her chin went up. "I said I was sorry."

Okay, enough of this charming repartee. "You're forgiven, my child. Go in peace."

She went, but not in peace. The happy clam lady shut the door firmly. She was probably mentally listing the ways she'd like to do him in.

"Nice meeting you, clam girl." And good riddance.

Chapter Five

After her unpleasant exchange with the jerk in room twelve, Celeste was more than ready for an afternoon beach walk.

"At least you know he's not a murderer," Jenna had said when Celeste told her about him.

Only a murderer of dreams. She was still smarting over the way he'd sneered at her children's book idea. He'd probably approve if her clam met its death during the razor clam festival and wound up in some kid's chowder.

Actually, she wasn't sure *what* kind of story she could write about a clam. What did they do, really, but lie around in the sand until somebody harvested and ate them? Still, it was a cute title and there had been an idea in there somewhere. And writing something sweet for children had to beat bumping people off.

"He's still a jerk," she'd insisted, slipping her feet into her flip-flops.

"I don't care, as long as he pays for his room," Jenna had said. Her sister had become downright mercenary since taking over the Driftwood.

The June afternoon was warm and the sky was the kind of summer blue that would have made Monet weep for joy. Celeste soon forgot her irritation as she walked along the beach, looking for agates. Who cared about the jerk in room twelve? Who cared about anything on such a beautiful summer day?

She abandoned the agate search, kicked off her flip-flops and allowed herself a run at the water's edge, enjoying the feel of the cool water on her bare feet. Suddenly, she heard a *woof* and found herself joined by a friendly yellow dog. He was some sort of mixed breed, probably part golden retriever, judging by his coat and friendly personality.

She stopped to pet him and he rewarded her with a vigorous tail wag and another bark, then jumped up and put his front paws on her white "I Heart Moonlight Harbor" T-shirt.

"Okay, manners," she said, removing the paws and returning him to all fours. He barked and wagged his tail and she bent down and rubbed behind his ears. "Who are you, fella?"

"Orrroarorr," he replied and tried to lick her face.

She checked him for a collar and dog license and found nothing, not even a flea collar. "Did you run away from home?" He must have. He was too friendly not to belong to someone. But whoever he belonged to sure wasn't taking very good care of him. He needed a brushing, maybe a bath, too.

She straightened and looked up and down the beach, hoping to see a sign of the dog's owner. Not a soul in sight. "You must be lost," she said.

He wagged his tail once more as if to say, "Who cares? Let's play."

There were several vacation rentals and hotels along her stretch of beach. The dog must have wandered away from one of them. Hopefully, he'd find his way back.

After a final ear rub, she told him, "You'd better go on home, boy." Then she continued on down the beach, this time at a walk.

Her new furry friend fell in step next to her.

She stopped.

He stopped.

"You need to go home."

He wagged his tail.

Okay, she was going to have to get stern. She clapped her hands, then gave him the time-honored gesture for shoo. "Go home!"

He leaped, then bowed, tail still going, and barked. Obviously, he had no intention of shooing.

Best to ignore him. She turned around and started back to the house.

So did the dog.

She was nearly home and her new friend was still with her, demanding nothing more than to walk by her side. "You need to go home," she said again. Firmly. Very firmly.

He kept walking along next to her, tongue lolling. She could have sworn he was smiling.

Okay, she'd reached her destination. Time to part ways. Of course, the dog had no intention of leaving her side.

"I suppose you're thirsty," she said.

The tail swept back and forth. *Yup. How'd you guess?*

"I can't keep you," she informed him. "I don't live here. And that's not my house."

The tail kept wagging.

"Okay, I'll give you a drink, but that's it." She probably shouldn't even do that. But he did look thirsty. And hungry. They went up the back steps together. Good buds.

"Stay," she commanded as she opened the door.

That word was not in the dog's vocabulary. Before she could stop him, he'd pushed his way into the kitchen, trotting up to where Aunt Edie stood rolling out pie crust and jumping on her.

Aunt Edie yelped and dropped her rolling pin. Roger, who'd been seated on his kitchen perch, let out a squawk and took off for the living room. Meanwhile, the dog, mistaking the rolling pin for a stick, got it between his teeth.

"My rolling pin!" cried Aunt Edie.

"Oh, you bad dog," muttered Celeste, starting for him. "Give that here."

Now the game was on. The dog bolted away, rolling pin in his mouth, and raced from the kitchen to the living room with Celeste in pursuit.

Sabrina had been sitting on the couch, reading a book. She broke into a smile at the sight of their uninvited guest. "A dog! Come here, boy."

The animal dropped the rolling pin, bounded over to the couch and jumped on her, barking a greeting.

Meanwhile, Roger had climbed into his cage and pulled the door shut after him. "Call the cops! Call the cops!"

"He's so sweet," Sabrina cooed as the dog tried to lick her. "Where did you get him?"

Aunt Edie chose that moment to march into the living room, frowning. "What is this animal doing here?" she demanded, retrieving her slobbered-up rolling pin.

"I'm sorry, Aunt Edie," Celeste said, dragging their four-legged visitor off Sabrina. "He followed me home."

Sabrina bent to pet the dog and he reached for her face with his tongue, making her giggle. "Who does he belong to?"

"I don't know," Celeste said. "He doesn't have a collar."

"He needs to leave," Aunt Edie insisted.

"Maybe he doesn't have a home," Sabrina said hopefully.

Celeste couldn't imagine that. "He's too pretty not to belong to someone. Come on, boy," she urged, patting her leg.

The dog bounded away from Sabrina, tail swinging hard enough to knock a candle from the coffee table.

"Oh, dear," Aunt Edie fretted.

"Oh, dear," echoed Roger from the safety of his cage. "Oh, dear, oh, dear. Give me whiskey."

Aunt Edie was going to need some whiskey herself at the rate they were going. Celeste managed to get the dog out of the house and onto the back porch, then slipped inside before he could figure out he'd been tricked. With a doggy sigh, he slid down against the door and settled in.

Sabrina was in the kitchen now. "What if he's lost?" she asked, looking out the door window at him.

"He'll find his way home," Aunt Edie assured her. She stood at the sink, squirting bleach on her rolling pin.

"He's thirsty. I should at least give him a drink," Celeste said, and dug a big metal bowl out of one of the cupboards.

"Give a mouse a cookie," Aunt Edie warned. She added dish soap to the bleach and began to scrub vigorously.

Celeste knew that children's book. "Just a drink, Auntie," she pleaded. "You'd never refuse a drink to a stranger, would you?" After all, she'd taken in Pete.

"I would if he had four legs," Aunt Edie replied. "Dogs are messy."

Not like parrots who spread birdseed everywhere and sometimes pooped on your shoulder.

"All right," Aunt Edie relented. "Give him a drink, dear, but he can't come in." She rinsed off her rolling pin and applied more bleach, lamenting, "My rolling pin will never be the same."

Jenna entered the kitchen. "Who's getting a drink?"

"We have a visitor," Aunt Edie told her, sounding none too happy about it.

"Aunt Celeste found a dog," Sabrina said, an eager smile on her face. "We don't think he has a home."

"We don't know anything about him," Aunt Edie corrected.

Oh, boy, thought Celeste. She'd brought home a problem. Aunt Edie was not in a welcoming mood and it was obvious Sabrina would like nothing better than to instantly adopt the dog. Which put Jenna uncomfortably in the middle.

"I'm sure he's got an owner," Celeste said, hoping to both placate her great-aunt and keep her niece's hopes from rising any higher.

"But he didn't have a collar," pointed out Sabrina.

Jenna poured herself a glass of lemonade. "Sometimes people just dump their pets and leave."

"That's outrageous!" Celeste couldn't restrain her disgust.

"Who'd dump a sweet dog like that?" Sabrina asked.

"He's not very well-mannered. No wonder he got dumped," Aunt Edie said as Celeste opened the door to put down the bowl of water for the dog, who was dancing around her in eager anticipation.

As soon as the bowl was down, he dove his face into the water and began to lap it up. That at least allowed Celeste to shut the door and keep him out.

Jenna looked at him through the back door window. "He's really scruffy."

"But pretty," Celeste said. Once he was well groomed, he'd be gorgeous.

"Since we found him, we could name him Nemo, like the fish in the movie," Sabrina said, joining them at the door.

Celeste saw the glance that shot between Jenna and Aunt Edie. *We're picking names.*

"I'm sure he has an owner," Jenna said. "Maybe he's chipped."

"What if he's not?" Sabrina persisted.

"He has to belong to *somebody*," Jenna said.

Yes, he did, but whoever it was didn't deserve him.

"We should take his picture and put it up on Facebook," Jenna continued. "We should probably make some flyers, too."

"We should take him to the animal shelter," said Aunt Edie.

Sabrina looked aghast. "If nobody adopts him, they'll kill him!"

Aunt Edie's stern expression melted. *Way to find the chink in Auntie's armor,* Celeste thought with a smile. Aunt Edie was far too tenderhearted to want a stray dog's death on her conscience.

"Let's take this one step at a time." Jenna pulled her phone out of her back pants pocket and opened the door to go out and take the dog's picture.

Seeing the open door as an invitation, he squeezed past her and reentered the kitchen, his tail doing the hula, and began sniffing the floorboards.

"That dog cannot be in my kitchen," Aunt Edie said firmly.

"He's gotta be hungry." Sabrina pulled some bologna from the fridge and held it out to the dog. It was gone in a snap and a slurp. "He's starving," she said in shock.

"He can't be starving in the kitchen," Aunt Edie

said, and Sabrina got the message and coaxed the dog into the living room.

"I'm sure he's just lost," Jenna said to Aunt Edie once they were gone.

"More like someone left him behind," Aunt Edie said with a frown.

"Hard to imagine," Celeste said. "He really is a handsome dog."

"Okay, then. He's yours," Jenna told her.

"Mine? Why me?" She wasn't in a position to take a dog.

"Because you're the one who found him," said her sister. "Finders keepers."

"I have an apartment. Remember?"

"You said they take dogs," Jenna reminded her.

"It's obvious Sabrina's fallen in love with him," Aunt Edie said, sounding none too happy about the love affair.

"Do you think you could put up with him for a couple of months if we kept him outside?" Jenna asked her. "He could sleep on the back porch. Then we can send him home with Celeste when she goes back to school. And Sabrina can have visiting rights," she added with a grin.

"Thanks a lot," Celeste said.

Except she was already getting attached to the dog. They'd never had one growing up. Their mom hadn't wanted the extra expense. Celeste had always vowed to have a dog or cat once she was on her own, but her first apartment hadn't allowed pets.

That wasn't the case where she was now. If the dog turned out not to have an owner, she could adopt him.

And leave him stuck alone in the apartment all day during the school year? That wouldn't be fair. Maybe she could find a doggy daycare for Nemo to go to while she was at work. It would be nice to have the company when she got home from school, and dogs were loyal. Which was more than you could say for a lot of men.

"This may be a moot point anyway," Jenna said. "There might be someone looking for him even now."

Celeste thought of the deserted beach. "Probably not, but we should at least try and find his owners. Have you got a local vet? I could take him in tomorrow before I clean rooms to see if he's chipped."

"Dr. Gladwell can check him out," Jenna said. She shook her head. "I'd be surprised if he is, though. Someone has not cared for that dog in a while. Look how skinny he is." She turned to Aunt Edie. "This is your house, Auntie. If you don't want the dog here, say the word and we'll take him to the shelter, and I'll tell Sabrina we found a home for him. Someone's sure to fall in love with him."

They could hear Sabrina laughing in the living room. "Someone already has," Aunt Edie said. She heaved a sigh. "Looks like we're stuck with him." She pointed her rolling pin at Celeste. "But you have to promise to take him home with you. And while he's here, I can't have him scaring Roger."

"We'll make sure he doesn't," Celeste promised and wondered how they'd manage that.

Pete walked in the back door. "What's with the bowl on the porch?"

"It's for our newest guest," Celeste told him. "A dog followed me home."

"And you gave him something to drink?" Pete asked in disbelief.

The poor animal had been about tripping over his tongue. What was she supposed to do? "He was thirsty."

Pete shook his head at Celeste's foolishness. "Now he'll think he belongs here."

"He does for the moment, until we can find his owner," Jenna said.

"Has he got a dog collar?" Pete asked.

"No," Jenna said.

"Good luck with that. Somebody probably dumped the beast. Whatever you do, don't feed him. Then he'll really stick around."

It was all Celeste could do not to giggle. From what she'd heard, that was pretty much how they'd wound up with Pete. He and her aunt had met at The Seafood Shack and he'd followed her home.

"Sabrina already gave him some bologna," said Aunt Edie.

"Well, then, you're stuck," Pete told her.

"We're going have to feed him something," said Jenna. "It could be a while before we find his owners."

"I'll go to the store and get some dog food," Celeste volunteered.

She was about to run upstairs and grab her purse when the doorbell rang.

"I've got it," called Sabrina.

Celeste came out into the living room in time to see that Sabrina wasn't the only one answering the door. The dog had appointed himself a member of the welcoming committee and was now jumping on Pastor Paul Welch.

Finding the dog's paws on his chest, Paul blinked in surprise and took a step back, and the animal joined him in the little dance. "Whoa," he said, removing the paws.

"No, Nemo," Sabrina scolded. "Come here."

Nemo looked from her to Paul, tail going like a metronome, and barked.

Paul glanced down at his polo shirt, then back up at Celeste, a weak smile on his face. The shirt was a little dirty, but not half as dirty as Celeste's T-shirt. Or Aunt Edie's blouse.

"Sorry," she said. "We just got back from the beach. Sabrina, why don't you take Nemo for a walk?"

Sabrina nodded, and she and Nemo vanished.

"So you have a dog?" Paul asked as the front door shut behind them.

"Not yet. I found him on my beach walk. We're hoping to locate his owners. Would you like to come in?" She motioned to the living room couch.

"Sure," he said, and the smile gained in strength.

"I'll get Aunt Edie."

Paul cleared his throat. "Actually, I wasn't coming to see your aunt."

"Jenna's in the kitchen."

Now he looked genuinely amused. "I came to see you, Celeste. I wanted to see how you liked the service."

"Oh. Well, I liked it fine. By the way, I managed to stay awake for all of your sermon," she teased.

"You're swelling my head," he teased back.

"It's been a while since I've been in church," she added. Full disclosure.

"A lot of people take a sabbatical now and then. I hope you'll come back."

Was he only here to see if he had a potential new member?

"Okay," he admitted as if reading her mind. "I'm not here strictly as a pastor. Although I do call on all our visitors."

He had a warm smile. She decided she liked Pastor Paul Welch.

Jenna was in the room now and wearing the speculative expression of a matchmaker. "Hi, Paul. What brings you over?"

"I thought I'd see how your sister's settling in."

"She can always use someone to show her around town," Jenna said.

"'Cause it's so big and easy to get lost in?" Celeste cracked.

"Something like that," Paul said. "How about it?"

"That could be arranged," Celeste replied with a flip of her hair.

What was she thinking? She'd just come out of a relationship. The last thing she needed was to jump into another one, especially with a pastor. Once Pastor Paul learned how...romantically active she'd been, he'd run faster than a man from a burning building. Yeah, bad idea. Pastors had high standards.

Time to get moving before she was tempted. Could pastors tempt you? With a smile like that, yeah. "But right now I've got a date."

He looked surprised.

"With a bag of dog food. Can't have my new friend starving to death."

Paul's smile faltered a little and she could tell he was trying to figure out whether she was on an urgent mission or had decided to stop him from starting anything. Maybe a little of both.

Aunt Edie appeared and was already inviting their visitor to stay for some coffee or tea. He had Aunt Edie, he had Jenna, he didn't need a third woman at this address. Celeste beat it before she could yield to temptation.

"You'd be a bad influence on him anyway," she told herself once she was in her car. She'd have the poor guy guzzling wine and going to the casino before he could say "fallen angel." No, they wouldn't be a match. She loved to dance and party. She was sure his social life never got wilder than a church picnic.

No, Pastor Paul visited little old ladies and did good deeds.

Perhaps he took walks on the beach, too. He was kind and patient. Had to be; it went with the job. And considering what he did, the odds were high he wouldn't cheat on a woman. He probably even wanted to settle down and have a family. A couple of kids, a dog. The man might not be into some of the frivolous trimmings she was, but darn, he knew how to smile so he had to have a sense of humor.

More important, he had to have principles. Did she want a man who was good on the dance floor or good at life? Maybe she shouldn't rule out Paul Welch.

Except he'd surely rule her out long before she would him.

Paul sat on the couch in Edie Patterson's living room, making conversation with her and Jenna, and thinking about Celeste Jones.

She'd looked so cute in those shorts and that muddied-up T-shirt, her hair mussed from the beach breeze. She had great legs, a great smile. Great everything. And personality. He'd barely talked to her, but he could tell she had a sense of humor, a sure sign that she had a zest for life.

He needed that in a woman, needed someone who could balance his more serious nature. Celeste was like the froth on the waves as they curled onto the beach. They added beauty to the power of the water. She was obviously kindhearted, too, since she'd adopted a stray dog.

A dog in need of obedience training.

"Pastor?"

His thoughts had wandered off after Celeste like that stray dog. He jerked them back into the moment. "Hmm?"

"We were wondering if you'd like to join us for dinner tonight," Jenna said.

"I'm afraid I can't. I've got a meeting. But I appreciate the offer. In fact, I'd better get going." He took a last gulp of his coffee and thanked his hostess, then stood.

Jenna stood, too. "Don't be a stranger."

"Thanks." How soon before he could come back?

Jenna had picked up a pen. "Give me your hand."

What? He held out his hand.

She took it, turned it palm up and began to write, saying, "I think you might want this."

It only took a second to see that she was writing a phone number. "How'd you guess?" Was there drool on his chin?

"I'm smart that way. Don't wash your hand. And don't wait too long to call her."

He wouldn't.

Chapter Six

Come morning, Nemo the dog was still happily camped out on the back porch on an old blanket Jenna had found and folded into a bed for him.

"Poor guy," Celeste said as she poured dog food into an old mixing bowl. Aunt Edie would bleach that to death when she got it back. "What's your story anyway? Did you get lost? I can't believe anyone in their right mind would desert you."

But then she'd never believed any man in his right mind would dump *her*. You never knew.

"Don't worry. If you do have a mommy and daddy, we'll find them," she promised as the dog tucked into his breakfast.

To that end, as soon as he was done eating, she loaded her furry new friend into her Prius and drove to the local vet's office.

Dr. Gladwell had a full schedule but had been willing to accommodate Celeste when he learned the situation. The good doctor's assistant took her to an exam room, past an incensed-looking older woman sitting in the lobby with a Chihuahua that barked irritably at

Nemo, making him jump as they passed. For a moment Celeste thought the woman was going to snap at her as well for having the nerve to get in to see the doc first. She wasn't positive, but she thought she heard the woman growl. They passed an exam room just as a cat inside let out a hiss and Nemo jumped again.

"That's Sweet Pea," said the assistant.

"I guess she doesn't like being examined." What was Dr. Gladwell doing to that cat anyway?

"Oh, doctor's not in there yet. She's with her owner. They don't get along very well. Some people should not be allowed to have pets," the woman added under her breath. She opened the door to a sterile-looking room with a cement floor and a big metal exam table. Framed posters of dogs, cats and bunnies decorated the walls, along with a diagram of doggy working parts and a poster that encouraged pet owners to bark less, wag more. "Doctor will be with you in a minute," his assistant said, then left them.

Nemo paced around and began to whine.

Celeste squatted in front of him. "Does this bring back bad memories?"

The dog licked her face. *I love you. Don't leave me.*

She rubbed behind his ears. "It's gonna be okay. Trust me. Whatever your past has been doesn't matter anymore. It's the present that counts, and you're here with me and it's all good."

The door opened. Nemo looked up and his tail managed a tentative wag.

"Well, now, here's a handsome fella," said Dr. Gladwell.

Which was, sadly, more than she could say for the vet. He was a tall, older man with a long face and jowls and eyes that drooped at the corners, making him look like a Basset Hound. A cute look for a dog. For a human, not so much.

"You must be Celeste," he said as she stood. He held out a paw, er, hand, for her to shake.

"I am. Thanks for making time for us."

"Always happy to help. I take it this is Nemo." He squatted in front of the dog. "Hey there, boy. How are you doing?"

Well enough to want to give the doctor a kiss.

But Dr. Gladwell was adept at avoiding sloppy dog kisses. He gave Nemo some nice ear rubs, then lifted him onto the table. "You're okay, young man," the doctor said as Nemo began to squirm, and ran a calming hand down the dog's back. "A lot of Golden in this boy, which, of course, explains the sweet temper. Let's see if we can find out who owns you," he said to Nemo, pulling out a chip reader.

"No chip," he said a moment later, shaking his head at people's irresponsibility. "Looks a little underfed, but other than that he appears to be in good shape. At least he's been neutered. Pet adoption agencies insist on that these days."

"So where are his owners?" Celeste asked.

"Your guess is as good as mine. Some people just dump their animals and leave them. It's a shame. This guy isn't more than a year old."

Barely out of puppyhood. Who'd leave a sweet dog

like this one? "I guess we'll put up some flyers around town," Celeste said. "He's got to belong to somebody."

"If he winds up belonging to you, bring him back and we'll check him for worms and we'll chip him and make sure he gets his shots," said the vet.

It was looking more and more like the dog was going to belong to her. She was smiling as she drove away.

She was even smiling when she knocked on room twelve later that morning. "Housekeeping."

"Come in," called a male voice, sounding irritated. Some invitation.

She came in and, just like the last time, found Henry Gilbert seated on his bed, this time wearing nothing but a pair of jeans, his legs stretched out in front of him, his laptop on his lap. He had long legs and his feet… She wasn't particularly fascinated by feet, but his were thin and elegant. For one insane second she caught a vision of one of those feet sliding up her calf as they lay side by side on that bed.

Oh, good grief. She'd obviously gone too long without sex.

"Just clean towels," he muttered as he typed away.

"And manners," she murmured, grabbing some towels off her cart.

He looked up at her as she came back in. "Seriously? You're gonna diss *my* manners? I'm not the one who goes around snooping through other people's things."

She left his clean towels and picked up the old

ones. "Okay, how long are you going to keep bringing that up?" she demanded.

He didn't reply, merely grunted and kept typing away. "Trying to work here."

"So am I. And I'm changing that bed tomorrow whether you like it or not," she informed him.

"Hard to do if I'm on it," he said, fingers clacking on the keyboard.

"Not really. I'll wrap you up in the bedspread like a giant spring roll and pull you off the bed. Don't mess with me. I dated a cop."

His fingers paused in mid-clack and he looked up again, considering her.

She raised her chin and considered him right back. He had hazel-colored eyes, although, at the moment they were half-hidden behind glasses with serious brown frames. What was it about glasses that when you saw a guy wearing them, you always assumed he was smart? Glasses didn't mean you were smart. They only meant you couldn't see.

"Do you have multiple personalities or something?" he asked.

"What?"

"Well, one day you're in here being Harriet the Spy, the next you're Suzie Sunshine who wants to write about happy clams and now you're Debbie Dominatrix, promising to get forceful and yank me out of bed and throw me on the floor. So which are you?"

"One thing I can tell you I'm not, and that's rude. You, on the other hand, are consistent. Always rude."

She used that as her parting shot and left him to type away on his laptop about killing people. If only he wasn't staying all summer. Henry Gilbert was like ants at a picnic, ready to swarm anything sweet and ruin it.

Well, she wasn't going to let him ruin her day. She finished up, then showered and changed and, after dropping Sabrina off at her driver's ed class for Jenna, who had a lunch date, she made her way to the local pet supply shop.

Rian LaShell, the owner of Sandy Claws, was appropriately feline, sleek with taupe-colored hair and charcoal eyeliner that accented the exotic catlike tilt of her eyes. She was wearing white capris and a dark, clingy top and she cocked a questioning eyebrow as Celeste entered the store.

"Can I help you?"

"I found a dog," Celeste explained.

"Ah," Rian said and nodded. "You look familiar. Have you been in here before?"

"I'm Jenna Jones's sister."

"I think I saw you on the Driftwood Inn float at the Seaside with Santa festival," Rian said, her smile more impish than sympathetic.

"That would be me," Celeste said. "The woman freezing her mermaid tail off."

"Some ideas work better than others," Rian murmured. Then, all business, she said, "So the dog you found, boy or girl?"

"Boy."

Rian picked up a shopping basket from the pile near the door and handed it to Celeste. "Did he have a collar?"

"Not even a flea collar," said Celeste, and Rian led them over to the collars.

"Talk to the vet about your options, but meanwhile, this will work." She selected one of the higher-priced flea collars from the display and dropped it in the basket. An equally expensive dog collar went in next, followed by a leash. "You'll need that when you take him to the park."

But not when they were on the beach, Celeste vowed. Dogs needed to be able to run free to chase waves.

Next came a rawhide bone. "Good for their teeth," Rian explained.

A squeaky toy was needed for keeping dogs entertained—a much better option than chewing up socks. Celeste also bought a brush so she and Nemo could do some serious grooming. As for the dog dish, that was too cute with all those little black paw prints all over it. Nemo deserved something cute.

Celeste needed to develop stronger powers of resistance, she decided later as Rian rang up her purchases. She'd already spent an arm and half a leg, and she hadn't even gotten him chipped, caught up on shots or purchased a dog license yet. This new relationship could wind up being very costly.

She considered the high price she'd paid in the end for her last human relationship and decided Nemo the dog was a much better emotional investment.

* * *

Jenna was surprised when she and Brody walked into Sandy's restaurant for lunch and found Tyrella and Nora seated at the table, waiting for them. Not that she didn't enjoy eating lunch with her two best beach buddies, but when Brody invited her to lunch he usually planned on lunch for two.

"Hey, ladies," he said, pulling out a chair for Jenna.

So this was planned. Jenna looked questioningly at him. "Is it someone's birthday and I don't know about it?"

"No, we just thought it would be fun to get together," Nora answered airily.

Yeah, because they never saw each other. Only every Friday evening in her aunt's living room and once a month at the Chamber of Commerce meetings. Not to mention church and any time Sabrina had a hankering for ice cream. It was an easy practice drive with a reward at the end—a win-win for mother and daughter.

"Something's going on," Jenna said suspiciously. She caught a conspiratorial smile flashing between Brody and Nora. Yep, something was definitely going on. "Okay, you guys, give."

"Let's order a drink," Brody said as Annie Albright approached them. "Annie, you're looking especially lovely today," he greeted, making her blush. "Can you bring me an iced tea?"

"Sure," Annie said. To Jenna, "Lemonade?"

She needed to branch out. She was becoming predictable. "Make it a raspberry one." Walking on the wild side.

Annie nodded and disappeared.

"The shrimp louie looks really good," Tyrella said.

"Never mind the shrimp louie. What's going on?" Jenna demanded.

"Not much," Brody said. "Just meeting to catch up on the local gossip."

Which meant there *was* local gossip. "Who's embezzling?" Jenna kidded.

"Me," Nora said with a grin. "I robbed my cash drawer again. I swear, I wish Elizabeth and K.J. had never opened that craft store in town. It's dangerous."

"I won't turn you in," Jenna promised. She, herself, was fast getting addicted to the MacDowell sisters' shop. "What else is going on?"

"Rick Rogers is calling it quits this fall," Tyrella said casually. "His wife is tired of never seeing him and she wants to travel."

"So Position Three on the city council will be open," Brody added just as casually.

"Have you thought about running?" Jenna asked him. "Everybody in town likes you." Including her.

"Right now between my business and the chamber, I've got my hands full."

"What about one of you?" Jenna asked the other two.

"Bill would hate it," Nora said. "We're too busy with the business and the family."

"And I'm too busy with the hardware store and church," put in Tyrella, and they all looked at Jenna.

"I'm a little busy, too, guys. I've got my massage business and the Driftwood and Sabrina and Aunt Edie."

"Yeah, but you're young and you've got energy," Nora argued.

"Not that much energy. I'm sure someone else will run."

Nora's mouth turned down at the corners. "Someone's already talking about it. Susan Frank."

"Susan?" The walking rain cloud. "She has no vision."

"She has no anything," Nora said. "But she'll get elected if nobody opposes her."

Which was, of course, where Jenna came in. She held up a hand in protest. "Oh, no. I've never held public office."

"You've got a kid. I bet you've been on a few school committees over the years," Nora said.

"And you know how to run a business," added Tyrella.

"And look what you've accomplished with the Driftwood," Brody said. "Plus, you have vision. No one else thought of having a winter festival."

"Which was an abysmal failure," Jenna reminded them.

"No, which turned out to be great for all of us," Tyrella corrected her. "You could do a lot for this town."

"Yes, remember your idea about building a convention center? If you were on the council, you could propose that," Nora said.

They made it sound so easy. But... "I've got too much on my plate. I'm sure someone will step forward."

"You'd better pray it's someone other than Susan," Nora told her.

Annie arrived with Jenna's and Brody's drinks and took their lunch orders. Once she left they turned the conversation toward the upcoming Fourth of July celebrations, and Jenna breathed an inward sigh of relief. Bullet dodged.

Unless Susan did decide to run for Council Position Three. Ugh.

Even if she did, someone else would have to bring her down.

Shopping done, Celeste got busy with Nemo's bath. The day was balmy, promising a long, sunny summer, and perfect for giving a dog a bath. And getting drenched.

Which happened very quickly. Nemo wasn't all that excited about being bathed and Celeste was struggling to keep him in the giant aluminum tub of water when Seth Waters walked by with his paint supplies, ready to tackle another portion of Aunt Edie's house.

Of course, the dog had to jump out of the tub and gallop over to greet him.

"What's this?" he asked, stopping to help put Nemo back in the tub.

"This is the newest guest of the Driftwood Inn," Celeste informed him. "We're going to see if we can find his owners."

"Did you check to see if he's been chipped?"

"Took him to the vet this morning. No such luck."

"Then I'm betting you're the new owner."

"I can live with that," Celeste said. "He's better company than most of the men I've dated."

Seth gave a snort, wished her well and went on his way.

The man was a walking piece of art. And he seemed to fit with the Driftwood Inn. Was he a fit for her sister?

A little later as Celeste worked to get the tangles brushed out of the dog's fur, she couldn't help watching as Jenna paused to visit with him when she got back from lunch with Brody. There was definitely a connection.

Brody, on the other hand, had shown no desire to hang around and visit with Seth. Instead, he'd frowned and zoomed off in his sexy red convertible. There was also a connection there. Two smart, decent, sexy guys. How was her sister ever going to decide?

"Seth's making it easy. His attitude has cooled considerably," Jenna said later as the two of them sat on the front porch, nursing glasses of pop, Nemo sitting between them, looking doggy-dashing with his clean, brushed coat.

"The way he looks at you is not exactly frosty," Celeste pointed out. "Show up at his room in nothing but a towel and invite him to go skinny-dipping in the pool after it's closed for the night and see what happens."

Jenna shrugged. "If something's going to happen it'll happen. I don't have to be in a hurry."

"Yeah, you do. You're not getting any younger," Celeste teased.

Neither was she. Suddenly, that crack wasn't so funny. She needed to do something about her own non-love life.

Could she do something with Paul Welch? He was friendly and smart, and the fact that he was also hot enough to be on a book cover didn't hurt. Not that looks mattered, Celeste reminded herself. Gorgeous on the outside was useless if the inside was rotten.

Nothing rotten about Paul, though, she thought as she sat next to her sister in church on Sunday, half listening to his sermon. It was hard to concentrate on what he was saying when her mind kept wandering to happy future scenarios. The two of them walking down the beach, hand in hand, Nemo racing ahead. Going with Brody to look at houses. Paul down on one knee, holding open a ring box like a hero in some sappy, old movie.

She'd never met her father, but the way her mother always talked about him, he had to have been someone special—loving, kind, considerate. Oh, how she wanted that. Surely, now she was looking in the right place.

"What do you think?" Paul asked from the pulpit.

Think? She pulled her attention back to the sermon.

"When you see someone who looks…a little scruffy, a little scary, maybe. Do you think, 'That person isn't my kind of person' and move away as fast as you can? Or do you ask yourself, 'What would Jesus say to this person?' If you see someone driving a nice car or wearing expensive jewelry, do you automatically think rich and selfish? That rich person might give a lot of money to good causes and that scruffy person could be a man who lost his job and his family. Someone who seems cold and unfriendly might really be shy. We all tend to make judgments about people, but remember that while people look at the outside, God looks at the heart. Let's try to focus this week on seeing the best in other people."

Willing to see the best in people. Oh, yeah. How could you go wrong with a man like that?

The service ended and the congregation drifted out into the foyer for coffee and cookies. "You guys are gonna sign up to work the booth after the Fourth of July parade, aren't you?" Tyrella prompted them as they grabbed their coffee.

"Sure," Jenna said, answering for both of them.

"What do we have to do?" Celeste asked.

"Dish up strawberry shortcake. It's for a good cause."

Strawberry shortcake, yum! "Free samples?" Celeste asked.

"No," Jenna scolded. "If you let her have free samples, she'll eat up all the profits and nobody will be going to summer camp," she said to Tyrella.

"Don't worry," Tyrella said to Celeste. "Sign up to work when I'm there and I'll make sure you get some strawberry shortcake."

"All right. It's a deal," Celeste said.

"You shouldn't indulge her," Jenna said to Tyrella.

"We have to keep our volunteers happy."

"Which is more than someone I know does," Celeste put in. "My sister's sticking me on a float again and what am I getting out of it?"

"Fame," Jenna retorted.

"At least you won't freeze this time," Tyrella consoled Celeste.

"No, this time she's threatening to put a white wig on me and make me look like Martha Washington."

"It *is* the Fourth of July," Jenna said. "And besides, Aunt Edie has a costume readymade."

Tyrella's mouth quirked up. "I wonder if it smells like mothballs."

Mothballs? "What?" Celeste demanded.

"Inside joke. Don't worry," Jenna said, linking arms as they made their way to the sign-up table. "Nobody will be able to smell you way up there. And Sabrina and her girlfriends and Aunt Edie will be with you."

"What will they smell like?" Celeste asked, still hung up on the whole mothball thing.

Jenna ignored her, leaning over the sheet of paper with rows of available time slots. So far only a few had been filled in.

Hyacinth was in charge of the table. She managed a weak smile for the sisters.

Oh, wait, what was this? All of a sudden a genuine smile? Celeste turned to see who rated such a sunny welcome. Of course. Pastor Paul.

"How are the sign-ups coming?" he asked.

"We're working on them," said Hyacinth, beaming at him.

"You just got two more victims," Celeste informed him. "Jenna, because she's noble. Me, because Tyrella promised me free strawberry shortcake."

He chuckled. "I like your honesty."

Not everyone did. Celeste was aware of Hyacinth's frowning at her.

Paul drew Celeste a little distance away. "What do you say to dinner tomorrow night?"

Oh, yes. "I say sure."

He beamed. "Great. Can I pick you up around six?"

"You can."

"See you then," he said.

He gave her a parting smile that made her heart jump like a fish on the line, and moved off to talk to other members of his congregation.

"Did he just ask you out?" Jenna asked as Celeste turned back to the table.

"He did."

Jenna smiled approvingly. "Smart man."

Hyacinth, on the other hand, looked anything but approving.

Smart man? Hyacinth thought. *More like stupid, taken-in-by-a-pretty-face man.* What was Paul thinking? Had he paid no attention to his own sermon?

A new person stepped up to the table to volunteer for the food booth on the Fourth. Hyacinth forced herself to smile. This was wrong. Really, really wrong.

Paul wasn't looking at Celeste Jones's heart. He was being…a man, only looking on the outside.

Yes, outside, Celeste Jones was all pretty and bubbly. But Hyacinth knew the type. She'd encountered it often enough when she was a teen. The outside appearance was like a candy wrapper, enticing and promising delicious things. Inside was a selfish woman who would break a man's heart, a woman who only wanted a good time. Once the good time ended, she'd be gone.

Hyacinth watched as the sisters moved through the post-service crowd, Celeste making her way toward the door with a smile and a laugh. She didn't have to ask what Paul saw in the woman. She knew. A pretty face, a great body, a flirty smile. Men, even the spiritual ones, the ones who should know better, were all alike. So easily deceived. Like Samson with Delilah.

The Bible taught that you should pray for each other. She intended to pray for Celeste. She was going to pray that the woman went far, far away. Celeste was obviously looking for love, and Hyacinth hoped she found it—someplace nowhere near Moonlight Harbor.

Chapter Seven

After lunch Celeste cleaned the rooms the guests had checked out of, and visited the others to make beds and clean bathrooms. Henry Gilbert's was the last one on her to-do list. Then she was free for the rest of the day. She wasn't looking forward to encountering him and making good on her threat to roll him out of his bed, so she was relieved to see the Do Not Disturb sign on his door.

Okay, *do not disturb* meant *do not disturb*. He could just stay in his room collecting dust on his glasses and writing his heinous story. And using dirty towels.

She did find herself wondering how that story was coming along. What made a person decide to write about serial killers anyway? It was so…creepy. So was he. She was glad to wheel her cleaning supply cart past his room. She stuck a load of sheets in the washer in the laundry room, then went to fetch Nemo for a beach walk.

Sabrina was with her dad for the weekend, and Aunt Edie was taking a nap. But Jenna was ready for a break, so the two sisters set off down the beach, Nemo loping ahead of them.

"No response from Facebook and no calls from the posters I put up," Jenna reported. "I have a feeling he's yours."

"I have a feeling you're right," said Celeste. "But that's fine with me. At last," she joked, "a man who'll be loyal."

"You have more than one option down here when it comes to that. By the way, Victor will be at The Drunken Sailor tonight."

"I am not falling for another cop."

"That isn't even logical," Jenna argued. "You got one loser. You know they're not all like that. In fact, who wouldn't want a cop? They're noble and self-sacrificing and sexy, and they all have handcuffs."

"Okay, you go out with him."

"He's not interested in me."

"You have enough men interested in you anyway," Celeste teased.

"You're not doing so bad yourself. When are you and Paul going out?"

"Tomorrow night. We're doing dinner."

"Well, there's one man you won't have to worry about cheating on you. Paul's probably as noble as they come."

Celeste picked up a stick and tossed it for Nemo, who went racing after it. "I've got to admit that kind of bothers me."

"What?"

The dog came back with the stick, but when Celeste went to take it, he dodged her. "Good grief, nobody's even taught you how to play fetch?" she lamented. She and Nemo got into a tug of war over the stick and she gave up, letting him have it. Of course he promptly dropped it and stood there, wagging his tail. "You don't know what you want," she informed him. But then, neither did she.

"Come on, urp it out," Jenna prompted as Celeste threw the stick again.

"I'm not exactly pastor girlfriend material. He's all…and I'm…"

"You're what?" Jenna looked genuinely perplexed.

"I'm not exactly Miss Snow White."

Jenna's eyes widened. "You mean just because you've been with other men? Come on, by this age nobody expects you to be a virgin."

"How do I know Paul doesn't? At any rate, he's going to want a woman who's got her life together."

"Yours is," Jenna said, ever the loyal sister. "You just haven't picked good men in the past."

"That's called not having your life together."

"Trust me. Paul's not the kind of man to hold people's pasts against them. And if the worst you've ever done is love someone too much, I don't think you're in bad shape."

Celeste sighed. "I hope you're right. I'm definitely interested, although, really, I can't even imagine what we have in common."

"That's why you're going out to dinner, to find out."

They caught sight of people approaching from the

other direction—an older woman, a woman somewhere around Jenna's age and two little girls, both racing along the beach. Nemo had spotted them, too, and bounded off to meet the strangers.

"Susan Frank! What's she doing away from her shop?" Jenna mused. "You'd better call him back. If he jumps on her, we'll never hear the end of it."

"Nemo!" Celeste called. "Come here, boy!"

Nemo had selective hearing. He charged forward, anxious to make new friends.

"Nemo!" Celeste injected more authority into her voice. Of course the dog wasn't listening. She ran after him, hoping he wouldn't jump on anyone.

Too late for that. By the time Celeste got to them, he'd jumped on one of the little girls, pushing her down and making her yelp. And then cry. Oh, great.

"Nemo, bad dog," Celeste said, grabbing his collar and pulling him off.

"Is this your dog?" Susan asked Jenna, who'd come up behind Celeste.

"No. He's a stray," Jenna sad. "He followed my sister home and we're trying to find out who he belongs to."

"He's got a collar," pointed out the woman with Susan. There was enough of a resemblance between her and Susan to know that this was her daughter.

"I bought that for him," Celeste said.

"So you're in charge of him?" Susan demanded.

"I guess so."

Nemo was straining to get to the kids. Tail wagging, he let out an eager bark.

The little girl he'd knocked down wanted nothing to do with him and was crying and hiding behind her mother. The other child reached out to pet him, but her grandmother took her arm and pulled her away.

"Don't touch him," Susan cautioned. "He might bite."

"Oh, honestly," Jenna said in disgust. "He's more likely to lick them to death."

"He's really friendly," Celeste insisted. "Are you okay, sweetie?" she asked the crying child.

"Of course she's not okay," Susan snapped. "That mongrel scared her to death."

"Sorry," Celeste muttered.

"Come on, girls," said the other woman. "Let's go back. We need to start home anyway."

"If you're going to keep that dog, you need to get a leash," Susan informed Celeste. They turned to leave, and Nemo broke free and began to trot alongside them. "Go on, get out of here," Susan yelled, shooing him away.

Nemo still didn't understand the whole shooing-away thing. He barked and wagged his tail, bowing in an effort to get Susan to play with him.

"Nemo, no!" Celeste grabbed the dog's collar again. "Now, stay with us," she commanded, turning him around.

"Yeah," Jenna added as they walked away. "You don't want to hang out with Susan Frank."

Celeste picked up another stick and threw it, distracting the dog. "Does that woman ever smile?"

"It's rare. Maybe if her business did better, she'd have something to smile about."

"Courtney oughta buy her out."

"I think if Susan would ever sell, she would. She doesn't show any signs of leaving, though. She'll be here forever, just like sand fleas."

"Oh, well, at least Aunt Edie isn't shopping there anymore."

"Thank God for that," Jenna said. "Now the only places I have to see Susan are at chamber meetings and church."

"People like that give church a bad name," Celeste said.

Jenna shrugged. "You know the saying—if you find the perfect church and join it, it won't be perfect anymore. We all have flaws."

Which made Celeste think of Pastor Paul. What were *his* flaws? And how accepting was he of other peoples'? She hoped he practiced what he preached.

He didn't seem to have any flaws, she thought the next evening as they settled at a table in Sandy's restaurant. It wasn't as impressive as The Porthole, which offered more expensive food and great views of the ocean, but oh, well. He was probably on a budget.

A man on a budget wasn't a problem for Celeste. Her family had never had a lot of money when she was growing up. But her mom and grandparents and Aunt Edie and Uncle Ralph had all made sure that she and Jenna had a happy childhood. Other than a weakness for purses, she still wasn't a big spender and was content to go dancing with girlfriends or curl up on the couch on a rainy night with a good book or a movie or play around with a craft project. She didn't need fancy trappings to be happy.

"I hope you like seafood," he said as they opened their menus.

"Absolutely. How can you come to the beach and not like seafood?"

He smiled at her. "Are you normally this easy to please?"

"I like to think so. Are you normally this nice?"

"I like to think so."

Yes, she could get used to Paul Welch.

Their waitress appeared. "Can I start you off with a drink?"

A drink. Priests drank. What about Protestant pastors? A glass of wine sounded really good to Celeste. If she ordered one, would he think she was a lush? But if she couldn't be herself and order a drink…

"Would you like some wine?" he offered.

"You drink?"

"Not very often," he admitted.

"Oh." Okay, that was awkward. "Lemonade," Celeste told the waitress.

"Make that two," said Paul. "Would you have preferred a glass of wine?" he asked as their waitress left.

She sighed. "I don't think this is going to work."

"What?"

"Lemonade."

"Is the fact that I'm not a big drinker a deal-breaker?"

"Well," she said, considering.

"I like a beer once in a while, but for the most part

I avoid alcohol. I have an uncle who's an alcoholic and watching all the chaos that came with that was enough to keep me away from booze. Anyway," he added with a shrug, "I try not to do things that might offend a member of my congregation. And I wouldn't want someone to start drinking because he saw me doing it and then end up with a problem."

Very noble but… "You must not have much fun," Celeste said. Not that she was a big drinker, but who didn't like a mojito or a glass of good wine now and then? This was definitely not going to work.

"I don't know. I think I manage to have plenty of fun."

"Doing what?" she challenged.

"I like to hike, play a game of pick-up basketball once in a while, go to baseball games, mountain bike, watch a good mystery on TV. I even eat chocolate."

"At least that's something I wouldn't have to give up if I started hanging out with you."

"I wouldn't want you to give up anything," he said. "Life's for living, Celeste."

"So if I wanted a glass of wine?"

"Jesus's first miracle was turning water into wine."

Even so, people at her mom's church didn't drink it, not even at communion. For that they used grape juice. "You really are not a normal pastor," she said, shaking her head at him.

"I didn't know there was such a thing."

"Pastor," called a voice.

Celeste turned to see Susan Frank approaching,

along with Hyacinth and another woman she'd seen at church. Oh, joy.

He raised a hand in greeting. "Hi, ladies. How are you doing?"

"Fine," Susan answered for all of them. "Did you find that dog's owner yet?" she asked Celeste, her tone of voice making it sound more like an interrogation than a question.

"No. I'm going to adopt him."

"Then I hope you take him to obedience school," Susan said, her mouth turning down at the corners.

She wasn't the only one not looking all that cheery. Hyacinth didn't seem very happy to see Celeste, and neither did the other woman.

"You ladies enjoy your dinner," Paul said. It was done with a smile, but it was a dismissal all the same, and the women had no choice but to move on.

"I guess you can't go anywhere without running into someone from church," Celeste said, and she wasn't sure how she felt about people always checking them out—it could feel like living in a fish bowl. Or like being examined for cooties, which was a little how she felt at the moment.

"I don't mind," he said. "I like people."

"Me, too." There was something they had in common, and a very important something. Celeste liked to have friends over; she liked to party. Her sister used to joke that Celeste had never met a person she didn't like.

The women had taken a table not far from them, and she was aware of all three looking speculatively in her direction. One in particular wasn't looking too friendly. Maybe Jenna was wrong about Celeste never having met a person she didn't like, because she wasn't so sure she liked Hyacinth.

She knew why Hyacinth didn't like her. Competition.

It wasn't the first time another woman had given Celeste the stare of doom. She had good friends who would always be there for her, no matter what, but she'd also experienced the animosity of insecure women who viewed her as a threat. She was enough of a people-pleaser to want everyone to like her, but there was no way this woman ever would.

Hyacinth could shoot death stares at her until her eyes burned up, Celeste decided, but if she wanted to spend time with Pastor Paul she darn well would. So there. *You had your chance to snag him, little flower, and you failed. You snooze, you lose.*

And as she and Paul talked, getting to know each other, she decided he was worth hanging on to. She didn't feel that undercurrent of danger and excitement she'd felt when she was with Emerson, but she'd seen where that led. Paul had principles, and she was sure whomever he ended up with, he'd be loyal to until the day he died. Now, that was a turn-on.

They chatted easily through the rest of dinner. He regaled her with stories of church programs that didn't go according to plan, including a New Year's Eve service where he'd had the congregation write down their worries and then burn them in a metal urn.

"Great symbolism," she said.

"Yeah, it sounded great, but in reality we about choked to death. The smoke was so thick we set off the fire alarm and had to hold the rest of the service out in the foyer," he said, shaking his head. "At least the party before was a success. We rang in the New Year on Eastern time so all the kids could stay up, dropped balloons from a net in the ceiling. It was great."

"You *are* a fun pastor," she told him.

"Life can be hard. It's important not to let that overshadow what's good."

It was all Celeste could do not to say, "Wow." Instead, she said, "I like that saying. I think I'll tweet it."

"Go for it," he said with a smile. Then he sobered. "It looks like you're not doing badly yourself. Jenna tells me you're a really good teacher. You're obviously also a good sister, down here helping out at the inn."

So her sister had been bragging about her. Celeste couldn't help smiling. Still, once Paul got to know her better… "I'm not perfect."

"What a coincidence," he said with a grin. "Me, neither."

Although he sure seemed close. He took her home and walked her up the steps of Aunt Edie's house to the front door. "Can we do this again?"

"Definitely," she said, giving him her most charming smile. Now he'd kiss her.

He nodded. "Okay. I'll call you." And with that, he turned and ran lightly down the stairs.

No kiss? She stood on the porch for a minute, trying to take that in. What man didn't want to kiss a woman good-night?

Pastor Paul, obviously. So he didn't kiss on the first date. She could respect that. It was actually rather sweet. Finally, a man who didn't want to get in her pants before they'd gotten to know each other. She opened the door with a smile.

But by the time she'd gotten inside the house, the smile was fading. What on earth was she doing? Paul wasn't the kind of man who went out with a woman simply for a good time. Any relationship he got into, he'd be getting into with an eye to making it permanent.

It was what she'd been wanting, of course. But what if things did turn serious? People had certain expectations when it came to pastors' wives. A pastor's wife had to walk the talk. She had to be noble and selfless and...

Oh, boy. What was she thinking anyway?

That she wanted to be noble and selfless. She liked being back at church, and she wanted to get her life right, settle down and have a family.

But could she do that with Paul? Could she handle it? At some point they needed to have a talk about her not-so-perfect past.

Sabrina came home from spending the weekend with her father all smiles. Jenna concluded that, as with every visit to the ex, Grandma and Grandpa, who picked up a lot of the slack for Damien, had taken her somewhere fabulous.

It turned out, however, that her high spirits had nothing to do with her grandparents. "Daddy and Aurora broke up," she announced as she and Jenna worked in the kitchen, assembling goodies for a Sunday-night movie binge.

Come to think of it, Jenna hadn't seen any sign of the "other woman" when she'd driven Sabrina up to Seattle on Friday to her former in-laws' house, where Damien had his struggling artist suite in the basement. Aurora was often the one opening the door to let Sabrina in before Jenna drove off. Jenna had finally reached the point where seeing the two cheaters together didn't bother her. They could have each other.

The one thing that did bother her was the two cheaters having each other, plus a portion of her earnings. It would be nice if Damien would hurry up and become the Dale Chihuly of junk sculpture. Then she could come after him for support.

Still, even though she didn't care anymore that he'd replaced her with a new soul mate, she couldn't help feeling a little twinge of satisfaction on hearing her daughter's news. The cheater got left. Poetic justice.

Jenna opted for mature and didn't gloat or so much as crack a smile. It was hard not to.

"I'm glad she's gone," Sabrina said.

Celeste walked into the kitchen, bearing a grocery bag with root beer and ice cream for floats. "Who's gone?"

"Aurora." Sabrina said the name as if it was synonymous with feces. Actually, it kind of was.

"You're kidding." Celeste pulled glasses down from the cupboard. "What happened?"

Yes, do tell. Jenna hadn't been about to ask—that maturity thing again—but she was glad her sister had.

"Daddy said she didn't understand him."

Who did?

Jenna set a dish of chocolate-covered raisins on the tray, along with smoked almonds and Skittles. She was aware of her daughter's speculative gaze as she put the popcorn in the microwave. Oh, boy.

"I think Daddy misses you."

Yep, she'd been afraid that was coming. Of course, like many children of divorce, Sabrina wanted her parents back together.

"Oh, I doubt it," Jenna said, trying not to let her dread of the looming conversation bleed into her voice.

"Did he say that?" Celeste asked, incredulous.

"Not exactly. But I know he does."

Her daughter, the teen psychic. "Honey, Daddy didn't want to be with me anymore." Okay, that still bruised her pride a little. "Sometimes two people think they're right for each other and later find out they were wrong."

"But you *loved* each other," Sabrina protested.

Jenna and Celeste exchanged glances. How did you explain to a girl madly in love with her boyfriend that love was a flower that sometimes died in spite of how much you watered it?

"We did," Jenna said. "Sometimes things happen."

"Yeah, like Aurora," Sabrina said bitterly.

"Daddy made a mistake." *Daddy was a shit*.

"He could change."

If he had a lobotomy. Jenna reached over and hugged her daughter. "Honey, your dad and I—we've both moved on." A tear leaked out Sabrina's eye and Jenna wiped it away. "I know that's hard for you. I'm sorry you're getting shuffled back and forth all the time. I'm sorry we're not together as a family anymore. But too much has happened between your father and me for us to be able to build the kind of relationship we once had. The good news is that we both love you and we always will."

"If you stopped loving each other…" Sabrina bit her cheek and looked at the floor.

She didn't have to finish her sentence. Jenna knew what she was thinking. "That doesn't mean we'll ever stop loving you. Parent love is totally different from grown-up love. It stays forever." She kissed the top of Sabrina's head. "So let's keep on the way we are and think of the times you get to see Daddy and your grandparents as vacations."

"I wish I'd had vacations that many times when I was your age," Celeste said. She handed a carton of ice cream to Sabrina. "Open."

Sabrina obliged and almost managed a smile as Jenna put an arm around her.

"You have so many people who love you, it's ridiculous," Celeste told her. "They just happen to live all over the place."

Sabrina nodded to indicate the message had been received. Reluctantly, but received all the same.

The microwave dinged. "Okay," Celeste said. "Popcorn time!"

Jenna handed the tray of goodies to her daughter. "Why don't you take these out to Aunt Edie. She's probably thinking we all died in here."

Sabrina nodded and left the room, and Jenna let out a breath.

"You handled that well," Celeste said as she returned to making their root beer floats.

"I tried." Jenna got the popcorn from the microwave and put it in a bowl.

"What do you think really happened with Damien and Aurora?"

"Who knows? Maybe she was hoping for something more serious than what they had."

"Or maybe she got tired of living in his parents' basement," said Celeste with a grin. "She probably found somebody else with money. Of his own," she added with a sneer.

"I wish *he'd* find somebody with money," Jenna said.

Celeste rolled her eyes. "He did. You."

"Someone with more money than me. Wouldn't that be nice? He could have his own personal patron of the arts."

Sabrina came back into the kitchen to fetch the floats, and that ended the conversation. Which was fine with Jenna. Damien had taken enough from her. Was still taking from her. She wasn't about to let him steal her good mood.

"Come on, gang," she said and picked up the popcorn. "Let's go watch a movie."

They all settled on the couch and Celeste started *Ocean's Eight*.

There was a time when Jenna would've sat stewing over her ex-husband's antics, unable to enjoy herself. That time was not now or ever again. She sprinkled a handful of chocolate-covered raisins on her popcorn and settled in to enjoy the movie.

Chapter Eight

"*Please, no,*" *she pleaded.*

As if begging would make a difference. As if he could stop what he'd started. She'd asked for this and now it had to play out. He looked at the knife, so sharp. Then he looked at her and said...

"Housekeeping."

Henry blinked. "What?"

"Housekeeping. I'm changing that bed today whether you want it or not." The door opened and in walked Clam Girl, clean sheets in her arms.

"I'm right in the middle of something here."

"Me, too," she said. "Now, come on. Move your something over to the desk while I change the sheets. It'll only take a minute, I promise."

Henry scowled at her. "I can't believe your timing."

"Did I save someone from being murdered?"

"No. The murder will happen," he said, relocating to the desk.

"That's so creepy," she muttered.

"It's fiction. It's not real."

"But just thinking about it." She shuddered as she yanked back the bedspread. "I don't know how you can sleep at night with all those gory images in your brain."

He slept just fine, thank you. She walked to the bed to pull off the top sheet and he caught a whiff of perfume. Who wore perfume to clean rooms? She leaned over and yanked off the sheet from the other side of the bed. The woman had a cute ass.

Never mind her ass, he told himself and turned back to his laptop.

Now she was humming.

"Do you have to do that?" he snapped.

She straightened and looked at him, brows knit. "Do what?"

"Hum."

"Oh. Sorry." She stopped humming and got back to work.

But a moment later she was doing it again, and it sounded a lot like "Happy" by Pharrell Williams. Good grief. How was he supposed to write something serious and suspenseful when the maid was in his room, humming pop songs?

"Look, what's your name?"

"Celeste," she said. "Celeste Jones. My sister owns this place."

So her sister had felt sorry for her and given her a job?

"Celeste. I'm trying to write here. I can't write with you making noise."

"Oh. I was doing it again?"

"Yes."

"Sorry. I get a song stuck in my head." She yanked off the last sheet and rolled it up.

He slammed the laptop shut. "I can't work with you in here humming."

"I'll only be another minute," she promised.

"Never mind. Take as long as you want," he said irritably. He picked up his laptop and marched out of the room. He'd go sit on a log somewhere and work.

Even after he found a log to lean against and had nothing but the gentle whoosh of the waves to listen to he couldn't recapture the mood. He wanted to write about his killer slashing and bashing, and all he could think of was Celeste Jones, the maid with the perky, round posterior. And those spectacular lips. What would it feel like to kiss her?

It would feel great, of course. But the Henrys of this world weren't meant to have the Celestes. Celestes went for sports pros, actors, rich dudes.

Hey, he wasn't poor. So what if he didn't drive a Lexus or own a house in some exclusive Seattle neighborhood like the Highlands. Someday, once he made it big, he could. If he wanted to. Not that he wanted to. The world was full of greedy bastards and pretentious shits. He didn't need to join that club. His Jeep was paid off, he had stock in his former company, which was doing just fine, and he had money in the bank. And he was perfectly happy with his houseboat.

But no dog. No woman.

He shut the laptop and sat watching the waves.

A gull soared past, coasting on the wind. The sky was cerulean, the air clean. The sound of the waves washed over him like a caress. He wished he wasn't sitting here on the beach alone. Did Celeste Jones have a man in her life?

Who cared? *You're not her type. Remember?* And she wasn't his.

Not that he was sure what his type was anymore. When he was younger, someone who was simply breathing was his type. Then he started watching reruns of *Friends* and decided he wanted a girl like Jennifer Aniston, someone cute and bubbly. Yes, he liked bubbly, outgoing women, women who had the kind of social confidence he lacked. Nikki had been outgoing and bubbly.

He frowned. No, that wasn't the kind of woman he wanted now.

Yes, it was. He wanted someone who was easy to be with, someone who could pull him out of himself once in a while.

Not that he didn't love that interior world of imagination, but he also wanted to live in the real world, have sex with a real woman, have someone to talk to besides himself.

"You're deep, Henry," his mom used to tell him. "You need a woman who can appreciate that."

"Your mother doesn't know what she's talking about," his father would say. "You need to be out there living. Find a woman who'll make you go and do things."

"You just need to get laid," said his big brother, Joe.

Nikki had come along, and she'd been that woman, the one who'd made him feel he was really living, the one who had appeared to appreciate his so-called depth. And as far as getting laid went, that had been stellar. She'd ticked off all the boxes. She was The One. Or so he'd thought. Turned out he'd thought wrong.

As far as his mom was concerned, Nikki's departure proved her point. He needed a woman who understood his mind, his artist's soul.

Wasn't there a woman out there somewhere who could understand the call of a good book and be a Jennifer Aniston, too? Someone who appreciated both imaginary and real worlds, who could put a foot in both?

Celeste the maid, the happy clam girl.

No. Even though he wasn't sure anymore what his type of woman was, one thing he did know. She wasn't it. She was Nikki the Second. Nikki the First had been enough.

He forced his attention back to his work in progress, his masterpiece of mayhem. The real plus about being a writer was that you could control everything that happened in the story. You were the master of that universe. Unlike real life, where nothing went according to plan.

This was his killer's first big scene, what he'd been leading up to for so many pages. He was going to relish every moment, every word, every syllable.

An hour later Henry had one paragraph to show for his efforts and he wasn't convinced that it was very good. The muse, unfaithful bitch that she was, had deserted him.

There was one cure for that—barbecue potato chips. He'd have to make a run to the store.

"Can I drive?" Sabrina asked as they walked to Celeste's car. Sabrina had her afternoon driver's ed class and Celeste was chauffeuring her. "I have to get in more driving time," she added.

Jenna hadn't officially given Celeste a thumbs-up for riding with Sabrina, but really, what did it matter? What could happen between Moonlight Harbor and the Safety First Driving School in Quinault anyway?

"Okay," she said and handed over the keys.

They eased out of the parking lot and Sabrina turned onto Harbor Boulevard like a pro. As they tooled down the road, Celeste didn't even have to remind her to keep to the speed limit.

She was doing well with her driving; so well Celeste felt she could take her eyes off the road long enough to find some music on the radio.

"Oh, here, we can use Spotify," Sabrina said, reaching for her purse, which was between them. "We can get it from my phone."

"I'll do it," Celeste said. "You just watch—" the deer strolling onto Harbor Boulevard. Aaack! "Deer!" she cried and jerked the steering wheel to the left, into the other lane going in the same direction.

"Car!" Sabrina shrieked.

Too late. They bounced off the car in that lane like bumper cars in Nora's funplex. This wasn't fun, though. The deer bounded away, unhurt, and a shaken Sabrina pulled off to the side of the road, the other car right behind them.

"Oh, no, it's Mrs. Frank," Sabrina said, panicked.

Why wasn't Susan Frank at her shop anyway? Oh, yeah. It was Monday. Since weekends were prime tourist business days, a lot of the shop owners closed on Mondays. Still, shouldn't Susan have been in her subpar clothing shop, making up for the time she'd spent playing hooky on the beach?

"Mom's gonna kill me," Sabrina whimpered.

"Let me handle it," Celeste said.

The poor kid was white as a seagull's feather and looking as if their car had been surrounded by cannibals. She nodded, eager to have someone take control.

Celeste got out of the car to find Susan Frank already out of hers and marching toward them. Out of the corner of her eye she caught sight of a Jeep across the grassy median, pulling over on the side of the road. Good. If Susan took a swing at her, she'd have a witness.

Except... Wait a minute. She'd seen that Jeep in the Driftwood Inn parking lot, right in front of room twelve. Great. The terror of room twelve would have some rude remark about this the next time she saw him.

Now was not the time to think about him. Celeste stepped around her car and headed Susan off, asking, "Are you okay?"

"Hardly! I think I've got whiplash. And it's a wonder I didn't have a heart attack with you two coming over in my lane like that."

"We had to swerve to avoid the deer," Celeste said.

"You should have hit the deer. You could have killed me!"

Susan Frank was like a zombie, impossible to kill. She had her cell phone in hand and began punching in numbers. "I'm calling the police."

For just scraping her car? "We could settle this by exchanging insurance information," Celeste said. Oh, boy. Jenna was going to blow a gasket. Celeste had a sudden vision of the famous painting *The Scream*. That would be her sister. At least they hadn't been in Jenna's car.

"I think not," Susan said firmly. "You should always call the police when there's been an accident." Someone had answered her call and she went into Drama Queen mode. "This is Susan Frank. Someone ran into me on Harbor Boulevard and we need a policeman here right away. Injured?" She shot a glance in Celeste's direction and had the grace to look sheepish. "I probably am," she said, lowering her voice as she walked back to her own car. "And my car has a terrible scratch on it."

Yes, a real police emergency. Celeste returned to her niece to find her crying.

"I almost hit a deer," Sabrina wailed.

"It's okay. You didn't."

"And now Mrs. Frank is mad and Mom's gonna be *really* mad."

"It was an accident," Celeste told her. "Accidents

happen, even to people who've been driving a long time." That didn't stop Sabrina from crying.

Celeste wanted to cry herself.

Here came the patrol car, and behind the wheel sat Victor King.

Okay, they were line dancing buddies now. Maybe he'd let her and Sabrina off with a warning, tell Susan not to make such a big deal of this.

He was hardly out of his patrol car before Susan had him cornered and was launching into her tirade. "They drove right into my lane and sideswiped me," she said, pointing to Celeste as she hurried over. "You need to give that child a ticket."

"She's only learning," Celeste argued. "And we swerved to avoid a deer."

"She swerved into me!"

"Ladies, I need you both to get back in your vehicles," Victor said sternly.

So much for being friendly line dance buddies.

"Are you going to give them a ticket?" Susan demanded.

"Ma'am, I need you in your vehicle. Now," he said in a tone of voice that made Celeste blink.

Susan's head snapped back as if he'd slapped her. "Well," she huffed. But she obeyed.

So did Celeste. Where was the friendly, blushing Victor King who'd helped her with her dance steps the night before?

At the driver's window, talking to Sabrina. "I need to see your driving permit," he said to her, and now his voice was gentler.

Still sobbing, she handed it over. "Are you going to take it away?"

"No. But I'm afraid I'm going to have to ticket you for inattention to driving. You were clearly at fault."

"What about the deer?" Celeste protested.

He shook his head. "She hit a car."

"But I'm the one who grabbed the steering wheel," Celeste said.

Victor King pinched the bridge of his nose.

Celeste pressed her point. "It really wasn't her fault. Isn't this sort of thing up to the discretion of the officer?"

Susan Frank was back. "I hope you're going to give this girl a ticket, Officer."

"Ma'am, for the last time, I need you to get in your vehicle."

"We have to exchange insurance information," Susan insisted. "And yours deserves to go up," she said to Celeste, which made Sabrina cry all the harder.

"Ma'am, I'm not going to tell you again," Victor said.

His stern tone of voice was enough to scare Sabrina. Susan merely sniffed. "Fine," she said and marched back to her car. "But don't you be letting them off just because they're cute or I'll be talking with the police chief," she called over her shoulder.

The muscles in Victor's jaw twitched. Sabrina continued to sob, and Celeste wished she'd never allowed her behind the wheel. To cap off the whole experience, here came Henry Gilbert.

He introduced himself to Victor, then said, "I saw the accident. Do you need a witness?"

"What did you see?" Victor asked.

"I saw a deer jump in front of the Prius. They swerved and scraped the side of the Toyota, which was close to being over the line."

Victor nodded and made notes. "Can I get your name and address, sir?"

Sir Galahad, thought Celeste gratefully.

Victor took Henry's contact information, thanked him and sent him on his way. Then he walked along the road, measuring and making more notes. After he'd gathered the information he needed, he handed Sabrina an official warning, had a talk with Susan, which left her red-faced and huffing, made sure both drivers had each other's insurance information and then he, too, went on his way.

And Celeste drove Sabrina to her driver's education class. She was almost as shaken as her niece and wound up going ten miles under the speed limit.

It wasn't easy telling Jenna about what had happened when Celeste returned to the Driftwood.

Jenna's nervous tic surfaced and her right eye began to blink. "How could she not see a deer? I keep telling her she has to pay attention."

"I didn't see it, either, until it was almost too late."

"Neither of you saw it? They're pretty hard to miss."

"I know."

"Why didn't you see it?" Jenna persisted.

Oh, boy. Moment of truth. "I was trying to find some music on the radio."

"You were supposed to be watching the road," Jenna scolded.

"I know. She was doing so well, I..." Screwed up. She decided it would be best not to mention that Sabrina had been about to dig in her purse for her phone. *She'd* been the responsible adult. She should've been more vigilant. If she hadn't started to turn on the radio and channel surf they'd have been fine.

Jenna groaned. "And of all the people to hit." She ploughed a hand through her blondish hair. She needed to get to the hair colorist. Celeste would offer to take her once she'd calmed down. Penance for what had happened.

"I'm sorry," Celeste said. "I really am. But at least we didn't hit the deer."

"That's something." Jenna didn't sound very mollified.

"And Henry Gilbert being a witness helped. The deer really did jump out at us. And Susan was darned close to the line. She didn't give us much wiggle room."

Jenna sighed. "Well, I'm glad you're all okay."

"It won't happen again," Celeste promised.

"You got that right. I'll drive with her from now on."

That was fine with Celeste. She left the office, shaken. She watched over entire classrooms of children and was always on the lookout for potential problems. Why hadn't she taken that same vigilant attitude when she'd been with her niece? Victor King should have given *her* a ticket.

She went from the office to room twelve and knocked on the door.

A moment later Henry Gilbert opened it. He was wearing the same jeans and T-shirt he'd been wearing when he stopped at the scene of the accident and was holding a bag of potato chips.

"I wanted to thank you," Celeste said. "For stopping."

He shrugged. "No big deal."

"You saved my niece from getting a ticket. She's just learning how to drive."

"And you say what I write is scary," he joked.

She couldn't help smiling. "She'll be the most careful driver on the planet now." Come to think of it, so would Celeste. "Anyway, it was nice of you."

"It's usually good to have an unbiased witness."

"I can tell you, Mrs. Frank sure wasn't unbiased."

"The other driver?"

Celeste nodded.

"She looked pretty pissed. You two probably gave her a few new gray hairs."

"Oh, well, she'll color them," Celeste said, and he grinned at that. He had a cute smile. He looked like an oversize Boy Scout, standing there with his bag of potato chips.

And she wanted to reward him with a badge. Or a kiss.

Okay, this felt awkward. It felt like being actors in a play and having the director change their roles but forget to give them their new lines. She backed away. "I'll let you get to work."

For a minute he seemed about to say something, but then he adjusted his glasses, nodded and shut the door.

Celeste hurried across the parking lot to the house, to Aunt Edie and Jolly Roger and Nemo the dog, and the world of normal. She hoped next time she went to clean room twelve Henry Gilbert wouldn't be in it. She'd just seen a softer side of him, and how could you not like a man who liked potato chips? But he also spent hours thinking up ways to kill people. Even though she knew it was only fiction, and fiction that a lot of people read, she still found the idea of a man wanting to write about that stuff a turnoff.

A vision of Henry the first time she'd seen him wearing nothing but a towel sprang to mind. Hmm. Not a complete turnoff. What was she doing, feeling even the tiniest bit attracted to a man who seemed to live in the minds of serial killers?

What was Paul doing right now? She climbed into her scratched Prius and drove to the church.

His secretary called him out of his office and he looked happy to see her. "This is a nice surprise."

"Thought maybe you'd like to get a latte."

"Sure," he said with a smile.

Ten minutes later they sat at a table in Beans and Books with large coffee drinks, surrounded by shelves offering a variety of books, coffee mugs and other coffee-lover paraphernalia, along with bags of coffee beans and grounds. She told him about Sabrina's close encounter with Susan Frank and then happened to mention Henry Gilbert's stopping to save the day.

"He's a writer," she added.

"Oh? What's he write?"

"Novels about serial killers."

Paul nodded, taking that in, and took a sip of his drink.

"What do you think it says about someone who writes that kind of stuff?" she asked.

Paul shrugged. "That he's got a wild imagination."

"Don't you think it's…kind of sick?"

"Not necessarily. I assume the killer gets caught in the end?"

"I hope so."

"I'm betting he does. When you write certain books, you're making a deal with the reader. If it's a romance, the reader expects you to deliver a happy ending. You write a mystery or a crime novel, the reader expects the bad guy to get caught and justice to be done. So if he's providing justice in the end and giving someone a good scare along the way…" Paul let the sentence hang unfinished.

"I guess I'm being a Suzy Sunshine," she confessed. "I just don't like stories where people are being murdered and dismembered." Happily for her, Emerson hadn't talked about any of the bad things he encountered as a cop, and while he'd enjoyed movies where cars went flying through the air and spies kicked and karate-chopped each other, they'd never watched the kind of creepy stuff that Henry was writing. And she certainly hadn't read books of that type.

"What do you like to read?" Paul asked.

"Give me a good romance novel with a happy ending any day," she said.

"If the bad guy gets caught, that'll be a happy ending. Hopefully, he'll meet a fitting creepy end."

"I'll never read the book to find out," Celeste said with a shudder.

How *was* that book of Henry's going to end?

Chapter Nine

Room number twelve was vacant the next day when Celeste arrived to clean it. She found herself wondering where Henry had gone. Just curious, of course. Not that she really cared. Maybe he was making a potato chip run.

She went into his room after cleaning for the nice middle-aged couple next door. As usual, they'd left a dollar on one of the pillows, about the average tip for guests of the Driftwood Inn.

If they tipped at all. So far Henry Gilbert hadn't given her a single tip. Of course, he was staying at the Driftwood for a long time and that could add up. Not that she was cleaning rooms for tips, anyway, or even for pay. She simply wanted to help her sister. Still, it irked her when people were cheap. Henry Gilbert was cheap. And rude.

But he'd also taken the time to stop and act as a witness at a car accident.

Lo and behold, what was this? A five-dollar bill lying on a pillow. And a note on the motel stationery. *So, change the bed already.*

She found herself smiling. *Well, Henry, maybe you're not such a bad guy after all.*

She encountered the middle-aged couple returning from a walk on the beach as she wheeled her supply cart from his room. "Our room always smells so fresh and clean when you're done," the woman complimented her after she'd thanked them for the tip. "And I love the decor. Those seashell lamps are adorable."

"I'll be sure to tell my sister," Celeste said. "She decorated all the rooms."

"Ours is certainly charming."

Jenna had done a great job of making the whole place charming. Yes, it lacked many of the modern amenities people had come to expect, such as king-size beds and fancy showers. No hot tubs, not even out at the pool. Although Jenna was budgeting for one. But the pool had been improved and now had that mermaid painted on the bottom. The rooms were kitschy yet delightful, and the beach was a quick walk through the dune grass. The price was right, too. Business had picked up with the nice weather, and Jenna was solidly booked through the Fourth of July.

She was doing as good a job of putting her life together again as she was bringing the Driftwood Inn back to its former glory days. Watching over Aunt Edie, working hard to guide and protect her daughter, making new friends—she was carving out a truly satisfying life for herself in Moonlight Harbor. Celeste suspected it wouldn't be long before her sister had her love life sorted out, as well. Oh, to be able to follow in those footsteps.

"How are you settling in?" Patricia Whiteside asked Celeste as the Friday-night gang settled in Aunt Edie's living room with wine, some of Aunt Edie's cookies and an appetizer concoction of brie cheese, shrimp and puff pastry that Annie had brought. The evening's entertainment was creating seashell-trimmed picture frames, and seashells were scattered everywhere, two glue guns plugged in and lying on plates on Aunt Edie's coffee table.

"Great," Celeste said, setting a tiny sea snail shell in place. "I love it here."

Aunt Edie smiled. "The beach, fresh air, wonderful friends—how could you not?"

"One thing I'm betting," Tyrella said as she helped herself to more of Annie's appetizer, "she's doing a good job of unsettling some of the men, including our pastor."

"A pastor?" Courtney Moore sounded almost shocked. "What are you doing with a pastor?"

Jenna jumped in. "Why shouldn't she be with a pastor?"

"Okay, maybe that didn't come out right. Somehow I can't see you baking brownies for the church potluck," Courtney said to Celeste.

"You haven't seen our pastor," Tyrella said.

"I've seen him around," Courtney told her. "And I'm not saying he's not cute. Or nice. But you like to party, Celeste. Is he going to do that with you?"

"There are all kinds of ways to party," Tyrella argued.

"And I bet he won't cheat on me," Celeste muttered.

"May the odds be ever in your favor," Courtney sneered, quoting from the popular *Hunger Games* movies.

"They are with Paul," Tyrella said.

"So you're going for a sure thing," Courtney deduced.

Again, Jenna jumped in. "There's nothing wrong with that."

True, especially considering how unsure Celeste's love life had been. So what if she was hedging her bets? "I'm ready for someone steady and dependable," she said, rubbing Nemo's ears. He let out a doggy sigh of happiness and slumped against her.

"You have him," Courtney said, pointing to the dog. "I say, when it comes to men, the last thing you want is boring."

Celeste remembered the scene in Emerson's apartment. That had been anything *but* boring.

"Paul's not boring," Jenna insisted.

"At least give some other guys a chance," Courtney said. "But not Victor," she hurried to add, making the other women chuckle. It was no secret that Courtney would be more than willing to take a trip around the world in Victor's squad car.

Nora held a small clamshell up to a corner of her picture frame to see if it would fit. "You'll end up with whoever you're supposed to. And whether you want exciting or not, we all wind up the same way, eating dinner in front of the TV and going to bed at ten."

"Yeah, sign me up for that," Courtney said in disgust.

"No matter what you sign up for, that's what you eventually get," Nora told her. "Which is why I have an ice cream parlor. A woman needs to get her kicks somewhere."

"Do you really think that's how we all end up?" Celeste asked her sister later, when it was just the two of them camped out on the living room couch.

"I hope not. I hope there's more to love than that."

Their conversation was interrupted by a text coming from Celeste's phone. Emerson.

Been thinking about you a lot. I miss you.

"Is he serious?" Jenna demanded, reading over her shoulder. "Tell him to go shoot himself in the foot."

I made a mistake.

"Is that what they call it now?" Jenna scoffed.

He'd made a mistake. He wanted her back. Like a genie popping out of a bottle, here came memories of all those good times they'd had, dancing over to Celeste, promising her a golden future with a reformed man.

"Men like that don't stop making mistakes," Jenna said. "What do you want to bet he's between women?"

Her sister was right, of course. And how dare he come slinking back after the way he'd disrespected her?

Celeste's fingers flew over her phone keyboard.

Are you serious?

As a heart attack. We were good together. You know you miss me.

"Talk about arrogant," said Jenna.

I'd have to be brain dead to take you back, Celeste texted.

"Good for you," her sister approved.

Come on, babe. I get that you're pissed, but give me another chance.

For a second, only a second, Celeste hesitated. Until her sister added, "To break your heart again."

And he would. Of course, he would.

Maybe in a parallel universe, Celeste texted.

She told him to go pistol-whip himself, then she turned off her phone and tossed it aside, proud of herself for not buying the fool's gold he was selling.

Oh, yes, she was definitely moving in the right direction. But, "You know, for a minute there, I almost believed him."

Jenna nodded. "You get that rosy picture in your mind of what could be, if only. But *if only* isn't real life."

Celeste sighed and took a thoughtful sip of her wine. "Do you think the women in our family are cursed?"

Jenna blinked. "What?"

"I mean, look at us. Dad died when we were really little and Mom never remarried. Aunt Edie's first husband was a wife-beater."

"Yeah, but Uncle Ralph made up for that. And Dad was a great guy according to Mom."

"We lost him all the same. And then there's Damien."

Jenna frowned at her empty glass.

"Sorry." What was she doing, bringing up Jenna's ratty ex?

Except that Jenna had already alluded to him with her talk of *if onlys*. Sometimes Celeste wondered if, in spite of how much her sister professed to despise him, she was still a little in love with him. Was that the real reason she was finding it so hard to move on with someone new? Love and hate, as the saying went, were two sides of the same coin.

"I don't believe in curses," Jenna said firmly. "Sometimes we just don't think when we're man-shopping. I sure didn't."

"If Damien asked you now," Celeste began.

Jenna held up a hand. "Don't go there. Even if I

completely lost my mind, I'd still instinctively know to run away as fast as I could. That man was a waste of love." She set her glass aside. "Come on. Let's go to bed."

Celeste had done her share of wasting, letting herself get swept away, seeing what she wanted to rather than what was real.

She was so done with that. Courtney could joke all she wanted about church potlucks, but church potlucks trumped a broken heart any day. And Paul Welch was not a heartbreaker. If a woman was looking for a man, she probably couldn't find a better one than him.

But, she wondered as she followed her sister up the stairs, if he really knew her, would he say the same thing about her?

"Why would you think that?" Jenna scolded when she brought up her concern.

Celeste shrugged. "I don't know." Yes, she did.

"Please don't tell me you're circling back to the men in your past."

Celeste plopped on the bed. "Trying not to." But it wasn't easy. Those past relationships were Ghosts of Stupid Past, delighting in haunting her. Where had all those "this is it" false starts gotten her? Then there'd been Emerson, the grand finale of stupid. He hadn't been a start at all. He'd only been using her.

"Hey, you fell in love. You gave your all. Granted, you gave it up to some real losers, but that's on them."

Celeste frowned at her painted toenails. "Is it?" She was the fool who kept rushing into relationships.

"Of course it is. It's not like you went out and hooked up with a different man every weekend."

"It's not like I sat home on a Saturday night with my legs crossed, either."

Jenna shook her head. "You're worrying for nothing. I mean, what do you think Paul's going to do? Grill you about your past? Who does that?"

"Someone who doesn't want an STD."

"You don't have one, so that's not an issue. Everyone has a past."

True. And if he were any other man, she wouldn't be worried about measuring up. "But he's a minister."

"And they understand human nature."

"They may understand it, but that doesn't mean they want to get serious with…" She stumbled to a stop.

"With a sweet, fun woman who has a big heart?"

Celeste had to smile at that. Her sister would always be her best advocate. But still… "Ministers have high standards. I don't know if I can measure up."

"You measure up fine," Jenna insisted. "Talk to him. He might surprise you."

How the heck did one bring that up? *By the way, if you're worried about having fun on our wedding night, don't. I've got it covered. How do you feel about sex? How do you feel about women who've had sex with more than one man? A bunch of them, even?*

She had to find out. There was no sense seeing Paul Welch anymore if her past sex life was going to be a deal-breaker.

When he called the next morning and invited her

to lunch on Monday, she suggested he join her for a picnic on the beach instead. A beach picnic would be the perfect setting for a cozy conversation about her past. Yeah, right.

Well, things would work out one way or another. Meanwhile, she had rooms to clean.

Happily, there was no answer when she knocked on the door of room twelve and called, "Room service." Good. Talking to Henry Gilbert always seemed to unsettle her.

She finished her cleaning and then, because it was such a fabulously hot day, she put on her bikini and hit the beach, Nemo happily tagging along. She caught sight of a man sitting a little farther down the shore. He was on a blanket, leaning against a log, and he had a laptop. Only one man would sit at the beach with a laptop. Henry Gilbert.

Nemo looked ready to trot on over and say hi, but Celeste grabbed his collar. "Not him. He's busy killing people. Anyway, we're here to swim, not schmooze." She dropped her towel and diet pop and ran for the water. "Come on, boy, surf's up."

He'd been following her for three weeks. Patient. You had to be patient. When you were, the universe rewarded you. And he was having his reward now as his hands tightened around her throat. Too bad he had to take precautions and wear surgical gloves. How he'd have loved to feel his flesh directly on hers. But this was close enough. He was close enough, close enough to see the terror in her eyes. He'd watched her in the club, tossing her hair, flirting, laughing. She wouldn't be laughing anymore.

Laughter from down the beach pulled Henry out of the scene. He looked up to see Celeste, the maid from the motel, splashing in the surf with a dog bounding beside her. She was wearing a bikini that showed off a perfect body, curved in all the right places.

"Never mind her," Henry muttered and turned his attention back to the screen.

But now, instead of picturing murder and mayhem, all he could picture was the happy clam girl in her bikini, the sunlight making her hair sparkle. He sneaked another look in her direction. She'd dived into the water and was swimming. The woman was nuts. That water was arctic.

He watched as her arms cut through the waves. She was fit, that was for sure. Thoughts of murder and mayhem melted away, to be replaced with thoughts of the happy clam girl. What would she look like out of that bikini?

Why would he care? He wasn't interested.

Except in a way he was. She wasn't a total airhead. She wanted to write.

Yeah, so did half the world. So what?

She wasn't swimming anymore. She seemed to be stalled out. Didn't the woman know better than to stay in such cold water that long? What was she thinking?

Her top. She had to get her top. The stupid thing had come off—with a little help from Nemo, who'd mistaken one of the strings tying it on for... Who knew what he'd mistaken it for? He'd sure found it fun to tug on, and between his tugging and her swimming she'd swum right out of the thing. Every time Celeste grabbed for it, it dodged her. Now it was floating away, just out of reach.

"Fetch, Nemo," she said through gritted teeth.

Fetch was not in Nemo's vocabulary. He trotted out of the water and stood shaking himself dry. Woman's best friend.

Her leg was cramping. She knew better than to stay in the water this long, even in summer. If she wasn't careful, the undertow was going to catch her and she'd really be toast.

She was already in the toaster. She tried to kick, but her cramped leg wouldn't cooperate. She thrashed her arms. They felt like lead. This wasn't good. She tried again. Her whole body refused to cooperate. A wave washed over her, making her choke. *Surface, Celeste. Surface!*

She willed her head back above water but she couldn't get enough momentum to make it to shore. Like her bikini top, it was becoming increasingly out of reach.

Oh, Lord. She was dying. It was true. Your life did flash before your eyes. She could see Jenna and her playing dolls; and saw herself climbing into bed with Mom during a thunderstorm. There she was, throwing a hopscotch game so her sister could win. The images kept coming, faster and faster. Jenna socking a mean girl who'd picked on Celeste. There were the two of them, Jenna starting middle school, she still in grade school, at Aunt Edie's house in the bedroom with all the dolls, making silly faces by the light of a flashlight. She saw little Tommy Driscoll from last year's first-grade class, holding out an apple. "You're so pretty, Miss Jones." And here came her first boyfriend from middle school. "Wanna go to the movies?" This was followed by, "Wanna make out?" The string of bad boyfriends flashed past, ending with Emerson, who seemed to be calling her.

No, not Emerson. Someone else. "What were you thinking?" demanded a voice she knew all too well.

A pair of sinewy arms hooked around her shoulders and started towing her out of the water. "No!" she screeched. Sort of screeched. She could hardly talk.

"You're gonna drown, you idiot," snapped her rescuer.

She tried to point to her runaway top, but couldn't raise her arm. She tried to say something but her teeth were clacking together too hard.

Henry Gilbert finally got them to where the water was waist-high and hauled her up. His eyes bugged out at the sight of her bare chest. "Shit."

Her teeth were chattering so hard her jaw ached. "My t-top," she stammered.

"Forget your top. It's gone. Some kid will find it washed up on the beach."

She looked in the direction of where the top had been. Where would it wash up? Who would find it? Who knew?

One thing she knew for sure. People were coming.

Two women, walking along the beach. One of them she'd seen with Hyacinth. *Oh, no!* Celeste let out a squeak and turned toward Henry.

He'd seen the people, too, and pulled her against him, all the while trying to struggle out of his wet T-shirt. "Shit. Shit, shit, shit."

Chapter Ten

They stayed in the water, Henry holding Celeste against him and fumbling with his T-shirt as the women walked past. One was goggling like a kid at the zoo. The other, Hyacinth's friend, was frowning and pretending not to see. This would be all over the church by Sunday morning. Ugh.

He finally got his T-shirt off and shoved it at her. "Here. Put this on."

Better late than never. Yeah, right. What idiot came up with that saying?

She was barely into the thing before he was towing her along the beach, Nemo trotting alongside. He stopped where she'd left her towel and wrapped her in it, then dragged her down to where his blanket was. He set his laptop and glasses on the log and wrapped her in the blanket, as well, then began rubbing her arms.

Pins and needles. She whimpered.

"Your dog makes a lousy rescue dog," Henry said.

"I recently adopted him," she explained through chattering teeth. "I think he's undereducated."

"He's not the only one. I wondered what you were doing staying in the water so long. That was stupid."

"Well, what was I supposed to do?" she stammered. It was hard to talk when your teeth were clattering against each other.

"Pretend you're on a nude beach somewhere and get out of the water."

"You're right. I was just…so embarrassed."

"Better to be embarrassed than wind up as crab food," he said, his voice gentler.

"Celeste Sushi," she joked. "Jones Jojo's."

That pulled a grunt and a half smile out of him. "You normally this funny?"

"No. Sometimes I'm funnier." Although there was nothing funny about nearly drowning.

"Glad to see you've managed to keep your sense of humor."

"I guess that'll be the last thing to go." To go. She'd been almost gone. The shivers intensified.

"You'd better get into a hot shower," he said. "You live around here, Celeste Sushi?"

"In the house next door with my sister and great-aunt and niece."

"Tell 'em to give you a stiff drink," Henry advised.

She stood up and handed him back his soaked blanket. "I will. In fact, I owe you a drink. Well, a lot more than that, considering that you saved my life."

"You don't owe me anything. Other than undying gratitude."

"You're kind of funny yourself."

"Nah, I'm just a smart-mouth."

"Whatever you are, I'm glad you happened to be here."

"Your lucky day," he said, and this time he gave her a full-on smile. "Now, either go get that shower or enter a wet T-shirt contest."

"I'll take the shower," she said. Then, with a final thank-you, she hurried down the beach toward home, shivering all the way.

"Did you have a nice swim?" Aunt Edie asked when Celeste walked in, wrapped in her towel, hair dripping.

She decided not to tell her aunt about her beach adventure. Aunt Edie would go into worry mode, imagining all the terrible consequences that never came to be. "Very refreshing," she said.

Pete was in the kitchen, too, pouring himself a cup of coffee. "You look like a drowned rat."

"You look like a drowned rat," echoed Jolly Roger from his kitchen perch. He cocked his birdy head as if trying to assess whether or not Celeste was telling the truth. "Very refreshing," he added. "Very refreshing."

Yes, very.

She told Jenna about her close call later when they were making a run to the store for groceries.

"Oh, my gosh, you could have died!" Jenna said, her eyes big.

"My bikini did."

"Better your bikini than you."

"All I can say is I'm glad Henry Gilbert was there."

"The crazed murderer?" Jenna teased.

"Okay, I was wrong about that."

"Good thing he's not as sick and warped as you thought. If he was, he'd have let you drown," Jenna said and got out of the car. "Think he's interested in you?" she asked as they walked into the store.

"What? No." Celeste frowned and grabbed a shopping cart. He might have saved her but that didn't mean he wanted to start something with her—or vice versa. The idea that he was a writer fascinated her, even though she didn't care for the type of story he wrote. But she knew better than to indulge her fascination. After all, Emerson's being a cop had been equally fascinating, and look where that fascination had gotten her.

"Just wondering."

Celeste caught the hint of worry in her sister's voice. "You don't have to go wondering in that direction. I've already found the perfect man. Remember?"

Jenna nodded. "Yeah, it's hard to get more perfect than Paul. I'd love to see something work out between you two."

Celeste didn't see that happening if Hyacinth's friend told him what she saw.

"They were playing in the water and she was topless," Bethany Stone finished and took another drink of the lemonade Hyacinth had poured her.

"Are you sure?" Hyacinth asked. What woman in her right mind would run around topless with some man when she had Paul Welch drooling after her?

Their friend Treeva Mills served herself more of

the shrimp salad Hyacinth had made them for dinner. "It's true. I saw them, too."

Bethany pointed her fork at Hyacinth. "Somebody should warn Paul."

As in her? Hyacinth pulled back. "I can't."

"Why not? He needs to know," Bethany argued.

"For sure," agreed Treeva. "Anyway, this is your chance. Once he learns what Celeste Jones is like, he'll come to his senses and see what's right under his nose. And that would be you."

There was nothing Hyacinth would've liked better than for Paul to finally see her, *really* see her, but tattling on some other woman didn't sit well and she said as much.

"All's fair in love and war," Bethany said. "That's what my mom always used to say."

Hyacinth shook her head. "I don't know."

"Do you want the man or don't you?" Treeva pushed.

"Of course I want him. But I want him to fall in love with me. I don't want to manipulate him."

"How do you think I got Brian?" Bethany asked.

"He fell in love with you," said Hyacinth.

"After I took out the competition."

"How'd you do that?"

Bethany shrugged. "Told him what a lush she was."

"Was she?"

"Close enough," Bethany said evasively.

"I don't know," Hyacinth said again. She didn't want to see Paul with Celeste Jones, but she didn't want to spread gossip, either. "I wasn't even at the beach."

"We were."

"Then you tell him."

"Maybe we will," Bethany said. "Someone needs to watch out for our pastor."

"He has God for that," Hyacinth retorted.

"God helps those who help themselves," Bethany told her. "Something you should keep in mind. Honestly, Hy, it's a good thing you've got us on your side."

Was it?

Chapter Eleven

Even if her mean-girl radar hadn't been operating on high, Celeste would've known she was being talked about when she glanced across the church foyer to where Hyacinth's two friends stood talking to Paul after church. The looks they kept sneaking in her direction were a dead giveaway. *See? There she is, a modern-day Hester, waiting for her scarlet letter.*

Paul frowned and turned toward her, and she quickly switched her attention to Tyrella, who was describing the interesting man she'd met online. "Except he's clear over in Tacoma. I doubt he'll want to drive all the way to the beach for a date," she concluded.

"If I was a man I would," said Jenna. "You're worth twice the drive."

"Aww, sweet," Tyrella said, smiling at her.

"No, true."

"We'll see. One thing I know for sure," Tyrella said. "I'm not goin' anywhere. Any man who wants me better want to live at the beach. You gotta keep your standards high," she told Celeste with a wink.

Not something Celeste had done much of.

And what about Paul? He probably had high standards. What was he going to make of this latest tale? Maybe she'd cancel their beach picnic.

Oh, no. He was coming their way. Celeste's heart rate picked up.

"Are you coming to fish for compliments on your sermon?" Tyrella teased him.

"No," he said with that beatific smile of his. "Just wanted to make sure we're still on for tomorrow, Celeste."

After what he must've heard? She blinked.

"Aunt Edie's already baking cookies for you," Jenna said, since Celeste was having trouble finding her voice.

She recovered enough to joke, "Aw, now I can't pretend I made them."

"The truth always comes out," he said, still smiling.

She hoped he wasn't simply talking about cookies.

There are other men in Moonlight Harbor besides Paul Welch, she reminded herself that night as she and Jenna twirled and stomped with the other line dancers. Victor King was still happy to help her with her dance steps and would probably be more than happy to handcuff her to his bed. A new man had joined the dancers, and he was also single. His name was Jonas Greer and he was a firefighter.

"There's another possibility," Courtney said to her. "If things don't work out with the pastor. In that case, I'd take the fireman if I were you. He's hot. No pun intended."

But Celeste didn't want a fireman. Or a cop. She wanted Paul. If things worked out with him her love life—her whole life—would finally be on track.

Henry Gilbert wasn't in his room when she came to clean it on Monday. She returned his laundered T-shirt and left the six-pack of beer she'd bought him on his bed, along with a note thanking him for saving her from becoming crab food.

She was leaving the room with a stack of dirty towels when he walked up, holding a take-out box from Sandy's. He was wearing jeans, flip-flops and a T-shirt that warned *Be Nice to Me or I'll Kill You in My Book*. And he had on his glasses, which accented that Stephen King look.

She frowned and pointed to the T-shirt. "Did you have that specially made?"

"My brother gave it to me. He's my number-one fan," he added with a smirk. When she didn't respond, he prompted, "*Misery*? Stephen King?"

"Your father?"

He shook his head in disgust. "Never mind."

"Happy to. By the way, I left you something," she said. "A thank-you."

"Yeah?" He looked into the room, saw the six-pack on the bed and grinned. "I should save your life more often."

"Once was enough." She didn't want to come that close to meeting the Grim Reaper again for a long, long time. "I'm glad you did, though."

"Gotta keep you alive. Who else is going to make sure I have clean towels?"

She made a face. "Funny."

"That's what you said yesterday. Glad to meet a woman who appreciates a clever man."

"Who said I appreciated you?" she said with a sarcastic smile. "That would be a stretch."

He didn't smile in return. "Ha-ha."

"Oh, hit a sore spot, did I?"

"Nope. No sore spots here."

But there obviously were because the moment of friendly repartee was gone. Someone had underappreciated Henry Gilbert. "I was kidding," Celeste assured him. "Really."

"Yeah, yeah. Thanks for the beer," he said, then slipped into the room and shut the door.

"Sorry," she muttered.

Obviously, Henry Gilbert had a past. Well, who didn't? Welcome to the club.

She didn't have any more time to consider Henry Gilbert's past. She had her own to explain. She put away her cleaning supplies and hurried to the house to freshen up and get her picnic ready for Paul.

An hour later they sat on a blanket on the beach behind the house, with Paul attempting to keep Nemo from trampling him and gobbling his tuna sandwich and her trying to decide how to bring up the subject of her beach adventure with Henry.

She finally concluded that the best way to tackle the problem was to dive in. "I saw you talking to some of the women at church yesterday," she said.

"I talked to a lot of people."

She didn't let him sidestep the issue. "I'm not sure what they told you, but it wasn't the whole truth."

"I don't listen to gossip, Celeste."

"Don't you want to know what happened?"

"Do I need to?"

"You need to understand that I don't cheat on men I'm dating."

"I never thought you did."

Okay. Maybe she didn't have to share all the embarrassing details. But she had to share more about herself. "You should know, though. I've got a past."

"Most people do." He frowned at Nemo, who was clambering on him in an attempt to get to his sandwich, and moved him off. "Trying to eat here."

That made her smile. But only for a moment. "Look. I've slept with other men, had relationships that didn't work out." Several.

He blinked at that, gave up on his sandwich and let the dog wolf it down. "Why are you telling me this?"

"Because I suspect you're interested in me."

"Of course I am. Otherwise, I wouldn't be here with you."

"Well, then. You need to know. I have baggage."

"Like I said, most of us do."

"Yeah, but doesn't it bother you that…" The rest of her sentence fizzled and she fed the rest of her sandwich to Nemo, as well.

"Celeste, I didn't have the most stellar life before I became a pastor. I was a frat boy and I had my share of sexual encounters. I did some drugs when I was in high school, stole a neighbor's car and went joy-riding. The only thing that kept me out of juvie was that the neighbor and dad were friends and the guy didn't press charges."

"Whoa, you were busy."

"You going to hold it against me?"

"Of course not. That was a long time ago."

"Then why should I hold *your* past against you? When it comes to people, I'm more interested in what they're doing in the present and what they plan for the future. I connected with God when I was a senior in college and I'm glad I did. I want the rest of my life to have meaning. If that's the page you're on, then we're good."

Celeste suddenly felt as if something heavy had slid off her shoulders. Paul Welch was truly special. And inspiring. "You are fabulous," she said and leaned over and kissed him.

Nemo, wanting attention, too, jumped between them, spraying sand on their laps and what was left of the food and bringing back Paul's frown.

"Do you mind?" he said irritably, pushing the dog away.

"Sorry," Celeste said. "He's a little rambunctious."

"He needs to go to obedience school."

"I take it you don't like dogs," she said, grabbing Nemo by the collar and hauling him to her other side. This could be a problem.

"I like dogs, but not the out-of-control kind."

Hers certainly fit that description. He'd have to go to obedience school, no doubt about it.

Paul began brushing the sand off his pants. The frown hadn't left.

It looked as though she'd found his one flaw. Paul Welch was not an animal lover.

"Sorry about the sand," she said.

"We're at the beach. Sand happens. I just don't like it in my food."

"Or on your pants?"

"I'll admit I'm a neat freak."

And she tended to let dishes pile up in the sink and never dusted. Left her clothes lying around. But that was minor stuff. Neat and sloppy could find a way to compromise. The dog thing, though. Hmm.

"So really, you and dogs…?"

"I got bitten when I was a kid. It kind of turned me off the whole man's-best-friend idea. And they're messy."

Now she was the one frowning.

"But Nemo here could change my mind. If he doesn't make a habit of getting sand in my food. Anyway, I have a feeling you two come as a set, right?"

"We do."

"Then I think I'm going to learn to like your dog," he said.

At that moment Henry Gilbert jogged past, sloshing his way along the edge of the water. Nemo barked excitedly and rushed off to join him, kicking up more sand.

"Nemo, no!" Celeste called. "Come here, boy!"

Nemo's selective hearing had kicked in again. He

was far too busy tail-wagging and greeting Henry, who'd stopped to rub behind his ears.

"Be right back," she said to Paul and ran over to where Nemo and Henry were having their love fest.

"Nemo, come here," she commanded.

Tail still wagging, the dog turned to her, a doggy smile on his face, tongue lolling.

"He's a good boy," said Henry, his voice softening. "Goldens are the best." He nodded toward Paul, who was now standing up and shaking out the blanket. "Looks like you've got more than one good boy in tow. Boyfriend?"

"We might be headed that way." She hoped.

Henry frowned. "He looks like a priss."

Just because he was wearing nice shorts and a polo shirt as opposed the ratty T-shirt and torn cut-off jeans Henry was in? And didn't like sand in his food? Nobody did.

"Well, he's not," Celeste insisted. "He's a really good man. And noble."

Henry gave a snort. "What is he, some kind of philanthropist?"

"No. He's a pastor."

Henry grunted.

"You don't approve of pastors?"

"I didn't say that. Never would've taken you for the pastor type is all."

She frowned at him. "What type would you take me for?"

"I don't know," he said.

"Nothing comes to mind? You're not very creative

for a writer," she taunted, falling back into their pre-rescue rhythm.

"I save my creativity for killing people. Better get back to your pastor. He looks like he might be thinking bad things about you," Henry said as a parting shot, then took off down the beach.

Celeste grabbed Nemo's collar before he could run after Henry. "Yes, I know. You want to be friends. But we're not going to start anything with him. We've already started something with someone else."

They returned to Paul, and the rest of their picnic passed pleasantly. He was easy to talk to. Comfortable.

Comfortable was good. Celeste said as much to her sister later that evening as they sat sprawled in front of the TV. Who needed to be like a teenager anymore, crazy for the guy, wanting his hands all over you, hardly able to breathe when you saw him?

She thought of Sabrina, lingering at the front door with her boyfriend earlier in the evening, squeezing in as many kisses as she could before Jenna put an end to the fun. He would be leaving for college at the beginning of September and Sabrina was already agonizing over their upcoming separation.

Meanwhile Jenna watched them like a mother hawk and worried that they'd do something rash. Jenna was a born worrier. Celeste, on the other hand, understood how her niece felt. She'd felt the same about Emerson.

And about every man she'd dated, for that matter.

Her friend Vanita was right. She was, indeed, a pushover for a great body and a nice smile.

She was done being a pushover now. She was going to be smart.

"Except do I only want to be comfortable?" she mused.

"So Paul doesn't do it for you? Is that what you're saying?" Jenna asked.

"No, he does. I really like him. It's just that, well, it feels different than it did with Emerson."

"I'd think you'd be grateful for that," Jenna said.

Celeste let out a sigh. "Yeah. With Emerson it was all sex and adrenaline highs."

"You can't live your whole life like that. You'd die of exhaustion."

"But I'd die with a smile on my face," Celeste cracked, then couldn't help wondering, *Would a pastor's wife say something like that?* Of course, she decided. Pastors' wives had sex, too.

"I remember what it was like with Damien and me," Jenna said. "He was so cool, so sexy, so everything I wanted. But not what I needed. He turned out to be shallow and selfish. I wish when I was dating I'd thought about the long haul. It can't just be about attraction. You want someone who'll be there to listen when you've got a problem, someone who's willing to pull his share in a relationship. Someone who gets the concept of commitment."

That was Paul. He was smart. And good-looking. And yes, she was attracted to him.

But not the way she'd been to Emerson. "I just feel there should be more…sparks."

"Has he kissed you yet?"

"No," Celeste replied. "I kissed him."

"Well?" Jenna prompted.

"That doesn't count 'cause it was a quick thank-you kiss."

"Thank you for what?"

"For being so understanding." She sighed. "He is such a sweet man. But am I falling in love with him?"

"You want to see him again?"

"Absolutely."

"I'd take that as a sign that you are. Or at least falling in like, and that's a good beginning."

"I'm ready for a good beginning," Celeste said. "And a good ending."

Which was exactly what she'd get with Paul, so bring it on.

Chapter Twelve

It was late afternoon on the third of July, and Jenna had just taken a reservation when the office door opened and Lisa Whitaker made a grand entrance, arms extended. "We're here," she declared as her sister Karen walked in behind her.

The sisters had stayed at the Driftwood Inn over the holidays and shared many a storm adventure with Jenna, and she'd been looking forward to having them and their husbands back at the Driftwood as much as they'd been looking forward to coming. She hurried around the reception desk to give them both hugs.

"It's good to see you."

"It's good to be back," Karen said.

"When the sun is shining," her sister added with a wink as their husbands joined them in the lobby.

"Aunt Edie's been baking up a storm and has big plans for a beach fire on the night of the Fourth," Jenna told them all. "I hope you'll be there."

"We wouldn't miss it," said Lisa.

"I hear it's crazy down here on the Fourth," her husband put in.

"Nothing can rival the fireworks show you get on Moonlight Beach. Thousands of people all come to set off their fireworks. You have to see it to believe it."

"I hope you have your fire department on standby," said Karen's husband, Doug.

"Oh, yes," Jenna assured him.

"So what rooms are we in now?" Lisa asked. "I hope you were able to put Dean and me in the one Karen and I had last time."

"Absolutely. And Karen, you and Doug are right next door," Jenna said. "Let's get you checked in."

That didn't take long, and the four of them left, each with a peanut butter chocolate chip cookie in hand, Aunt Edie's offering for the day.

"It looks like the sisters are here," Courtney said when she showed up for her turn at the desk.

"Yep. We have two late check-ins, and then we're full for the Fourth."

"No vacancies. All right!" Courtney said and they bumped fists.

"Yep, it's going to be a fun time. Oh, and speaking of, Aunt Edie's planning a beach fire for tomorrow night. Hope you can come."

"Gee, let me check my social calendar," Courtney joked. "Yeah, I'm free. Who all's gonna be there?"

"The sisters, of course, and the Marshes. All the other usual suspects—Nora and her husband, Tyrella…"

"Any singletons coming?"

"Brody for sure," Jenna said.

Courtney rolled her eyes. "Well, he's taken. And Seth? I assume you've invited him?"

"Haven't seen him much lately, but yes, he's on the list."

"Alas, he's also a Jenna fan." She sighed. "If only the police and fire department weren't going to be busy."

"If you're wanting to see Victor or Jonas, I guess we can always set your hair on fire," Jenna teased.

"I may get desperate enough to do that at some point."

"Meanwhile, come party with us."

"You know I will."

With Courtney ably handling the evening shift, Jenna left the office, headed for the house. She saw Seth's truck in the parking lot and decided to detour past his room and invite him to come enjoy the fireworks with them the following night.

Fireworks on the Fourth? Seeing him answer the door in jeans and shirtless was enough to set off sparklers in her chest right then. She could hear the shower running in the bathroom and he had the musky smell of a man who'd been working outside all day.

"Hang on," he said and went to turn off the shower. Seth Waters had a gift for filling out a pair of jeans, she thought, watching him walk away.

"So what's up?" he asked once he returned.

Besides her libido? "A party on the beach. Aunt Edie wants us all to watch the fireworks together."

He nodded. "Who's coming?"

"The usual gang," she said evasively.

"Yeah? Who?"

She started naming names, not mentioning the one she knew would be a deal-breaker.

"How about the house peddler?"

"Well, he *is* one of our friends," she had to say.

"Sorry, I've got plans."

Seth Waters could be so irritating. Jenna tried another tack. "Aunt Edie will be disappointed."

"Just Aunt Edie?"

"You know I will be, too."

He leaned against the doorjamb.

A shirtless man leaning in a doorway—all those lovely muscles on display. Jenna's mouth went dry.

"You don't need me. You've got Green."

"Why are you always bringing him up?" she demanded.

"You can't tell me there's nothing between you two."

No, she couldn't. But she wanted there to be something between her and Seth, too, more than this animal magnetism dance they'd gotten so skilled at. Poor, confused her.

"You're together all the time."

"We have chamber business. And he wants me to run for city council."

Seth nodded, taking that in. "You're becoming a real mover and shaker. Green's a good match for you."

"Maybe he is," Jenna snapped.

"So you really don't need me there."

"Maybe I don't. A woman can only wait so long."

His easy expression faded. "I know about waiting, Jenna. I waited a long time to get out of prison. But I'm not..." He stopped and shook his head.

"Honestly, Seth, you make me crazy."

"Not half as crazy as I make myself sometimes. Answer me this. How do you become a winner?"

"By risking everything." *Even your heart.*

He shook his head. "By going with the sure thing. Enjoy the fireworks," he said, then, with a rueful smile, he slowly shut the door.

She should've pushed it open, rushed him, grabbed him by the ears and kissed him. But she didn't. What would be the point? Seth wasn't ready for commitment, at least not to her, no matter how many sparks flew back and forth between them.

"Fine," she muttered as she walked across the parking lot. "You aren't the only man in town who knows how to stir up a woman's hormones."

Halfway to the house, she met her sister and Nemo, who were about to take a beach walk. "You look like you're ready to murder somebody," Celeste said.

"I am. Seth Waters."

"Okay, spill. What's going on?"

"Nothing. And nothing ever will be. I'm not waiting for him to get his emotional act together any longer. It's Brody all the way."

"Brody's great."

From her sister's tone of voice, Jenna knew there was more. "But?"

"But are you sure?"

"Yes. I am officially no longer interested in that man."

"Then why are you so pissed that he's not coming to the beach fire?"

"Because he irritates me."

Celeste grinned. "Irritation. Definitely a sign of love."

Hmm. And how did that apply to her and the terror of room twelve? Celeste asked herself.

Henry Gilbert could, indeed, be irritating, but it wasn't the kind of irritation that turned into love like in books and movies, she decided. He was simply irritating.

Still, he had his good points. For one thing, he liked dogs. That was easy enough to see when she and Nemo met him on the beach. He'd been running and his ragged T-shirt was dotted with sweat. For a man who sat around writing all day, Henry Gilbert was certainly in shape.

"I'd better be careful," she said as Nemo flopped on his back for a belly rub. "My dog might leave me for you."

"Yeah, you'd better watch it. I might dognap him. He reminds me of my dog."

The Driftwood Inn was a pet-friendly establishment but there was no dog in room twelve. "Where is your dog?"

Henry frowned. "He crossed the rainbow bridge. My ex ran over him."

Celeste blinked. "Whoa. You not only write about creepy stuff, you live it."

"She didn't do it on purpose," he said. "She didn't see him."

"Poor dog." Celeste couldn't help asking, "Is that why she's your ex?"

"No. She's my ex because she got tired of waiting for me to become rich and famous."

"Real committed, huh?"

He shrugged and stood up. "Nobody wants to be with a starving writer."

"Unless he's going to be the next Stephen King."

He acknowledged that pearl of wisdom with a grunt. Nemo was dancing around him now and he gave the dog a playful shove.

"But only wanting you if you were going to be successful wouldn't make her much of a girlfriend," Celeste continued.

He shrugged. "I guess we're even. She didn't think I was much of a boyfriend. Anyway, my mistake for picking her. I got caught up with the surface stuff that didn't matter."

Celeste sighed. "Been there, done that."

"Is that why you're with the pastor now? Is he your sure bet?"

"Maybe."

"I guess being a pastor's wife beats being a maid."

Yes, Henry Gilbert was definitely irritating. "I told you. I'm down here helping my sister. I'm a teacher. I can afford to be with a starving writer." Now, why had she said that? That could be taken the wrong way. "If he wasn't warped," she added.

"Nobody calls Stephen King *warped*."

"Not to his face anyway."

Henry threw up his hands. "Genius is always misunderstood."

"Oh, so you're a genius."

"I wasn't talking about me. But hey, if I ever have even a tenth as many people reading my books as read his, I'll be happy."

"When's your book going to be finished?"

"End of summer. Kind of hate to leave when it's done. The beach is an inspiring place to write," Henry said. He picked up a stick and threw it into the water and Nemo dashed in after it.

"Then why not stay?"

"I might. If I make it big enough, maybe I'll buy a shack down here. I like this town."

"What have you seen of it besides the grocery store?" she challenged.

"I've seen the beach. That's all I need to see. Like I said, the beach inspires me. It's a good place for writers."

"It's a good place for everything." Even falling in love. With Paul, of course.

"Speaking of writing, have you started your book about the happy clam yet?" he asked.

"Not yet." Thinking about writing a children's book was so much easier than actually sitting down and writing one. "I'm waiting for inspiration."

He gave a snort "Good luck with that, especially if you're writing about clams."

It was a perfectly fine idea. "What have you got against clams, anyway?"

"There's no conflict. Every story needs conflict. Clams don't do anything but lie around."

"I'm sure I can find something for my clam to do."

"Put him in chowder," Henry said.

"That would be a sad ending."

"Not for the person eating the chowder."

"Thanks for the advice. I think I won't take it."

He shook his head at her. "You'll probably never get around to writing that book anyway."

"I will. Eventually. Maybe."

He cocked an eyebrow.

"Okay, what can I say? I'm easily distracted. I like to do crafts. I've got my family."

"All good stuff," he agreed. Nemo was back with the stick now, and Henry took it from him and threw it again, sending the dog charging off down the beach.

"And I've got a social life," Celeste continued. "Something you might try," she suggested. "There's more to do here than sit on the beach."

"Yeah? How do you know that's all I do?"

She didn't. "What *do* you do?"

"I hang out at that pub down the road sometimes. Shoot some pool."

"It's a start. You should watch the parade and do Fourth of July on the pier."

"Crowds aren't my thing."

"Oh, yeah, that's right. Writers are all introverts."

"How are you going to become a writer, then? You're obviously not an introvert."

"I intend to be the exception to the rule. Anyway, I want to write a children's book. Remember? We children's book authors are much more touchy-feely and fun than you brooding Heathcliff types."

"Hey, I can be fun."

"Yeah? Prove it. Get out there and mingle."

Nemo was back with the stick and Henry got busy playing tug of war with him. "I don't like mingling when I don't know anyone."

"You know me. My aunt's having a beach fire on the Fourth. A bunch of us are going to hang out and watch the fireworks. You do like fireworks, don't you?"

"Of course I like fireworks. I'm a guy," he said and threw the stick for Nemo again.

"Well, then, when it gets dark, come find us. We'll be on the beach behind our house. Look for the biggest bonfire and that'll be our party."

"Maybe I will," he said.

"You should. See you then," she said as if he'd committed himself. She called to Nemo, who'd abandoned the stick to sniff some seaweed, and they took off on their walk while Henry took off for his room. "There," she told the dog. "That shows how much Jenna knows. I have no interest in Henry Gilbert whatsoever because he no longer irritates me."

Hmm. He really didn't. She'd gone from suspecting him of being a murderer to inviting him to her family's beach party.

"What if he gets the wrong idea and thinks I'm interested?" she asked Nemo.

"Woof!" Nemo replied.

"Yeah, that was probably a stupid thing to do. But I can introduce him to Courtney if he hasn't already met her. They're both creative types. They might hit it off."

Except Courtney was crazy about Victor King, so it would be a waste of time to introduce them.

"Or am I just being like a dog with a bone?" she mused.

Nemo whined.

"Oh, sorry."

She was even sorrier when she remembered that Paul had invited her to another party to watch the fireworks. How could she have forgotten? She'd probably never make it to the bonfire.

But then Henry probably wouldn't, either. He'd avoided saying a definite yes to her invite for a reason. He'd pull a camp chair up outside his door and watch the show from the safety of the motel.

By the afternoon of the Fourth, she'd shoved all thoughts of Henry Gilbert out of her mind. Well, nearly. She had way too much going on to worry about whether or not he decided to be social. Her sister had her on the Driftwood Inn float yet again, along with Sabrina and her two girlfriends and Aunt Edie. The girls were in period costume gowns one of the moms had sewn and Aunt Edie had dressed like Martha Washington, which left Celeste stuck in breeches, a jacket and a ruffled shirt, playing George

Washington. It beat freezing to death in a mermaid costume, which was what had happened to her during the Seaside with Santa parade, but by the end of this one she was sweating and more than happy to lose the costume and get back into her shorts and top and flip-flops.

She'd barely changed before it was time to report to the church booth for strawberry shortcake duty. Tyrella, Hyacinth and a chunky older woman were there, serving the treat.

"I'm sure glad to see you two," Tyrella told her and Jenna as they entered the booth. "I never thought I'd hear myself say this, but I'm sick of the smell of strawberries. Come on, Georgia," she said to the older woman who was red-faced and sweating. "Let's go get some shaved ice."

"Wait," Celeste protested. "Aren't you going to, like, train us?"

"Nothing to it," Tyrella assured her. "Jenna will be taking the money and she doesn't need any training for that. You'll be dishing up orders. Just follow what Hyacinth does."

As if on cue, Sabrina and Tristan showed up. "Two strawberry shortcakes, please," he said to Jenna, and handed over a twenty. According to Jenna, Tristan made a ton of money creating websites for local businesses and helping frustrated seniors when they managed to mess up their computers. "I think he makes more than I do," she'd said.

"All right." Celeste rubbed her hands together. "Two strawberry shortcakes coming up."

She turned to see that Hyacinth already had a disposable bowl and was putting a sponge cake in it. Aunt Edie, who firmly believed shortcake should be made with biscuits, would have been appalled. But it had probably been easier to buy up a bunch of the little sponge cakes.

She, too, put one in a bowl.

"One serving of strawberries," Hyacinth said, demonstrating with the ladle in the bin of semi-mashed strawberries, "and one squirt of whipped cream."

It was a quick, parsimonious squirt. Celeste made a more generous one and handed it over to Sabrina with a wink.

"We can't run out of whipped cream," Hyacinth cautioned.

"You've got to give people their money's worth," Celeste argued. "If it looks like we're running out, I'll go out and buy more."

Hyacinth didn't say anything. She didn't need to. Her disapproving expression said it all.

"We'll be fine," Jenna told her, and Hyacinth responded with a resigned shrug.

Karen and her sister Lisa stopped by the booth to buy some strawberry shortcake. "We're looking forward to your beach party tonight," Karen said to Jenna and Celeste.

"That'll bring back memories," Lisa added with a wink.

"I think I prefer to make some new ones," Jenna said to her.

"Don't worry, we will," Lisa said. "By the way,

we saw Taylor and Greg over by the rides. They're coming tonight. She's hoping to get Miranda to take a nap so she'll be able to stay up, but with all the sugar Greg's pumping into her, good luck with that."

"They'll get her all wound up, keep her up late and she'll sleep like a rock," Jenna predicted.

"Just like Uncle Ralph did with us when we were kids," said Celeste.

"You gotta celebrate," Jenna said.

"I'm glad you've finally figured that out." Celeste gave her a nudge. Brody was their next customer. "You coming over tonight to help my sister build the beach fire?" she asked him.

"Absolutely. I'm good at building fires." He waggled his eyebrows, making Jenna blush. "You gonna be there?" he asked Celeste.

"Maybe later. I have a party to go to." She was aware of Hyacinth, shamelessly eavesdropping, and suddenly, working in the booth together felt as awkward as she'd feared it would be.

"Are you going to the party at the Nobles'?" she asked Celeste as Brody moved on to the next booth.

"Um, yes. Will you be there?"

"Most of the church was invited," Hyacinth said. *So don't feel special.*

Celeste acknowledged that with a nod. "It sounds like fun," she lied. Yeah, with all the women from church who disapproved of her glaring at her. She should tell Paul she'd changed her mind and go hang out on the beach with her sister and people who really cared about her.

But Paul cared about her. And darn it all, she wasn't going to let a few snobbish, judgmental women drive her away.

"I imagine Pastor Paul will be there," said Hyacinth, obviously fishing.

Celeste nodded again and decided that was all the answer she needed to give. Hyacinth would find out soon enough that they were coming together.

Victor King stepped up to the booth, sparing her from further conversation. He was in civilian clothes, but she suspected he'd be working that night. Between people trying to blow off fingers, accidentally starting brush fires and driving neighbors to file complaints, both the police force and fire department were kept busy on the Fourth.

"Hi, Celeste. Saw you on the float. You make a cute guy."

"Ha-ha. Can I get you a strawberry shortcake… in the face?"

He chuckled and handed over his money to Jenna, and Celeste got busy dishing it up. Another customer arrived, and that put Hyacinth to work, too.

"I imagine you guys are going to have a beach fire," he said to Jenna.

"Of course. You're welcome to join us."

"I would if I wasn't on duty."

"If you just happen to stroll past, we'll give you some of Aunt Edie's famous baked beans," Jenna promised as Celeste passed him his shortcake.

"Beans, beans, the magical fruit," Celeste began to chant. "The more you eat the more you toot."

"Oh, stop already," scolded Jenna.

Victor smiled and strolled off, spooning strawberries and the extra whipped cream Celeste had given him into his mouth.

"Are you two dating?" Hyacinth asked Celeste, oh, so casually. As if she didn't know Celeste and Paul were dating.

"No. I'm not into cops. Been there, done that. I got tired of him using his handcuffs on me," Celeste quipped, dusting the ugly breakup with some humor.

Hyacinth didn't laugh. Didn't even crack a smile. "My fiancé was a policeman."

"Was?" As in not anymore? "What happened?"

Hyacinth suddenly looked as if she was going to cry. "He died."

Chapter Thirteen

"He died?" Celeste repeated. What to say to that? She looked to see if Jenna had heard, hoping she'd step in with something properly diplomatic and comforting. But she was occupied with counting out change for someone.

Hyacinth was on the verge of tears. "He was killed in the line of duty."

"Gosh, I'm sorry," said Celeste. Poor Hyacinth. "How long ago was that?"

"Five years ago," Hyacinth said softly. "He was so honorable and kind. I never thought I'd meet another man like him."

Until Paul. She didn't need to say it. Celeste knew.

Well, crud. "I'm sorry you lost him. That had to be hard."

"It was."

"I'm sure you'll get another chance at love." *With someone besides Paul.* "You never know where you're going to find the right person. Sometimes it turns out not to be the one you thought it would," Celeste continued, hoping to encourage her to look in a different direction. She felt bad for Hyacinth, but darn it all, she couldn't help it that the magic wasn't there between her and Paul.

Hyacinth seemed anything but encouraged by that bit of philosophizing. She'd obviously decided who her right one was.

A group of teenagers hit the booth, and for a few minutes both women were busy dishing up shortcake. Good. Maybe they could drop the subject.

Or not. "I'm sorry things didn't work out with you and your policeman," said Hyacinth.

"Oh, well. I thought he was the one. Turned out he wasn't," Celeste said and left it at that.

"So now you're here...?"

"Having fun." And working on getting her life together.

Hyacinth frowned. "It sounds like it."

Celeste flashed back on her embarrassing encounter with Henry that Hyacinth's squad had witnessed. Of course, Hyacinth would have heard about it.

She kept her tone light. "Isn't that what you're supposed to do at the beach?" She hadn't done anything wrong. No apologies needed.

And right on cue, here came Hyacinth's friends, stopping by the booth to order shortcake. They had sweet smiles and friendly words for her. For Celeste... *greetings from the Popsicle Twins.*

Hyacinth made no more attempts at conversation after they left and it started feeling pretty uncomfortable there in Strawberry Shortcake Land. They might have been volunteering for a good cause, but

there was no feeling of camaraderie. Celeste was relieved when the next volunteers showed up, and she
and Jenna could scram.

"For a moment I thought you and Hyacinth were
actually bonding," Jenna said as they walked away.

"It was a short moment. Did you know she was
engaged before she moved down here?"

"No. To who?"

"To a cop. He was killed in the line of duty."

"That's awful."

"It is," Celeste agreed. "So then she moves to
Moonlight Harbor and eventually finds another good
man only to lose him."

"But she never had him," Jenna pointed out, "so
no guilt because he's interested in you."

"Guilty? Me?"

"I know you. Look, I'm sorry for what happened
to her, but that's not your problem. If Paul ends up
with you, it only means there's someone else meant
for her. So no guilt."

"No guilt," Celeste echoed.

Yet, that evening when she walked into the party
with Paul, she did feel, if not guilty, at least mildly
undeserving.

It wasn't long before that was replaced by a new
discomfort. Their hosts were an older couple who
owned a house about a mile and a half down the
beach from the Driftwood, the beginning of a string
of two- and three-story homes, prime real estate filled
with retirees and large families with money to blow.
They welcomed Celeste, as did a couple of women

she'd met the week before—both of them married and not threatened by a newcomer. A middle-aged woman admired Celeste's red shorts, white top and star-spangled scarf and asked how she was settling in.

"I love being with my sister," Celeste said. "And what's not to like about the beach?"

"If you're looking to get more involved in the community, we can always use volunteers at the food bank," the woman said. "It's worthwhile work. Hyacinth Brown, Bethany Stone and Treeva Mills help us out. I think you're all about the same age."

As if all being Millennials meant they were destined for friendship. Nightfall was still half an hour away and there was plenty of light for Celeste to see the looks she was getting from Team Hyacinth as she and Paul made the rounds. *Who invited you, man thief? You don't belong.*

The kitchen table was laden with food—barbecued chicken, burgers and hot dogs, potato and broccoli salads and, of course, a number of seafood treats. Plus rolls, cake, pies—a carboholic's dream.

"Shall we fill our plates?" Paul suggested.

Celeste suddenly didn't have an appetite. "I'm not very hungry."

"Then how about something to drink? A pop?"

"Diet Coke."

"I'll get it," he offered, and she wanted to plead, "Don't leave me."

People were gathered in groups, talking with their friends, and for once in her life she lacked the confidence to join in. She followed him out onto the deck, hoping to find a chair next to a friendly face. It seemed as if out there, as well, everyone had already found someone to talk to. She'd hoped to see Tyrella, but then remembered she was partying with Jenna and the Driftwood Inn gang.

Which was where Celeste should have been. Everyone there would've been glad to see her. She should have suggested party-hopping when Paul asked her to this, instead of jumping on his invitation like a hungry dog. Speaking of dogs, she hoped Nemo would be okay. They'd shut him in the house with his favorite chew toy and given him a doggy tranquilizer, but she should've stayed close at hand to keep an eye on him.

She should've done a lot of things, but she'd been so happy when Paul asked her out—a sure sign that her love life was moving forward—that she hadn't thought beyond what to wear to impress him.

That was the *should haves*. Then there were the *could haves*. She could have told Paul that she didn't feel she was fitting in with some members of his congregation. Not a good thing if what was starting between them turned into something permanent. Weren't pastors' wives supposed to be loved by all? She could at least tell him she was feeling uncomfortable. But that would make her appear insecure. And she didn't want to get into the whole female dynamics situation. He'd probably think she was ratting out Hyacinth. And really, what had Hyacinth done to her? Nothing. The woman didn't like her. What could Paul do about that? What could anyone do about that?

He brought her a can of soda and she managed to smile and thank him.

He studied her. "Are you okay?"

"I'm fine." Sort of.

"You look like something's bothering you."

A sensitive man who actually noticed when a woman was feeling upset. Yes, Paul Welch was as close to perfect as they came.

But this wasn't the place to share her insecurities. In fact, this wasn't the place for her, period. She needed to return to her Driftwood Inn tribe.

"I've got a headache," she said. No lie. Her earlier discomfort was edging toward a throb in her temples.

"I can see if Dee has some aspirin," he said.

"No, don't bother her. I just need to go home."

"Okay, I'll take you."

"Paul," a hefty man in a Hawaiian shirt called from the far corner of the deck. "Come here. Joe wasn't paying attention to the sermon on Sunday. You need to settle this."

Paul held up a hand and nodded to acknowledge that he'd heard. "Give me a minute and I'll take you home," he said to Celeste.

"Don't worry about it," she said. "The Driftwood's just a mile or so down the beach. I'd rather walk. It'll be good for me."

"Then I'll walk with you."

"No," she said firmly. "You stay."

"I don't like to think of you walking all that way."

As if she didn't walk that far every time she was

on the beach. As if she hadn't walked by this very house before. "I'll be fine," she insisted.

"Are you sure?"

"I'm sure."

"I'll come by later to see how you're doing," he promised.

She'd be doing a lot better once she got back where she belonged. She thanked her hostess, then hurried down the beach to check on her dog and see her friends.

"I guess *that* party's over," Bethany said as she and Hyacinth watched Celeste vanish into the crowd on the beach.

And her date didn't look any too happy about it. Poor Paul, thought Hyacinth. Celeste Jones couldn't even handle a party with the members of his congregation. If that wasn't a clue that she wasn't right for him, Hyacinth didn't know what was.

He was moving in their direction, making his way to Jimmy Williams and Horace Ringwald, and as he passed with a pleasant nod for the two women, Bethany asked, "What happened to your date, Pastor?"

Hyacinth saw the disappointment on his face. He'd wear that expression a lot if he stayed with Celeste Jones. "She wasn't feeling well. She decided to go home."

"That's too bad," Bethany said, then the moment he'd passed them, she said to Hyacinth, "Trouble in paradise. I knew it wouldn't last. She's already tired of him."

"Or maybe she really doesn't feel good." Hyacinth had been hoping and praying things wouldn't work out between Paul and Celeste—selfish yes, but there you had it. Still, she doubted her prayers would be answered that quickly.

"She was okay when they got here," said Treeva. "That was a fake headache. They're not a fit, Hy. This proves it."

"So get over there and move in on him," advised Bethany.

Hyacinth balked. "He's in the middle of a conversation."

"He's always in the middle of a conversation. Honestly," Bethany said in disgust. "You have to put yourself out there so he knows you're interested. Send the right signals."

"I bet Celeste Jones didn't have to send any signals," Hyacinth muttered. *No bitterness here.*

"Are you kidding? She's a walking cell phone tower. Go make conversation," Bethany said and gave Hyacinth a nudge.

Hyacinth still resisted and Bethany turned the nudge into a shove, leaving her no choice but to move her legs. They probably looked like middle-school girls at a dance. This was stupid. What was she supposed to do, walk over and interrupt the men's conversation?

She took her time, stopping to get a soda, then asking one of the older women who was a frequent customer how her quilt was coming. That delayed her by a good fifteen minutes, because once avid quilters started talking about their projects, it was hard to stop. Quilting, gardening and baking—all topics Hyacinth could converse easily on. It made her hugely popular with a lot of the women in the church. And made her well qualified to be a pastor's wife.

"You look lovely today," Susan Frank told her as she walked past.

"Thank you," she murmured. She'd thought she looked pretty cute in her white jeggings and red top. Until she'd seen Celeste in her red shorts.

Paul had now moved away from the men he'd been talking to and was in the house. She saw him at the table, helping himself to a piece of barbecued chicken. Food. There was a topic she could manage.

Except when she was around Paul. She took a plate and edged up to him, her mind as empty as her plate. *Say something!* "This all looks delicious." Oh, that was witty.

"It does," he agreed and put a chicken leg on his plate.

"So you prefer dark meat?"

"Actually, I like white."

"But you're taking a leg."

"I think most people prefer white meat. I try to leave the breasts for others at a party like this."

"Gosh, that is so sweet."

"Not really," he said. "Speaking of sweet, I see someone brought chocolate chip cookies, and I'm not staying out of them."

"I made those." *Those are your favorites, which is why I made them.*

He smiled at her. "I should have known. That's your specialty, isn't it?"

One of them. I have many specialties. Hyacinth nodded.

She was on the verge of offering to make another batch just for him when a man came up and clapped him on the back. "Hey, Paul, how's it going?"

And there went her chance. It sure wasn't going great for Hyacinth. She left the salads and went straight for the desserts, determined to commit diet suicide and eat herself into a sugar coma. Paul's date had abandoned him. She'd had her chance and she hadn't taken it. She loaded her plate and returned to her friends.

Bethany's husband was with them now, his plate piled with chips, a hamburger and a hot dog, but she didn't let his presence stop her from questioning Hyacinth. "So how'd it go?"

"Fine," Hyacinth said, hoping Bethany would get the message and drop the subject.

"How'd what go?" asked Bethany's husband.

"Nothing," she said to him, then took Hyacinth's arm and turned away. "Why are you back?" she demanded. Treeva was on Hyacinth's other side, all ears. Too bad there was nothing to hear.

"Did you flirt with him?" Treeva asked.

Somehow, flirting with her pastor didn't seem right. Hyacinth bit her lip.

"Mission failed," Treeva said with a shake of her head.

"I don't know what happens. I get near him and I...fail."

"Honestly," Bethany said, "how did you ever manage to get engaged?"

Sometimes Bethany didn't think before she spoke. Hyacinth suddenly wanted to cry. "I don't know," she said and walked away.

"Way to go," she heard Treeva say to Bethany.

"Seriously, how did she?" Bethany said in her own defense.

Indeed. Hyacinth was shy, especially around men. She found it hard to put herself out there. If you asked her about quilting, she'd talk your ear off, reminiscing over how her grandmother helped her make her first quilt when she was sixteen. She could talk about her favorite foodie websites and HGTV shows, share the secrets of perfect pie crust—thanks, Gram!—and even give the stats on every member of the Mariners baseball team.

But someone had to prime the pump. She'd been shy as a child, struggling to get out from under the mighty shadow of two overachieving siblings. A common thread ran through her report cards. Her work was always satisfactory, but her teachers never failed to add comments such as, "Hyacinth needs to participate more in class discussions." Hyacinth often wanted to participate more, but while other students were raising their hands, jumping up and down in their seats, chanting, "I know, I know," a fear of somehow getting the answer wrong kept her hand down and her bottom glued to the seat. She was smart, but she never felt smart enough.

And she'd never thought she was pretty, which

didn't give her much confidence around the opposite sex. Her sister, who didn't want the competition, never said anything to assure her that she was. The few boys who showed interest lost it soon enough—too much work trying to pull any conversation out of her. And definitely too much work getting her to loosen up when it came to sex.

Then she'd met Andy. He'd come to their church one Sunday and her dad had invited him home for dinner. There'd been a baseball game on. Comfortable in the safety of her own living room, she'd been free to be herself. She'd joined in with the men, analyzing every play and every player and, without even realizing it, impressing Andy. He'd asked her out, done most of the talking, told her she was cute and then asked for another date. And that had been that.

Andy had been a kind man, a big man with an even bigger laugh. He'd been taken out by a punk with a gun who, along with some friends, was on a mission to kill cops. They'd gotten a twofer, because after losing him she'd turned into one of the walking dead.

Until she came to Moonlight Harbor and met Pastor Paul Welch. Hope had been resurrected and she'd fallen in love again. If only Celeste Jones hadn't come to town.

Celeste found Nemo stretched out on the couch, something Aunt Edie would not approve of, sound asleep, his doggy chew toy still clutched between his paws. Probably no need to worry about the fireworks scaring him. She left him to dream of chasing seagulls, then walked down the path through the dune grass to where Aunt Edie's beach party was in full swing, everyone gathered around the fire.

Many of Jenna's Moonlight Harbor friends were present, as well as some of the friends they'd made during the big holiday storm back at Christmas. All were happy to see Celeste. And there, to her surprise, sat Henry Gilbert on a log, talking with Tyrella. Celeste grabbed a wine cooler from the selection of drinks and joined them, taking the spot on Tyrella's other side.

"I thought you'd be at the Nobles' with Paul," Tyrella greeted her.

"I was."

Tyrella's eyebrows went up inquisitively, but Celeste shook her head and she dropped the subject. Instead, she said, "I've been talking with your guest here. Did you know he's a writer?"

"I do. Did he tell you what he writes?"

"He did. I am gonna buy me that book when it comes out."

Celeste stared at her. "You are?"

"Absolutely. I love books like that."

The smirk Henry gave Celeste said, "So there," and she couldn't help smiling.

Tyrella, who'd been looking back and forth between the two of them, got up and said, "I think there's a marshmallow calling my name. Henry, it was good talking to you. Come visit my church sometime."

"I'll have to do that," he said and scooted over next to Celeste. "See, even church ladies like what I write."

"I never knew what a sick puppy she was," Celeste said and took a draw from her wine cooler.

"Nice of you to invite me here when you had a date for another party," he said.

"Sorry about that. I forgot."

"You forgot you had a date?"

She shrugged.

"I can see things are really working out with the preacher."

"They are," she insisted. It was only some of the people around him who were giving her problems.

"So how come you're here?"

"I had a headache."

"A shrink would have a field day with that."

"It was only a headache."

"How is it now?"

"It's better," she said and downed more of her wine cooler.

"Why am I having trouble envisioning you with a minister?" he mused.

"Not enough imagination?"

"Yeah, right. So why did you really leave the party?"

"I told you. I had a headache."

"Sorry, not buyin' it."

"Too bad. That's all I'm selling," she said, irked. Henry Gilbert thought he was so smart. What did he know? "Anyway, why *shouldn't* I be with a minister? Aren't I good enough?"

He held up a hand. "Hey, I didn't say that."

"You might as well have."

Put in his place, he shut up and finished his beer, and she polished off her wine cooler.

"I'm getting another drink," he announced. He pointed to her empty bottle. "You want another?"

"Sure." She wasn't driving. She could have another.

The wine cooler went down fine. So did the hot dog he roasted for her.

"Celeste, I think we need an encore performance of 'Girls Just Want to Have Fun' from you and Karen and Lisa before the fireworks start," Taylor Marsh said from her side of the fire.

The last performance had been during their winter bonfire party. But they were missing a part of the act. "We don't have a guitar player," Celeste pointed out.

Where was Seth anyway? Not that Jenna seemed to be missing him. She and Brody were looking pretty cozy parked on a beach blanket, their backs up against a log. Not only did they appear to be a good fit, but his kids, who'd come down for the partying, also liked her. Of course, who wouldn't like Jenna?

"We don't need a guitar," Lisa told her. "We can sing by ourselves. Come on, sis," she said to her sister Karen.

"I haven't had nearly enough to drink for that yet," Karen protested.

"Sure you have," said Lisa.

"Come on, give us a warm-up act before the fireworks start," Tyrella said.

The three launched into their song, stumbling over the lyrics as always—why was it that the one thing you remembered was the "girls just want to have fun" line?—getting into their performance. Especially Celeste, who after a couple of wine coolers figured she was ready for *America's Got Talent*.

Henry Gilbert was certainly enjoying the show, smiling appreciatively. The smile turned even more appreciative when she went for a big finish, took a twirl and lost her balance, landing in his lap. She'd probably have kept falling and landed on her head if he hadn't put an arm around her and held her upright.

Her audience thought the whole thing was intentional and she got a good laugh.

From everyone but the newcomer. There stood Paul Welch at the edge of the group, and he wasn't even close to smiling.

Chapter Fourteen

Celeste hopped off Henry as if she'd been jabbed with a hot poker. Darn it all, she hadn't done anything wrong. She had no reason to be embarrassed.

Still, she was. She put a good face on it by calling a cheery hello and dashing over to take Paul by the hand and pull him into the group, introducing him to the ones who didn't know him.

"I thought you were at the party," she said to him.

"I thought you had a headache," he said to her.

"I did. It's gone now."

"Obviously." He didn't sound at all happy about her recovery.

"Would you like a hot dog?" she asked, moving toward the spot where the food was stashed.

"No, thanks. I already ate. At the party."

Okay, he was pissed. Pastors weren't supposed to get mad, were they?

The last of the light was vanishing and people were digging out their fireworks. At a nearby bonfire, a dad was lighting sparklers and handing them to his kids.

"How about a walk?" Paul suggested.

She wasn't sure she wanted one-on-one time with him right then, but she nodded and they left the fire.

"Why did you *really* leave the party, Celeste?" he asked as soon as they were out of earshot.

"I told you. I had a headache."

"Did you?"

"I did."

"But that wasn't the only reason, was it? If you'd wanted to go to your sister's party instead, all you had to do was say so."

"I know." She avoided looking at him, instead watching the first fireworks shoot into the sky.

"What's going on here? Be honest. Don't you want to go out with me?"

"Yes, of course I do," she said earnestly. "It's just..."

"What?" he prompted.

"Okay, if you want honest, here it is. I'm having trouble feeling like I belong."

"You don't feel like you belong?" He sounded honestly puzzled. "I don't understand."

Men were so clueless. "Some of the women don't like me."

"How could anyone not like you?"

"Well, duh. Competition, Paul. All the single women in your church have the itchy hots for you and only one of us is getting scratched."

"You do have a way with words," he said, and it didn't exactly sound like a compliment.

"I have a way with a lot of things," she said lightly. Then sobered. "What I don't have a way with is bitches." Uh-oh. That had definitely been the wrong thing to say. He looked…not so much shocked as dis-appointed. "Oh, this isn't going to work. You need some sweet woman who plays the piano and likes to visit the sick. I can't play a note and I break out in hives even walking into the lobby of a hospital."

"No one's asking you to play the piano or go to the hospital."

"But you are asking me to fit in. I get that. You need me to. The problem is, I don't feel I do. I usu-ally have no trouble talking to people at a party, but today…" She shook her head. "I felt like I was in a foreign country and didn't know the language. It was awkward. And I did have a headache."

"That was my fault. I should've done a better job of introducing you around."

"You were fine," she said. "The problem was me. Look, Paul, I haven't been in church for years, not since I was in high school."

"But now you're back. That's what matters."

She was back but not comfortable. Much as she wanted to think she was immune to the animosity of other women, the truth was that she was a people per-son, and being liked was important to her. She sure hadn't felt liked at the party, and how was that ever going to change?

"Oh, Paul, we're not a match. Can't you see that?"

"Do you want us to be a match?" he asked softly.

"Yes, I do," she said, barely able to raise her own voice above a whisper. "But the truth is, I think you're too good for me."

"Oh, brother," he said, closing his eyes.

"It's true. You are."

"Celeste, get that idea out of your mind. I'm no better than anyone else. I'm just a man who's trying to do what's right."

"Then do what's right and find someone who's better for you." Oh, what was she saying? Paul was the best thing that had ever happened to her and she was driving him away. She wanted to cry. So she did.

"Hey," he said gently, putting an arm around her shoulder. "Enough of this kind of talk. Celeste, I really like you. I like you more every time I see you. I know you're not perfect, but neither am I. I think we could have something good together. More than good, even. Something great."

"Do you?" She sounded like an eager puppy, like Nemo would if he could talk.

"Yes, I do. You're fun and kindhearted. You love kids and adopt stray dogs. You love your family. You're coming to church and getting involved, which, I'd say puts us on the same wave length spiritually. What more could a man want in a woman?"

"Someone his congregation likes."

"Most of them do like you. As for the ones who don't, that's their problem, not yours."

It sure felt like her problem. "You need someone who doesn't say bad words."

"I bet you could manage to lose a couple," he said, giving her shoulder a squeeze.

She wasn't convinced. Some words suited some people perfectly.

"Come on," he urged. "Let's give this a fair chance. Next time don't run away. Tell me how you're feeling."

She chewed on her lower lip. She *had* run away. Good grief. Most of her life she'd been running into relationships and now she was running from one that could possibly work. She had to be insane.

He put a hand under her chin and nudged her face up. His expression was so tender. She couldn't remember Emerson ever looking at her like that. She couldn't remember any man looking at her like that. Maybe her father had, but she'd been too young to store it in her memory bank.

Then, even better, Paul went from looking to kissing. The kiss was as sweet as the look, and she let him draw her close, slipping her arms around his neck. So what if Paul Welch wasn't the world's best kisser? He was surely the world's sweetest. He hadn't said it yet, but she could tell he was falling in love with her. And, unlike Emerson, she knew, just knew, that she wouldn't have to coax him into telling her he loved her. A man like Paul wouldn't kiss a woman unless he intended to follow up that kiss with a serious relationship.

He didn't go beyond the one kiss. Instead, he turned them around and led her back to the party, saying, "Come on. Let's have fun."

Oh, yes, in Paul Welch she'd finally found the perfect man.

Henry had watched Celeste and the boyfriend take off down the beach. Not even holding hands. Some boyfriend.

She'd left the other party early, left her date. Headache. Yeah, right. He had no idea what Celeste Jones was doing with that guy, but any fool could see she didn't belong with him.

It was starting to get dark and people were bringing out their sparklers and artillery shells. He heard a burst of laughter from another group having a bonfire a little farther down the beach. He'd had enough fun for one night.

He thanked Jenna Jones and her great-aunt for letting him crash the party and then left, although Edie Patterson pressed him to stay and enjoy the fireworks. "The show's just beginning," she said.

Henry declined. He'd seen more of the show than he wanted.

The sister, on the other hand, didn't press him to stay, and he was pretty sure he knew why. Celeste's grand finale that landed her in his lap had been a shock, a very enjoyable one, but Henry was a people observer and even with the great sensations Celeste was causing, he'd managed to catch the expression on Jenna's face. It said, "Oh, no. Not that lap."

He'd also seen the expression on the preacher's face. That one said, "Fire and brimstone for you, dude."

The vote had been cast. Unanimous in favor of the preacher; Celeste's future was already wrapped up. But if Henry was writing her story he sure wouldn't put the bubbly, bikini-wearing Celeste Jones with that guy. He wouldn't know what to do with a woman like that.

Oh, and you would?

"Yeah," he told himself. He might not have been as good-looking as the other guy but he was willing to bet he'd be ten times better in bed. Or on a blanket on the beach. Or leaning against a wall. Anywhere she wanted to do it. He was, after all, creative.

But there would be no getting creative with Celeste Jones.

Hank the happy clam... Celeste took a sip of her morning coffee and frowned at what she'd written on the legal tablet she'd snatched from Jenna's massage room. Hank—wasn't that a nickname for Henry? Not appropriate at all.

She scratched it out and tried again. *Horace the happy clam...* Okay, that was better. *Horace the happy clam lay in his clam bed, dreaming of being chopped up and put into someone's chowder. It was a terrible nightmare.*

And this was a terrible idea. She crumpled the paper, returned the tablet to the massage room. Maybe she wasn't cut out to be a writer. Not everyone was. Anyway, the world needed readers as much as it did writers.

Still, it would be fun to try and write a book someday. If only she had someone to help her. There *was* someone who could help her. He was staying in room twelve.

There were plenty of other writers out there. Paul wrote sermons. He could probably help her, too. And wouldn't that be fun to do together. There. See? Another reason Paul was the right man for her.

All the same, her heart fluttered a little as she approached room twelve with her cart of linens and cleaning supplies. She was relieved to find Henry gone. The incident the night before was one from which she'd just as soon distance herself. Anyway, with Henry gone, she could change the bed. Were writers good in bed?

Aack! What was she thinking? *New leaf. Remember?* She was turning over a new leaf and being smart about love.

To prove it she called Paul and offered to take him out to lunch.

She spared no expense, treating him to lunch at the Porthole and insisting they start with crab cocktails. The day was sunny and the view was lovely. So was Paul.

They chatted about their families. She told him about losing her father when she was a baby. "I wish I remembered something about him," she finished sadly. "Anything."

"I'm sorry," he said. "I have to admit I can hardly imagine what that's like. All I know is that I'd hate to lose my dad."

"So he's still alive?"

"Yep. He's a pastor, too." Paul gave a rueful smile. "I sure resented all the time he spent doing things for the church congregation when I was growing up. It seemed like everybody got more attention than my sister and me. She was an angel but I was a typical PK."

"What's a PK?" she asked.

"Preacher's Kid. Notorious for doing stuff to embarrass the old man. I did my best to turn his hair gray, figuring negative attention was better than no attention."

"I bet he's proud of you now."

"He is. So's my mom."

And what would they think of her? Would she give his father more gray hairs?

"He'd love you," Paul said as if reading her mind. "So would my mom. I hope you can meet them."

Already talking about bringing her home to meet the parents. That was a good sign. "I'd love to. Where do they live?"

"At the moment, in Burkina Faso, Africa."

"Africa?" She and Paul wouldn't be driving down to meet Mom and Dad anytime soon.

"They're helping an organization down there that builds wells for villages."

"Wow. And your sister? Where's she?"

"She works for that organization, too."

Of course. There wasn't anyone in Paul Welch's family who wasn't noble. Would they like her? Really?

And would she like them? What if Paul decided he wanted to go to Africa and build wells? "Would you ever want to live in Africa?" She'd heard Africa was beautiful, but she couldn't tolerate extreme heat and she didn't want to get malaria. Then there was the unrest and danger in so many parts of the continent. Was there unrest in Burkina Faso? She didn't know. And what about lions?

Gosh, she was a wimp.

"I'm perfectly content where I am," he said. "We have plenty of people who need help right here in this country."

She breathed a sigh of relief. Okay. That was settled. "I'm happy to help people here, too." Much as she admired his family and others like them she was sure she wouldn't be able to handle any place with so many challenges.

After lunch Paul returned to church to work on his sermon, while Celeste and Nemo hit the beach. And wouldn't you know it? There was Henry Gilbert, camped on a blanket, working away on his book.

Nemo was more than happy to run over and say hi, completely ignoring Celeste's commands to come back.

"Sorry," she said, hurrying up as Henry moved his laptop out of range of the flying sand. "I tried to call him back."

"Don't be," Henry said, giving Nemo's furry neck a good rub even as the excited dog tried to trample him.

"I need to take him to obedience school."

"Nah. A few lessons and you'll have him whipped into shape." He pushed on Nemo's rump and said, "Sit." The rump went down, and Henry rewarded the dog's obedience with an ear rub and a "Good boy."

"That was impressive," Celeste said, and she sat, too.

"That's how you do it. Show 'em what you want

and reward 'em when they do it. Positive reinforcement. He'll catch on fast, won't you, boy?" Henry said, rubbing the dog's ears again. Nemo leaned over and gave him a doggy kiss. "Man, I miss my dog," he said.

"You could get another," Celeste suggested.

"Not sure I'm ready for that yet."

"Well, then, how about if I share mine? You can help me train him."

"That's a deal," he said. "So did you patch things up with the preacher?"

It was pointless to pretend she didn't know what he was talking about. "I did."

Henry didn't look at her. Instead, he concentrated on scratching the dog's chin. "I still can't picture you with a guy like that."

"I'm not having any trouble. He's a good man. With principles. And that's a refreshing change."

"Yeah? Been burned, huh?"

"To a crisp."

"What happened?"

"He cheated on me." Even though she was over Emerson, the words still tasted bitter. She picked up a pebble and gave it an angry toss.

As if on cue, a text came in, and she knew without looking it was from Emerson. She didn't bother to take her phone out of her shorts pocket.

"Your fan club?" Henry guessed.

"He's banned from the clubhouse after what he did."

"I take it that was the cheater. Wants you back now, huh?"

"The day he gets me back is the day the tide stops coming in."

"Smart," Henry said approvingly. "I can't believe any man would be stupid enough to cheat on you," he added, keeping his gaze on Nemo, who'd lain down against his leg.

"There are a lot of stupid men out there."

"Stupid women, too."

For a moment he seemed so sad Celeste couldn't help saying, "Any woman who doesn't appreciate a man who can write doesn't deserve him."

Now he did look up at her and smiled. Since he was wearing sunglasses she couldn't see his eyes but she somehow knew that smile had reached them. "You think so?"

"I do."

"You flattering me so I'll endorse your book, Happy Clam Girl?"

"You're mocking me."

"No, I'm not."

"Don't judge. I may be the next Dr. Seuss."

"You're the wrong sex," he said, making her smile. "And much cuter than he ever was."

Henry was pretty darned cute himself.

But who cared? She wasn't interested in him. She wasn't interested in any man but Paul Welch. This time around Celeste was taking the sure bet.

"So any inspiration for your clam yet?" he asked.

She sighed. "I can't think of anything. You're right. Clams are boring."

"Maybe you should try writing about something with a little more energy."

"Crabs?"

"Uh, no. How about a dog?" he suggested.

"The Happy Dog!"

"Everything doesn't have to be happy, you know. You could have a lost dog or a lonely dog."

"Or a best dog. The Best Dog. What do you think of that title, Nemo?"

Nemo wiggled his ears at the sound of his name but other than that had no opinion.

"I could write about a child at an animal shelter, trying to choose a dog."

Henry shrugged and nodded. Not very enthusiastic.

"Wouldn't you want to read about a kid picking out a dog?" she asked.

"I'd rather read about a kid being lost in the woods with his—or her—dog and how they make their way back to camp."

"That could be a sequel," she said. "But first you have to find the right dog."

"Not much conflict there," Henry observed. "It's not hard to do that."

"It wasn't for me, was it, Nemo?" Celeste reached out and petted him, and he gave her hand a doggy kiss.

"Finding the right dog's a lot easier than trying to find the right person, that's for sure," Henry said.

"Hi, Celeste."

She turned from Henry to see Hyacinth's friend Bethany strolling past. She wore the kind of smug, gotcha look that movie bad girls wore when they were sure they'd one-upped the heroine.

Great. Just great. At least Celeste had her clothes on.

But by the time this got down the grapevine to Paul, would she have been seen wearing anything at all?

Chapter Fifteen

"I saw them, Hy," Bethany said, following Hyacinth down one of the aisles in her shop as she put bolts of fabric back on the shelves. "Sitting there all cozy. It was the same guy she was topless with. Do you really think Paul needs to be with her? You know she'll cheat on him."

"I don't know that. And there might be an innocent explanation."

"Seriously? If you believe that, I've got a two-carat diamond ring to sell you for a buck."

"They could be just friends."

"They were looking friendly all right. You oughta tell Paul."

"Why don't you tell him?" Hyacinth didn't want to see Paul get hurt, but she'd be much happier if someone else took on the unpleasant duty of bearing bad news.

"Treeva and I already tried to talk to him but he wouldn't listen. With everything you do around church, he's bound to listen to you."

"I'm not so sure." If Celeste Jones was really seeing someone besides Paul, he'd find out soon enough. He didn't need to hear it from Hyacinth.

"Suit yourself," Bethany said with a shrug. "But you know she doesn't deserve him."

No, she didn't, and Hyacinth knew, *knew* Celeste Jones would never love him as much as she did.

"And she's gonna get him."

Sadly for Hyacinth, it was looking more and more that way. Should she tell him or shouldn't she?

She wrestled with the dilemma all evening and into the wee hours. Finally, around 3:00 a.m. she reached the conclusion that she wouldn't say anything. Not unless she had a sign from heaven. Like a lightning bolt.

The lightning bolt came. Literally. Saturday found her dashing for the church side entrance with her flowers for the sanctuary, rain pelting her, thunder rumbling overhead.

She was struggling to get her church key when Paul opened the door, obviously on his way out. "Oh, Hyacinth. Hi," he said and held the door for her.

He was never around on Saturday mornings. What was he doing there? Was it a sign? Lightning crackled overhead, making her jump.

"Thank you," she murmured and walked in past him. Then, once inside, the words dried up.

"Those are pretty," he said, pointing to the lilies from the shore by her rental cottage on one of the town's two little lakes.

"They're my favorite," she said. *Say something more*, she urged herself. *Do you have a favorite flower?* No, that would sound stupid. Men didn't have favorite flowers. Did they?

"We all appreciate you sharing them with the rest of us. You do a lot to make things look nice around here."

"I try," she said.

"Well, I gotta go. The door's locked, so just shut it behind you when you leave."

The lightning crackled again, and the hairs on the back of Hyacinth's neck stood up. Okay, she knew a sign when she saw one. "Uh, Pastor."

He paused, looking at her expectantly, a smile still on his face.

How to phrase this? She had no idea. She caught sight of a stain on his shirt and stalled. "Did you know you've got a stain on your shirt?"

He glanced down. "Where?"

"Right there," she said, pointing to his chest. His left pectoral to be exact. Paul Welch had such a beautiful chest. Paul Welch had beautiful everything.

"I wonder where that came from."

"A little baking soda will take it out."

He nodded, obviously impressed with her knowledge regarding stains. When it came to neat and tidy, Hyacinth was an expert.

"Thanks," he said. "What would I do without you to watch over me?"

He needed watching over. She took a deep breath. It was now or never. "I was talking with Bethany yesterday." Was it her imagination or had his smile cooled? He didn't say anything to interrupt her, so

she was forced to go on. "I know you've been seeing Celeste Jones, and I don't want you to think…"
Oh, this was awkward. "Well, Bethany saw her on
the beach with another man." Paul didn't appear to
be taking this well. "I wasn't sure if I should tell you
or not. Bethany thought—"

This time he did interrupt her. "I don't care what
Bethany thought, Hyacinth, and you don't need to be
asking what she thought, either."

At his words she felt heat race up her neck and
across her cheeks. "No, you're right. She just felt
someone should tell you."

"And that someone should be Celeste, don't you
agree?"

"Of course," Hyacinth murmured. The thunder
rumbled and the lightning flashed outside, coming in
through a window and lighting up the hallway where
they stood. It reminded her of the photo-enforced traffic light that went off whenever someone was fool-
ish enough to run the red. She suddenly felt ill. "I'm
sorry."

"I know you thought you were helping, but spreading gossip never really helps."

"You're right. I just…" *Oh, spit it out.* "I guess I
like you too much to want to see you get hurt."

She couldn't believe she'd actually found the nerve
to say that. If this was a movie, Paul would say something like, "Hyacinth, do you care that much?" Then,
of course she'd say, "I do. In fact, I don't simply like
you. I love you. I've been in love with you for the past
year." Then he'd say…

"I appreciate that, but don't worry. I can take care of myself."

What happened to "What would I do without you to watch over me?" Apparently, that only applied to stains on his shirt. Sigh.

Hyacinth nodded, promised not to listen to any more gossip, then scatted. She was going to throttle Bethany.

Paul's sermon on Sunday was on the dangers of gossip. Celeste was sure it had something to do with her getting caught on the beach with Henry. She should have felt vindicated but instead she was embarrassed.

"We're supposed to love each other," Paul said, "be an example to others. Gossiping is not showing love. Gossip taints the person you're gossiping about, prejudices people against that person. It also taints you and makes you look small."

Celeste checked out Hyacinth, sitting with her friends Bethany and Treeva. Her cheeks were red and so were Treeva's. Bethany's husband watched her speculatively and she raised her chin as if to say, "Not me." Then she shot Celeste a look that threatened terrible consequences, as if Celeste was somehow to blame for their public scolding.

This was *her* fault? They were implying she'd known what they'd said or done and had sicced Paul on them?

"I feel like I'm on trial," she confessed as she, Jenna and Tyrella left the sanctuary.

"Don't," Tyrella said. "You're not the one who's misbehaving, girl."

Sabrina had joined them now. "Who's misbehaving?"

"No one," said Jenna. "You want to drive home?"

"Hudson asked if I can come over."

"Homework done?"

Sabrina nodded.

"Okay, then, go have fun."

And that left the sisters free to discuss the latest complication in Celeste's love life as they drove back home.

"He hasn't called me in two days," Celeste said miserably. "And he didn't talk to me after church."

"In case you didn't notice, he was surrounded by the entire building committee. I know for a fact he's been up to his ears working with them on the new addition."

"He has a cell phone. He could've at least called." Of course, she could have, too. "I think he's distancing himself from me." Another failed relationship. At the rate she was going, she'd make it into Guinness World Records.

"I'm sure he's not."

"Well, he should. Nobody wants us to be together. How's anything going to work between us if people don't like me?"

"One lovestruck woman?" Jenna scoffed.

"And her two deputy bad girls. And they're only the ones I know about."

"That's because there aren't any others. And those

three are such a small percentage of the people here, it's practically microscopic," Jenna said.

"Maybe I'm being paranoid," Celeste said with a sigh. "I just hate feeling like I'm back in high school. I mean, how old are we anyway?"

"Not everyone's going to like you. That's how people are. You know that. Don't worry about the ones who don't like you. They don't matter."

"You're right," Celeste said.

"Of course I am," Jenna said as they pulled into the motel's parking lot. "It's still no fun, though, especially when you've done nothing to deserve that kind of treatment."

Seeing the funky old place and Aunt Edie's house next door was enough to remind Celeste of the good things in her life. And the good people. She had family here, and friends whom her sister had kindly shared. She was having a great summer. Did she really need to let a trio of petty women ruin that? But...

"What if Paul and I do get serious, end up getting married?"

"Then I want to be matron of honor," Jenna said easily. "And we'll have a huge beach party to celebrate."

"That's not what I meant and you know it."

"The people who don't approve will leave and take their bad attitudes someplace else. Stop worrying and enjoy the ride."

"Enjoy the ride. That's what Emerson used to say," Celeste muttered.

"You're with Paul now. This ride's as safe as the bumper cars at Nora's funplex."

"Yeah, well, those can get a little bumpy," Celeste retorted.

"But they're fun. Come on, let's go make lunch."

They'd just finished making egg salad sandwiches when Celeste's cell phone announced a call coming in from Paul. She said a cautious, "Hi," her heart thumping. In spite of his sermon she knew he was going to dump her. She was too much trouble.

"I thought I'd see if you had plans for tonight."

He wasn't going to dump her? "Are you sure you want to hang out with me?"

"Of course," he said as if she was crazy to even ask.

She smiled. "As a matter of fact, I was going line dancing with Jenna. Want to come?"

"I've got two left feet. How about dinner instead?"

Celeste had gotten hooked on line dancing, but she could do that any Sunday night. "Okay."

"I'll pick you up at six."

"I'll be ready."

"Don't tell me, let me guess," said Jenna. "That was Paul."

Celeste nodded.

"Told you."

"Yes, you did," Celeste said and hugged her. "Thanks for always being right, sissy."

Jenna smiled. "Well, I *am* right about this. Paul is perfect for you."

It certainly seemed that way. He wanted all the things she wanted—a home, a family, kids.

"And a dog?" she prompted as they toyed with their desserts.

"You know I'm not big on dogs," he said, "unless they come with the right woman. And Nemo's beginning to grow on me."

If that wasn't further proof that things could work out between them, she didn't know what was.

After dinner they enjoyed a walk on the beach. He held her hand. This was what love was supposed to be like. She sent a quick thank-you heavenward that she'd finally found a man she could trust—and trust herself to fall in love with.

Back at the motel parking lot she made a half-hearted attempt to get out of the car and he got the message and kissed her. It was a lovely kiss, tender and so romantic.

"Celeste, it's probably too soon to say anything."

"Oh, go ahead," she murmured.

"You've got to realize I'm falling for you big-time. You're so easy to be around, so much fun."

"Girls just wanna," she quipped.

His expression turned more serious. "I know you have that lighthearted side to you, but..."

Uh-oh. She was afraid to ask. "But what?"

He suddenly seemed at a loss for words. Not normal for Paul Welch.

"Paul?"

"People shouldn't gossip, but it's also a good idea not to give them something to gossip about."

"If you're talking about me sitting on the beach with Henry Gilbert…"

He shook his head. "I'm talking about you sitting on the beach *on* Henry Gilbert."

"What?"

"At the bonfire on the Fourth."

He hadn't said anything about it and she'd forgotten. Well, almost.

She pulled away. "Oh, so we're finally getting around to that. I was goofing around, being silly and I tripped." And conveniently landed in Henry's lap. It sounded made up even to her.

Paul was silent a moment, digesting that. "I guess for me it's problematic, you being seen hanging out with someone else when we're seeing each other. We are seeing each other, right? I mean you're interested in taking this further, aren't you? If you're not, tell me now. Please."

"Of course I am," she said earnestly. "You shouldn't even have to ask."

"But I do have to."

"Why? Can't you tell how I feel about you?"

"I want to be sure, Celeste. After what I saw, what I've heard…"

"I explained about what you saw," she said stiffly. "And didn't you just preach a sermon on gossip?"

"Yeah, and I also said that when you hear things about people, it can color the way you see them."

A chill in the air suddenly diminished the warm, romantic glow. "How do you see me?"

"As a beautiful and desirable woman."

"Who can't be trusted?"

"I didn't say that."

"You didn't have to. Paul, I've been cheated on. I know how it feels. I would never do that to somebody."

He took in her words, nodding slowly. "I guess I'm a little jealous. Of course other men are going to want you. But I want to be the only one *you* want."

"You are," she said, taking his face between her hands. "I've fallen for some real losers. You're the best thing that's ever happened to me. So, final warning. If you feel you need to get out, you'd better do it now. Otherwise, I have no intention of letting you go," she finished with a grin.

"I don't want out," he said and kissed her again.

So there, that settled it. She'd met her perfect man at last, and that equally perfect life she'd envisioned was right around the corner.

Celeste was sure Henry would be at the beach by the time she got to his room to clean, but she found him stretched out on his bed, typing away on his laptop. In jeans and shirtless. Why wasn't the man civilized enough to wear a shirt, for crying out loud?

"How's the dog training going?" he asked, not looking up from the screen as she came in with fresh towels.

Dog training? She'd been too busy fixing her love life to deal with improving Nemo's manners.

"Not very well. I guess I'd better start working with him, though, huh?"

"Probably. You want to work with him while he's still young."

"Can't teach an old dog new tricks?"

"Something like that. Everything okay with the preacher?" he asked, still not looking up.

"Fine."

Now he did look up and his expression was almost cynical. "I guess the woman on the beach didn't rat you out for fraternizing with the enemy."

"Oh, she did. And Paul preached a sermon on gossip."

Henry did manage a smile at that. "Smart man."

Celeste had work to do. She didn't need to stand around all day talking with Henry Gilbert. Giving people something else to gossip about.

Despite that, she sat down on the other twin bed. "How's your writing coming?"

"Great." *Clack, clack, clack.* "I just finished a scene. Want to read it?"

She was curious to read some of his book. But not the gory parts. "Is anyone getting murdered in it?"

"No murder," he assured her.

"Okay," she said.

He handed her the laptop and settled on the bed next to her, his shoulder up against hers. Paul would not approve of this. She'd move away as soon as she was done reading.

"I'm afraid," she whimpered, and pushed closer to him as if she'd climb right inside him if she could.

"I know, but you don't need to be. I won't let anything happen to you. I promise."

"Is that what you said to those two girls who were murdered? Matthew, I don't want to die."

"You're not going to. Look at me," he told her. She did, with those beautiful green eyes of hers.

Celeste had green eyes. Well, that was a coincidence.

"My God, but you're beautiful," he murmured and touched a strand of her golden hair.

Celeste's hair wasn't gold. It was platinum.

Was Henry wearing cologne? He smelled good. She told herself she wasn't there to think about how Henry Gilbert smelled.

This wasn't appropriate, he knew, but he didn't let that stop him, not when she was looking at him the way she was.

"You're the only one who can save me," she said, and laid a trembling hand on his chest.

His well-muscled chest, with reddish hair. Celeste swallowed and read on.

He slid an arm around her waist and nuzzled her hair. She smelled like a summer garden. He wanted to stand there, holding her forever. No, he wanted to lay her down on a deep, soft bed and kiss every inch of her, make love to her every hour on the hour. Wanted to...

Aack! Celeste handed back the laptop. "This is a sex scene."

"No, it's not. It's a love scene."

Whatever it was, it had her stirred up in places that Henry didn't need to be stirring. "I thought you were writing about a serial killer."

"I am. But I have to have a detective, too. That's Matthew. And he's in love with the killer's next victim."

"Next victim? You're going to let her have sex and then kill her?"

Henry shrugged. "She must die. That's the title of the book."

"You are sick," Celeste said in disgust, hopping off the bed.

"Hey, maybe I'll fix it so she'll die with a smile on her face."

"Not funny," Celeste snapped and marched into the bathroom to replace the towels.

He followed her and stood leaning in the doorway. "Then maybe I'll let her live."

"Big of you."

"The killer's going to get caught, you know."

"I should hope so."

"He has to. Justice must be done and the story has to be satisfying in the end. In other words, order and optimism are restored to the characters' world. It's that way with all good stories."

"Not all. Some of them have sad endings," Celeste told him. She hated that kind of story.

"I like things to end well for the hero. And the heroine." She was about to walk past him, but he didn't move aside. "How's *your* story going to end, Celeste? Are you sure you picked the best hero?"

Her mouth felt like the Sahara. Her lips were desperate for moisture. She licked them.

He watched.

How had they wound up standing so close? Her heart rate went from a trot to a canter.

"Has he kissed you yet?"

The canter went to a gallop. "That is so none of your business."

"He has, hasn't he? But it wasn't that good. Otherwise, you'd be bragging."

"Only jocks do that in the locker room."

"That's kind of a sexist remark."

"I need to get back to work and you need to get back to murdering people," she said and brushed past him, making a dash for the door.

"Don't rush into anything, Happy Clam Girl."

"I'm not," she insisted. "I've found the perfect man."

"So I'm wrong, then? Is it perfect when he kisses you?"

His words stopped her in the doorway. It took a moment for her to nod.

"Yeah, right. I thought so," he sneered.

She didn't stay to clean or make his bed. She wasn't going near that bed with Henry Gilbert in the room. She wasn't going near Henry anywhere. If she saw him on the beach she'd walk the other way. If she called, "Housekeeping," and he said, "Come in," she'd move on to another room. She'd found the man for her, and she wasn't going to mess things up.

For once in her life, she was going to be smart when it came to men. And that was that.

Chapter Sixteen

"I'm not cleaning room twelve anymore," Celeste informed her sister later that afternoon.

Her conversation with Henry had unnerved her. The fact that she couldn't get him out of her mind unnerved her even more. She'd worked with Nemo on some commands but that had only made her think of Henry. His words kept coming back to taunt her. *Is it perfect when he kisses you?*

Yes, of course it was. So far Paul hadn't driven her wild the way Emerson used to. Not yet anyway. But you couldn't tell much from just a couple of kisses.

Or from reading part of someone's novel. So what if she'd about caught fire when she read what Henry had written? Who wouldn't? That didn't mean a thing, other than that Henry Gilbert had a way with words.

But she sure didn't want to find out what else he might have a way with. She wanted Paul, not Henry.

"Is he planning another murder?" Jenna teased.

"Ha-ha."

"Seriously, is there a problem?"

"No, I need a break. He's…" *Too cute for my own good.*

"Don't tell me you're interested in him," Jenna said, looking worried.

"No. He just… I just…"

Jenna frowned. "You are."

"I am not," Celeste insisted. "But I don't want to be around him." He was far too tempting, and Celeste had no intention of giving in to temptation.

"Paul is perfect."

Is it perfect when he kisses you?

Celeste batted the words out of her brain. "I know he is. I want Paul." No lie. She did. Paul was a great guy. He was kind and easy to talk to. Henry was… well, she didn't know what he was.

Yes, she did. He was not the right man. That was what.

"Henry Gilbert is cute, in a nerdy sort of way," Jenna said.

More than nerdy. Jenna hadn't seen him without a shirt.

"But you're smart not to get sidetracked." This from the woman who had men on two different tracks.

"You clean room twelve and I'll work the office," Celeste offered.

"Okay, deal."

And so the next day Jenna went into the lair of the Terror of Room Twelve. "Have you seen him without his shirt?" she asked Celeste when she came back to the office.

"Yeah." *Why do you think I'm here?*

"He's hotter than I realized."

"Don't get attached. You already have two men," Celeste said, but she realized she was only half teasing.

"No room in my life for another man," her sister assured her.

"What did he say when you showed up?" *Did he ask about me?* Oh, for crying out loud. What did she care whether he did or didn't?

"He asked if you were sick."

"What did you say?"

"I told him you were busy helping out somewhere else."

"Did he look disappointed?"

"Hard to tell. He just went back to typing on his laptop." Jenna's eyes narrowed, a sure sign she was about to go into big-sister inquisitor mode.

"What?" Celeste demanded.

"You're falling for this guy. What are you *thinking*?"

"I am not. Falling for him, that is. Well, maybe a little."

The expression on her sister's face said it all. *Here we go again.* "Celeste, you hardly know him."

"I'm aware of that."

"It's glamorous that he's a writer and all, but those creative types are flaky."

Thanks to her ex the artiste, Jenna was slightly

prejudiced. Celeste should have been, too, after dating Josh, the musician. He'd been completely undependable and constantly broke. But writers were different. Weren't they?

"Celeste?" Jenna prodded.

"Huh? Oh, yeah, you're right."

Now Jenna was looking truly concerned. "Don't do anything stupid, not when such a great man is crazy about you and you've got a chance for the kind of future you've always wanted."

"Don't worry, I won't," Celeste said.

She normally had terrible taste in men. The fact that she was seeing one who was actually capable of making a serious relationship work was practically a miracle, and she'd be a fool to blow that simply because some other man who was passing through wrote stuff that gave her hormones a whirl. And was easy to talk to.

But so was Paul. He never judged; he never shamed. He'd never cheat on her. And he was kind and encouraging.

Henry, on the other hand, came with baggage.

Paul had no baggage. Well, maybe a tiny carry-on hidden somewhere. But she had yet to find it.

Henry could probably use some help in getting rid of his baggage. The right woman...

Celeste frowned. What was she doing? It was pointless to have her sister clean Henry's room so she could avoid him physically if she wasn't going to avoid him mentally, too. No talking about Henry

Gilbert; no thinking about Henry Gilbert. No looking at Henry Gilbert if he happened to pass by.

Which he did a couple of days later when she was on the beach working with Nemo. She'd been trying to get him to stay when he gave a *woof* and took off.

"Nemo, come back!" she called irritably, and turned to see the cause of her dog's lapse. Here came Henry, running along the water's edge. Shirtless and wearing sunglasses instead of his regular ones. A writer shouldn't look that sexy. "Nemo, come!"

Nemo loped back to her, and directly behind him was Henry. She could hardly pretend she hadn't seen him. But she didn't have to hang around and talk with him. She snapped Nemo's leash on his collar and started walking toward the house. She'd say a passing hello and leave it at that.

She began walking at a determined clip. Surely, Henry would get the message and run on past, give her a friendly wave.

He didn't run on past. Instead, he ran right up to her.

"Hi, Henry," she said and kept on walking.

He fell in step with her. "Is it my imagination or are you avoiding me?"

"It's your imagination," she said, keeping her gaze straight ahead.

"Didn't you accuse me a while back of not having enough imagination?"

"I guess it's improved."

"It was the love scene, wasn't it? It got you all

steamed up and that freaked you out. Another minute and you'd have—"

Jerk! That simple reminder of what she'd read was enough to get her steamed up all over again. "Don't you have something to do besides bother people who are minding their own business and trying to take a walk on the beach?"

"It looked like you were trying to train your dog. I think you need help."

Boy, he could say that again. "I don't need any help," she said, for her benefit as well as his.

"I think maybe you do, Happy Clam Girl."

She scowled at him. "Will you please stop calling me that?"

"You know, that was a perfectly good scene," he continued. "Haven't you ever read a romance novel?"

"Of course I have! I love romance novels." And some of the scenes she'd read in those books got her pretty stirred up. But none of them affected her the way Henry's writing had.

"Well, then, if it wasn't the love scene, what sent you running?"

It was as much the person who'd written those words as the words themselves. If she'd read any further she would've wound up horizontal. With him.

"I didn't even get into any gory details," he continued.

She made a face. "Don't use that word." And what if she'd been reading one of the scary scenes? How would that have affected her? She'd probably have been terrified. But at least she would've had an excuse for running away.

"You want to know why I think you freaked out?"

"No."

"Because you were afraid of what would happen between us if you kept reading," he said with an irritating smile.

"You are so full of yourself," she said in her frostiest tone of voice.

"No, I'm not. Admit it. My love scene got you all primed for sex and that made you feel guilty."

"I have nothing to feel guilty about," she said, her cheeks simmering.

"Are you sure? I bet you were worried about what your boyfriend would think. Like I said before, he seems kind of prissy to me."

"Well, he's not. Anyway, I like prissy."

He gave a snort. "Yeah, right. You're delusional."

"Oh? And how is it you know so much?"

"'Cause I've been down that road. I was so sure I was with the right woman. I only saw what I wanted to see."

"I've been down that road, too. I've raced into love so many times, I should have owned a racetrack. But that's changed. I've finally gotten smart, and there's nothing wrong with my eyesight."

He shrugged. "If you say so. It's none of my business."

"That's right, it's not. And I'm not reading any more of your book."

"Okay, fine. Your loss," he said easily. "Look, I'm

not gonna stalk you, Celeste. If you want help training your dog, my offer's still good. And if your sister gets sick of cleaning my room you can come back and do it, and I'll go for a run or go to the store or something. I don't want to be the creep who scares the maid," he finished with a smile.

It was a boyish smile, a harmless, friendly, irresistible smile.

"I'll even let you change the bed," he added.

Bed, aack! *You are not interested in Henry Gilbert. You are not!*

"Come on, what do you say? You don't need to be scared of me. Let's call a truce and give Nemo an obedience lesson."

Paul would be happy if Nemo was better behaved. Surely, giving a dog an obedience lesson didn't count as hanging out with someone. Anyway, she now had her boundaries firmly in place.

But would Paul believe that? And what if somebody came along and saw them together?

"What do you say, Nemo?" Henry asked the dog.

"Woof!" Nemo answered, and wagged his tail.

"There you have it. Come on, let's give the boy a lesson," Henry said. Then, not waiting for an answer, he started working with her dog.

Well, Nemo did need help.

She did, too.

Jenna had opted for a quick beach walk to rest her tired brain after doing the books for the motel. The sun was out and the air was fresh and tinged with salt. She could hear the waves crashing. Ah, yes, there was nothing like a beach walk to bring out the happy in life.

She'd just cleared the dunes when she caught sight of her sister and their summer resident, Henry Gilbert, on the beach with Nemo. Henry was making a hand motion for the dog to stay. To her astonishment, Nemo stayed put. Then he called and Nemo came bounding toward him. Henry knelt to pet the dog and looked up at Celeste, who pushed back her hair and smiled down at him.

Even from where she stood, Jenna knew how to caption that picture. Good grief, her sister was a mess. She needed to pull Celeste away from Henry Gilbert before she did something stupid, drag her back to the house and…what? Lock her in their bedroom? Like she had any control over her sister's love life?

If only. Paul Welch was the smart choice. Celeste should concentrate on him instead of muddying the love waters with another man.

When it came to water-muddying, though, Jenna was hardly one to talk. She herself was having trouble deciding between two men. She abandoned the beach walk and went to the house in search of lemonade. She'd tried to help, given her sister advice, but in the end Celeste had to make her own choice. Jenna could only hope she chose wisely.

She soon had other things to think about besides her sister's love life, although that was never far from her thoughts.

"You have to run for that council position," Nora

told her when the friends met in Aunt Edie's living room for their weekly Friday night get-together. "Susan's declared her candidacy. The last person we need on council is her."

"Yes, please, save us from that," put in Courtney.

Jenna had hoped her friends would drop the subject of her running for council. Instead, they were gripping it more tightly.

"We need people with vision," Tyrella said.

Jenna took a sip of her wine. "I don't know. I don't think I'm cut out for that."

"Of course you are," Celeste told her. "You're good at running things."

"I think you'd be wonderful," Aunt Edie told her.

"I'm so busy here."

"We can pick up the slack at the Driftwood," Courtney assured her. "Can't we, Edie?"

"Of course we can. I can certainly put in more hours on the front desk."

Good old Aunt Edie, eighty-three going on thirty. At least in her mind. But no way was Jenna going to load any extra work on her great-aunt. Edie already did enough, cooking for everyone and baking cookies for Jenna to offer their Driftwood Inn guests.

"I'll think about it," Jenna said, and left it at that.

But there was no getting away from the topic. She and Brody were at Good Times Ice Cream Parlor indulging in sundaes the following day when he brought up the subject.

"Did Nora put you up to this?" she demanded.

Nora stood behind the counter, dishing up ice

cream for Sabrina and Tristan. She cast a look in their direction, a downright conspiratorial one.

"You should," he said, neither confirming nor denying.

"Why is everyone so anxious to volunteer me for this?" Jenna groaned.

"Because you'd be good at it," he said.

"You'd be just as good. Probably better. You're the king of schmooze."

"Yeah, but I don't have the vision you do."

"Okay, you run for the position and I'll feed you ideas."

He shook his head at her. "Don't be such a chicken. You were born for greatness. Accept it."

"Accept what?" asked Sabrina, plopping down on a seat next to Jenna.

"A bunch of us want your mom to run for city council," Brody told her.

"Wow, Mom, that would be awesome!"

"No, it would be work," Jenna corrected.

"You'd be really important," Sabrina continued.

"She already is," said Brody. "But Sabrina's right. You should run."

"Are you going to campaign for me?" Jenna asked him, half joking.

"Of course. I'll be your campaign manager."

"We'll help. Won't we, Tristan?" Sabrina said to Tristan, who'd joined them.

"Sure. Uh, help what?"

"My mom's gonna run for city council."

"Cool," Tristan said. "I'll build you a website."

"There you go." Brody nodded as if it was all settled. "You've already got a campaign manager and a website."

"And don't forget me," Sabrina said.

"It costs money to run for office, even a small one like city councilor, and in case you've forgotten, I don't have any to spare."

"Don't worry. I'll raise the money for you," Brody promised.

"I still have a business to run," she protested.

"So does everyone else on the council," he argued.

"Yeah, but their kids are all raised."

"I'm raised," Sabrina said, looking offended.

"And I have the Driftwood."

"I can clean rooms when Aunt Celeste leaves," Sabrina said, filling Jenna with motherly pride.

"That's sweet of you, but you'll be busy with school and extracurricular activities."

"Hey, if she's willing to help, take it. Not everybody's got such a great kid," Brody said and Sabrina rewarded his compliment with a smile.

Way to win points with the daughter, thought Jenna, and she, too, smiled.

"So what do you say?" Brody pressed.

With every objection being swept away she was getting closer and closer to the edge of commitment. "Oh, what am I thinking?" she fretted.

She knew what she was thinking. She was already considering all the things she could do to help the town, the contributions she could make. Moonlight Harbor was a wonderful place to live and to visit. It could be even more wonderful with a convention center and possibly that aquarium Kiki Strom had once proposed. Maybe she really could be a mover and a shaker. Maybe she could be someone important.

"Well," she said, waffling.

"All right," Brody said, translating that as a *yes* and rubbing his hands together.

Nora came around the counter and stood by their table. "Well?"

"She's in," Brody said. He looked at Jenna. "Aren't you?"

"Go for it, Mom," Sabrina said eagerly.

Jenna took a deep breath, then took the plunge. "Okay, I'm in." If she won, she'd know it was meant to be. If she lost, which she probably would, she could at least say she'd tried and that would make everyone, including her, happy.

Her announcement was met with much excitement at home. "All my friends will vote for you," Aunt Edie assured her.

"I can't vote, but I'll pass out flyers while I'm here," Celeste promised. "Oh, and we should make buttons. And you need a slogan. When does your team meet?"

"I'm not sure I exactly have a team yet," Jenna said.

"You have us," Aunt Edie told her. "And Brody as your campaign manager."

"That's team enough to start with. Let's meet right after you get signed up," Celeste suggested.

Which meant they met the very next day. Brody

went with her to City Hall and helped her fill out the necessary paperwork, and that evening The Jenna Jones for City Council campaign had its first meeting in Aunt Edie's living room. Her team consisted of her family, Brody, Nora, Tyrella, Ellis West, who owned the Seafood Shack, which was right next to the motel, and Courtney.

"How's this for a slogan? Jenna Jones: fresh face, fresh ideas," Celeste proposed.

"I like it," said Nora. "Makes it sound like something good will happen with you on board."

Hopefully, they wouldn't capsize with her on board.

Susan Frank was sure they would. "Honestly, Jenna," she said when they ran into each other in the grocery store a few days later. "What do you think you're doing? You've never held an office."

"Have you?" Jenna countered.

"I certainly have. I was on the council ten years ago. And I've lived here for years. I know how we operate in this town. You're still a newcomer. You have no idea how we do things."

"I think I'm learning pretty quickly," Jenna said.

Susan shook her head. "You're still too green. Withdraw, take a little more time to get to know the community." *Don't stand in my way.*

That confirmed it. Jenna had made the right decision when she decided to run. "Well, Susan, I think that even though I'm a relative newcomer, I have something to offer."

Susan rolled her eyes. "Go ahead, be stubborn. But I'm afraid you're going to be disappointed."

"I'll risk it," Jenna said and wheeled her cart away. She wouldn't be half as disappointed if she lost as the residents of Moonlight Harbor would be if Susan won.

Once she'd committed herself to running for office, her campaign hit high gear. Almost everyone on her team chipped in money for the cause and several of her friends from the Chamber contributed to her campaign fund, as well. Nora, Cindy Redmond and one of the older women from church hosted get-acquainted coffee hours for her, which brought in more contributions. Brody paid not only to have signs made—bright blue with Jenna's slogan on them—but buttons, too, that announced, *I'm Voting for Jenna.* Ellis found plenty of takers for the signs and got busy pounding them into front yards.

Then there was the doorbelling, which kept everyone busy. Celeste, who could talk the scales off a fish, reported positive reactions from the people she talked with, as did Brody. Sabrina got fussed over by plenty of residents, with comments such as "Good for you for being so civic-minded," and "Aren't you sweet to be helping your mom's campaign?"

Jenna, on the other hand, experienced a wider variety of comments, including "How much experience have you had?" and "Weren't you the one in charge of the Seaside with Santa festival?"

She tried her best to answer these comments in a positive way. "This would be my first involvement in local government, but I do know how to run a business, and I think some of the same principles apply." Or "The weather was unfortunate—" *that* was an understatement "—but many of our local businesses benefited from it." There, sounding like a politician already.

"I didn't benefit," said a woman who'd paid for a booth on the pier. "I'm voting for Susan."

"Don't get discouraged," Brody told Jenna at their next campaign meeting. "You don't need to convince everyone in Moonlight Harbor to vote for you come November, just a majority."

No problem.

The summer moved on, with schmoozing and doorbelling on her sister's behalf, cleaning rooms and helping Jenna by taking Sabrina for practice drives. Fortunately, Jenna had mellowed out and allowed Celeste and Sabrina together in the car again. Neither even mentioned the idea of having music on when they drove. Then there was line dancing, which Celeste still enjoyed doing when Paul was busy with his building committee.

She was also reading more of Henry's book. She'd vowed not to read so much as another page, but the rat had left some printed pages on his bed one morning when he went for a run and she was in there cleaning all by herself and, well, they were just lying there. And she'd gotten hooked.

"I thought you didn't want to read any more of my stuff," he'd teased when he came into the room and caught her. "You really are a snoop."

"You left them lying out," she'd said in her own defense.

"Uh-huh. So what did you think?"

"I was glad it wasn't a gory scene, that's what I thought."

"No, about the writing."

She'd laughed. "Are you fishing for a compliment?"

"Maybe. We writers are all basically insecure, you know."

And that was when the conversation had turned serious. She'd told him he was a very good writer and that she hoped he became a bestseller. They'd moved from there to sharing hopes and dreams. Henry wanted to succeed at his writing, to prove to his parents that he'd made the right move in quitting his job, and to keep up with his older brother, the jock, who was a babe magnet and made big bucks managing a sports store chain. And yes, to make the woman who dumped him eat her heart out.

"I guess that's the guy equivalent of the woman who wants to go to her ten-year reunion looking hot and making the old boyfriend jealous with the guy she's brought as a date," he'd said with an embarrassed smile.

"There's nothing wrong with wanting to prove you're worth the space you're taking up," she'd told him.

"Is that why you're with the preacher?" Henry had asked. "You wanting to be noble or something?"

Just wanting to be loved by a good man. And yes, she wouldn't mind living nobly. "Maybe."

"It's good to be noble. It's also good to be crazy

in love," he'd murmured, and the edges of the room had turned all soft and fuzzy and suddenly, it felt as if there wasn't enough oxygen. And hot. Was it hot in there?

Celeste had remembered she had other rooms to clean and scrammed.

Paul came over that same night and played Farkle with her, Jenna and Aunt Edie. They'd enjoyed lavender lemonade and some of Aunt Edie's sugar cookies, had laughed and teased each other. He'd smiled at her, and her heart had squeezed in response, and she knew she was with the right man. Finally.

She reminded herself of that on Sunday morning when Hyacinth and her friends gathered on the other side of the church foyer and gave her nasty looks. If not for the fact that they were all in church, she'd have sworn they were hexing her.

Hyacinth had tried, but she couldn't bring herself to like Celeste Jones. The woman was never serious. And Hyacinth was sure Celeste wasn't serious about Paul. But what more could she do? She'd tried to warn him and had gotten a lecture on gossip for her efforts.

It was early days, she consoled herself. They'd only been dating a few weeks. They were still in the infatuation stage of their relationship. At some point Paul would come to his senses and realize what a non-match they were. Celeste was only in Moonlight Harbor for the summer. In September she'd go back to her real life and he'd go back to his. And when he did, Hyacinth would find a way to make sure she played a more important part in it.

She was still thinking about that when she went to church on Saturday morning before opening her shop to arrange flowers for the Sunday service. She'd finished with the sanctuary and was in the women's restroom, placing a vase on the vanity counter, when she heard the sound of male voices in the foyer. One of them she'd have known anywhere. Paul.

The other voice, a deeper one, was laughing at something he'd said. Kenneth Edwards, one of the church trustees. He was retired and stopped by a lot to discuss church business and do handyman chores around the building. She'd just saunter out and join them, say hi to Paul.

She started to open the door when she heard Paul say, "So, is end of summer too soon to say something?"

Say something? What kind of something? They could be talking about anything. It didn't have to be what she thought it was.

She stood rooted where she was, the door barely open, holding her breath. She could feel her blood pulsing, her heart pounding like an angry prisoner banging to be let out of its cell.

"Do you think she feels the same way?" asked Kenneth.

Nooo.

"Yeah, I do," Paul said.

"Well, she seems like a nice young woman. Got a ready smile."

Too ready, if you asked Hyacinth.

"She'd be a good balance for you since you tend to be a little more serious."

No, she wouldn't!

"I've never fallen this hard for a woman," Paul confessed.

That's because she tripped you.

"I felt the same way about Bootsie," said Kenneth. "Asked her to marry me on our second date."

Paul chuckled. "And what did she say?"

"She told me I was nuts."

Just like Paul was.

"But six months later we were married. When it's the right one, you know. I say go for it."

I say don't listen to him.

"Good advice," said Paul and the two men moved on toward the front door.

Hyacinth shut the bathroom door and leaned against it. She was going to be sick. Or cry. Or both. Paul was making a huge mistake. What was she going to do about it?

Chapter Seventeen

Paul didn't want to do anything to crank up the gossip machine, so he drove to a jewelry shop in the nearby city of Aberdeen to look at rings. He wondered if he should be doing this so early in his relationship with Celeste, but decided that was nothing more than a bout of insecurity. Brought on partly by the small misunderstanding they'd had on the Fourth, but mostly from the bits of gossip that certain tattlers had embedded in his brain.

He was determined not to listen to it. He didn't want to rush into anything, of course, but by the end of summer Celeste would be gone and he wanted to settle things between them before she went back to school, make sure she was as serious as he was.

Come to think of it, why would she even need to go back to her old life? She was happy in Moonlight Harbor. She could stay right here and they could make wedding plans. Maybe for next spring. Or better yet, for fall.

"Are you sure this is the one?" his father had asked when he made a long distance call to his parents in Africa. "It feels rather fast."

Normally, Paul was a cautious man, taking time to pray and carefully consider any major decision. "Things are going along at a pretty good clip," he'd admitted. But that didn't mean he'd rushed into this relationship.

"Have you prayed about this?"

"Of course I have," he'd replied, insulted. He'd already seen enough of Celeste's character to know what a good-hearted woman she was. He'd asked God for a sign to help him know for sure, and nothing had stopped their relationship from growing sweeter all the time. As far as he was concerned, that was the best confirmation possible. So why wait? "You'll love her, Dad. She's wonderful."

Her dog, not so much. Dogs were smelly and infamous for their ability to demolish a couch in an afternoon when left unsupervised. And this one had no manners. But he knew Celeste and Nemo were a package deal, so he'd put up with the dog. They'd get Nemo better trained once they were married. And keep him outside.

"I'll take your word for it," his father had said. "But be wise, son. Once you make that vow, you're committed."

Paul was already committed and had said as much.

"All right, then. You know you have our blessing."

There it was, another sign that he could keep moving forward with Celeste.

He picked out a ring, not the biggest diamond in the world but it was the nicest one he could afford. Celeste wasn't so shallow that she'd care about the size of the diamond anyway. He put money down on it and left the store with a smile on his face. By the time he had it paid off, he'd be ready to propose.

The weekend of the second annual Blue Moon festival arrived. The church volunteers were planning another go at selling strawberry shortcake. This time around, Celeste didn't sign up to work the booth.

"Mom's going to be here," she told Tyrella. "I want to be able to hang out with her." And not with the resident church poops.

"And someone else, too, I imagine," Tyrella responded with a chuckle. "Looks like things are going strong with you and Pastor Paul."

They were. "He's the best," Celeste said.

"You're lucky to get him," Tyrella informed her. "I think all the single women in church wanted him."

One did, for sure. "Yes, I am lucky," Celeste said.

"You'd better dance with me at the street dance," she said to him as they walked along the beach the Monday before, Nemo racing ahead of them. It was Paul's day off, and they were spending it together. Beach walks, a picnic lunch. Later he was taking her to a movie. Her life had never been better.

"You know I can't dance."

"Okay, you stand there and I'll dance around you," she teased. "Or better yet, hold me in your arms and just shuffle around."

"That I can manage," he said with a smile.

There hadn't been too much of that holding-in-the-arms stuff. Only a few tender kisses. Paul had put the brakes down on his sex drive. "You deserve to be treated with respect," he'd said one evening after bringing her home from a drive along the coast.

No man had ever said that to her, and she'd nearly melted into a puddle right there in his car.

"Not that I don't want to do more with you," he'd added. "You're a beautiful woman, Celeste, both inside and out."

No man had ever said that to her, either. Paul was a gift, no doubt about it.

Celeste came to Henry's room to clean the Friday morning of the festival. "Are you going?" she asked him.

"Maybe," he said, clacking away on his laptop.

"You should. It's lots of fun. Booths with all kinds of great food, rides on the pier. There's a street dance Saturday night down by the pier. You don't want to hole up in here like an old hermit crab."

"You gonna be at the street dance?" he asked, eyes still on his laptop.

"I'm going to be at everything."

"With the preacher, I suppose."

"Of course."

Henry shook his head and kept typing. "Bet he doesn't even dance."

"Well, he's going to."

Henry gave a grunt. "I'd like to see that."

"What have you got against pastors anyway?" she demanded, irked.

"Nothing. I think they're great. Self-sacrificing,

doing good deeds, spreading the good word and all that." He finally looked up. "I just don't think he's the right guy for you."

"We've had this conversation before," she said and marched to her supply cart to deposit his dirty towels.

"Just sayin'. But what do I know?" Henry said when she returned with body wash, shampoo and fresh towels. "If he makes you happy, that's what's important."

"He does," she said.

"Lucky you. And he'll probably stay with you for the long haul."

"That's what I want." No, it was more than wanting. "What I need," she corrected herself.

"But you want both of you to be happy, right?"

"Of course. And we will be. We have fun together, Henry."

"You can have fun with anyone."

"I want to have fun with *him*. And I want more than that. I want a soul connection."

"Pastors are all about souls. I guess you're good to go there."

Yes, she was. Time to change the subject. "How's the book coming?"

"Getting close to the end. Just finished a scene. Want to read it?"

"Is it gory?"

"No." He held out his laptop.

She took it and sat down on the bed, and he moved next to her, looking over her shoulder as she read about the detective hero's strategy to protect the serial killer's latest target. The last time she'd snooped, er, checked, the killer had nearly succeeded in murdering the poor woman and now, like Henry's fictional cop, Celeste feared for the woman's life.

"I don't think I can take much more of this," she said as they went up the walk to his beach place.

He never brought women here, hardly came here himself anymore. But it was still a good place to stash someone. She'd be safe here. That was why he was bringing her. That was what he'd told himself. But he knew it was more than that. She'd become like air to him. The air he breathed. The air that kept him alive...

Celeste couldn't help sighing. "That is really romantic."

"That's how a man should feel about a woman," Henry said.

Celeste knew that was how Paul felt about her.

"And that's how a woman should feel about a man," he added.

Celeste kept reading.

"This won't last much longer," he promised. *"We're closing in on the sick bastard."*

"It can't be too soon."

He led her to the bedroom where she'd be sleeping, set down her overnight bag. The moonlight was flooding the room, washing over her pale skin and lovely golden hair.

"You're beautiful in the moonlight," he said.

Celeste was suddenly very aware of Henry sitting next to her. She could feel the heat of his body, feel his breath on her neck.

She cleared her throat, which was suddenly dry. "This is good."

"It was inspired by…"

Don't say it. Celeste held her breath. What if he said it was her? She was tingling all over and felt like she had a beehive in her panties.

"Someone," Henry finished.

She didn't ask who. She didn't have to. Feeling self-conscious and uncomfortable, she read on.

Maybe, once this was all over, he'd never see her again. But he had to have her, had to make her his.

The hero got busy doing just that and the bees got busy again. Oh, the things that cop was doing to that woman. It was getting very hot in Henry's room.

"You don't have to finish it," he taunted, breaking the spell.

Celeste frowned and shoved his laptop back at him. "That cop is just using her. I hope the killer gets him."

That made Henry grin. "Every writer wants the reader to have a visceral reaction to his work," he said lightly. "But I have to let my cop live."

"Yeah?" she retorted. "Well, I think *he must die.*"

He laughed. "That's not the title of the book."

"Change the title."

"Besides, how do you know he doesn't really love her?"

"I can tell. He only wants in her pants."

"Crude. What would your preacher say?" Then, before she could reply, his smile was replaced by a more serious expression. "Maybe my hero is afraid to tell her how he really feels," he said softly. "Maybe he doesn't think he has a chance."

It was definitely too hot in this room. "I have work to do," Celeste mumbled and beat it before they could take the conversation any further. The last thing she needed was Henry Gilbert saying what they both knew. They were drawn to each other—metal to magnet, moth to flame.

But attraction wasn't true love. Attraction was what had gotten her in trouble over and over again. She had so much more than that with Paul. No way was she going to do anything to lose it. And darn it all, wasn't it time for Henry Gilbert to check out?

Celeste was glad to see her mother when she arrived, not simply because she loved her dearly and was looking forward to spending time with her, but also because she wanted Mel to meet Paul.

He escorted all the Jones women and Aunt Edie to the festivities on Friday night, and they enjoyed the rides, the corn dogs and a concert by the Moonlight Harbor High a cappella singing group. After the concert he returned to the house to visit.

"What do you think of Paul?" Celeste asked her mom once he'd left.

"He's a really nice man," Mel replied.

"And perfect for her," put in Jenna.

"What do you think, sweetie?" their mother asked Celeste. "Is he the man for you?"

"He's the best thing that ever happened to me." So how could he not be?

"I must say, he's head and shoulders above the other men you've brought home," her mom said with a smile. "But there's more to finding the right partner than a checklist. You know that."

Yes, she did. Of course she did. "How did you know Dad was the right one?" she asked.

"I couldn't picture the rest of my life without him," her mother said simply.

"Yeah, well, I couldn't picture my life without Damien," Jenna muttered, "and look where that got me."

Her mother acknowledged Jenna's point with a nod, then said to Celeste, "I didn't say you shouldn't have a checklist. But the connection needs to be there, too."

"We have that," Celeste told her.

"If you do, then you're all set."

But what if you had a connection with another man, as well? Celeste decided not to ask. She wasn't even sure why. Because she didn't want to look like a flake? Or was it something else? Maybe she didn't want her mom advising her to wait and be absolutely certain. She'd waited long enough; she'd been waiting all her life. She was tired of waiting. Paul was the man for her.

Strolling through the crowd hand in hand with him on Saturday only confirmed it. She was so happy she couldn't stop smiling.

Until he suggested they go to the church food booth for some strawberry shortcake. There was Hyacinth, dishing up the treats and dishing up smiles for everyone who came by.

Everyone except Celeste. The smile faltered at the

sight of her. She did manage to be polite, though, and asked Celeste how she was enjoying the festival.

"I'm loving it," Celeste said.

"I wish you could have volunteered to help us out," Hyacinth said. "We could've used an extra hand."

They seemed to have plenty of hands on deck. What a cheap shot. She suspected Paul was now wondering why she hadn't been willing to do her part for a good cause. Maybe he was even wondering if she was unselfish enough for him. She felt a flush of shame creep up her neck.

Darn it all, she had nothing to be ashamed of. "My mom's in town. I wanted to spend time with her."

"Oh? Where is she?" Hyacinth asked and glanced around.

"Right now she's with my sister at the dunking booth, trying to dunk the mayor." *Too bad we couldn't put you in the dunking booth. I'd spend a fortune trying to drown you.*

Okay, that was not a nice thought. Celeste sent it packing.

Hyacinth, the relationship saboteur, nodded. "I'm sure she's having a good time." She might as well have added, "My job here is done."

"We all are." Celeste pulled out her wallet. "We'll take two strawberry shortcakes."

"I'm paying for that," said Paul, who already had the money out of his wallet.

"No, this one's on me. I want to do my part." *So there.*

He handed Hyacinth a ten anyway. Of course he

would because it was for a good cause. And because it was a Paul sort of thing to do.

"I did work the booth on the Fourth," she reminded him as they walked away.

"Why are you telling me that? Are you worried I'll think you're a slacker?" he teased.

He was so insightful, it was scary. "Yeah, as a matter of fact, I am. Paul, I'm not sure we're a fit." Would she ever receive the approval of his congregation? His *whole* congregation? That had to be important to him.

He slipped an arm around her and smiled. "You fit fine."

"You know what I mean."

"Yes, I do, and we've had this conversation before. You have got to stop worrying about what other people think."

"I can't help it."

"Yeah, you can. Every time you're tempted to go there, remind yourself that I think you're fabulous."

"Do you? Really? There's still so much you don't know about me."

"What don't I know?"

"I love margaritas."

"Olé."

"I love to party."

"I'll bring the balloons."

"Sometimes I have a potty mouth. Except you already know that." That alone should have been enough to disqualify her from being a pastor's girlfriend.

"I'll bring the soap."

"I'm being serious," she said, exasperated.

"You've got a dab of strawberry on your chin," he said. He removed his hand from around her waist and wiped off the offending dribble with his finger.

His touch should have sent a tingle down her neck. It didn't. It only irritated her. Another man would have licked off that bit of strawberry. Or not pointed it out in the first place. She pulled away.

"I've got faults, too," he said. "We all have faults, but we're all in this together. Come on, now, don't let your insecurities spoil our day."

Her *insecurities*. He said it so condescendingly. "I think my insecurities matter."

"Of course they do," he said, backpedaling. "But they're not based on anything real."

She didn't know if she liked that, either.

"What's real is what's happening between the two of us."

He said it so softly, so sweetly. Of course he was right. She was being insecure for no reason.

"We all change. We all keep working on becoming better people."

That was what she wanted.

"I know you'll do that."

She realized it was said to encourage her, but somehow his words left her feeling even more insecure. She felt an underlying message. *Keep working at it. You'll measure up eventually.*

She'd picked the right man for her. But now, suddenly, she was wondering whether he'd picked the right woman for himself.

Chapter Eighteen

The rest of Paul and Celeste's day together went so smoothly that it effectively smothered her moment of doubt. He even stayed long enough into the evening to dance one dance with her.

He was right; he couldn't dance. That was okay. She was happy to shuffle about with his arms around her. Very romantic.

But the romance ended too soon when the musicians paused between songs and he said, "I need to get home and get ready for tomorrow. Pastors only have Friday nights to be the life of the party," he added jokingly.

That would be the case with pastors' wives, too. But she didn't need to party every night. She wasn't a college kid anymore. She was ready to settle down, start a new life and a family. Down the road—hopefully, not too far—she'd be giving their kids a bath on a Saturday while Paul went over his sermon for Sunday.

"No problem," she told him. "I understand."

"I'm glad you do. Come on, I'll run you home."

Just because he had to leave didn't mean she had to. She wasn't a pastor's wife yet. The band had started a new song and some of the gang from The Drunken Sailor were lining up to dance.

"You go ahead," she told him. "I'm going to hang around. I'll get a ride home later with Jenna and Brody and Mom."

He nodded, his expression reluctant. "Sorry I have to leave you."

"That's good," she joked. "That way I'll know you miss me."

"I'll miss you every minute," he said and gave her a quick kiss. "See you tomorrow."

"Tomorrow," she repeated.

She sent him off with a finger wave, then joined the dancers.

Everyone was doing a dance she knew and she had no trouble jumping in. Too soon the music was over and she found herself wishing Paul could have stayed a little longer. Later on she'd try to talk him into taking some dance lessons with her. Oh, yeah. A tango, like those sexy ones they did on *Dancing with the Stars*.

The band started a fast number and she sighed. She sure loved to dance.

Emerson had been great on the dance floor. He'd had the moves.

He'd had the moves, all right, and he'd enjoyed doing them with more than one woman. So did she want a man who could dance or a man who would treat her with respect? The answer to that was a no-brainer. Still, her feet were itching to move and there was no stopping them. She found herself having her own little party at the edge of the crowd.

"Want to dance?" asked a voice at her elbow.

She wasn't given a chance to reply. The guy—oh, no, Henry!—already had a hold of her hand and was leading her into the throng. Next thing she knew, he'd put an arm around her waist and was putting her through some pretty sexy moves. He flung her out, brought her back in, dipped her, nearly made her dizzy. Definitely made her laugh from the simple thrill of it all. Who knew Henry Gilbert could dance?

"That was seriously impressive," she said when they were done.

"Yes, it was," he agreed, and the look he gave her…oh, no, here came the bees.

Time to go home, after all, especially since the band was launching into "Send My Love," a sexy Adele song. "Thanks," she said, and started to walk away.

"Oh, no," he said, catching her arm. "You don't want to miss this song. Know how to do a nightclub two-step?"

It was her favorite dance, one she hadn't done since she broke up with Emerson.

Henry moved like a pro, and it was a treat to dance with someone who was so good. The music got inside her, bubbling away. What a high.

Then the band went for something slower, and he slid his hand along Celeste's middle and settled it on her lower back. Buzz.

"You're a good dancer," she told him, trying desperately to distract herself from the sensations he was causing.

"You're an ideal partner," he said.

She could feel the heat coming off his chest. He had stubble on his chin. He was wearing some kind of citrusy aftershave. Did it have pheromones in it? Had to. She was being seduced by pheromones.

"Don't say stuff like that," she said.

"Why not? You are." Then he made a face. "Oh, yeah. You should only be an ideal partner with your preacher. Where is he?"

"He had to go home."

"He just left you here?"

"Of course not! He had to go and I wasn't ready to leave yet."

"You shouldn't, not when there's still music to dance to." Henry's hand splayed across her back and he pulled her close.

The heat between them was nearly killing her. She was going to melt right there on the street, under the moonlight. *There's more to life than sex*, she reminded herself. *And crazy, wild attraction is...crazy.*

"Forget this guy," he whispered, his breath ruffling her hair. "He's not the one for you and you know it."

"Henry, don't," she said. It was a pitifully half-hearted protest.

"Give me a chance. I could make you happy."

He probably could. Oh, what was she doing?

She was suddenly aware of him bending just

enough to brush his lips against her neck. Oooh, what was *he* doing?

She swallowed. "There's more to life than sex." There, she'd said it.

"Of course there is," he agreed. His hand slipped down to her bottom.

She was going mushy in all the right places.

"We have a connection. You know we do," he continued.

The song ended but they were still practically glued together. All Henry had to do was say the word, and she and her tingly mushy parts would go back to his room with him and let him do all those things to her that he'd inspired his hero to do. Her eyes drifted shut, imagining...

"Celeste!"

Her eyes flew open, and she saw Jenna, Brody and their mom. She stepped away from Henry, feeling like a sugar addict caught stealing from the candy bowl.

"Mom's ready to go home," Jenna said and glared at Henry.

"I can bring you back," he said to Celeste.

If she stayed, she knew what would happen. She'd be signing the death certificate on her relationship with Paul. Henry was there for the summer; he'd abandon her in the end. He'd become famous and have affairs with literary groupies or other writers. He'd be like Jenna's husband, finding a "soul mate" who matched his creative talents and leaving Celeste broken and bleeding.

"Thanks," she said to him, "but I'd better go."

Frustration and anger chased across his face. "Fine. Do what you gotta do."

Picking the right man was what she had to do. She said a quick good-night and hurried off.

Jenna didn't say anything as they made their way to Brody's car, but Celeste knew she would the minute they were in the house.

Sure enough, she began as soon as she'd shut the front door. "Look, I know you have to make your own choices, but I thought you and Paul were an item."

"We are," Celeste insisted.

"Then what were you thinking back there?" Jenna scolded.

"I wasn't thinking." That was for sure. "I was just dancing."

"Just dancing? You looked ready to peel your clothes off."

"Honey," their mom added, "if Paul's the one for you, you can't be dancing like that with other men."

"Dancing? That wasn't dancing, that was foreplay," Jenna snapped.

Yes, it was. But instead of making her feel penitent, her sister's words turned Celeste defensive. "Since when is that any of your business?" she demanded. "I can dance with whoever I want. I'm not married. I'm not even engaged."

"At the rate you're going you won't be," Jenna retorted. "You'd better hope nobody tells Paul about this. He'll dump you in a heartbeat."

"He doesn't own me yet." *Own* her? Where had that come from?

"Girls," Mel said, stepping into the fray, "let's calm down. Things will work out with the man they're meant to work out with."

So there. Celeste almost stuck her tongue out at her big sister.

Until her mother looked at her sternly and added, "But meanwhile, don't go rushing into anything with that man. That will only confuse you further."

It didn't seem she could get any more confused than she already was. She stamped upstairs to bed as irritated with herself as she was with her sister.

"I'll clean his room from now on," Jenna called up after her.

"Fine," she hollered back. "You can clean all the rooms."

By Sunday morning Celeste's brain had decided to function again. She apologized to her sister, sent her mother home with promises that she was going to be wise, then rented kayaks and took Paul kayaking out in the bay after church. The water was sparkling and the sun was out. The gulls were wheeling on the breeze, calling to them. Across the bay they could see Westhaven, catch a glimpse of a boat or two headed for open water to fish. It felt so…companionable.

After they returned the kayaks, she brought him back to the house to have dinner with the family. Tristan was present, too, and they all settled in to watch a vintage movie with Aunt Edie.

Paul said nothing to indicate that anyone had gossiped about her dancing with Henry after he'd left the night before, and she breathed an inward sigh of relief. By the time he'd kissed her good-night and gone home, she'd gotten her world back on its axis and all was well.

She assured her sister that she had her head on straight again and that she'd be fine cleaning Henry's room. But in spite of her assurances, she was very aware of her heart trampolining around in her chest as she parked her supply cart outside room twelve the next morning. The day before he'd hung a Do Not Disturb sign on the door. She wished it was still there.

She knocked on the door. "Housekeeping."

No answer. Good.

She went inside to find both Henry and his laptop missing. He'd gone somewhere else to write. That saved her from an awkward scene or, even worse, having the bees start buzzing again. The bees would wait. There'd be plenty of buzzing once she got together with Paul.

She couldn't help wondering why he wanted her when they were so different. He was more serious. She was more fun-loving, a little more out there. Okay, a lot more out there. Who would have thought they'd get together?

But what was it people always said? Opposites attract. They had definitely attracted and she shouldn't look that gift horse in the mouth, whatever that meant, but simply take what she'd been given—and be grateful for it. They would each bring something unique to the relationship, one complementing the other. They'd be happy together.

* * *

Henry camped out in Books and Beans most of the day, writing and drinking enough coffee to keep himself awake for the next forty-eight hours. He half wished he'd stayed in his room, confronted Celeste or at least given her another love scene to read. These days he was much more interested in writing those than in putting his killer to work. In fact, it seemed that sex was all he could think about. Sex with Celeste. He could have seduced her. If her family hadn't come along when they did, the two of them would have wound up in his room, and they wouldn't have been reading.

Oh, yeah, Don Juan him. He picked up his coffee mug. Empty. Just the way he felt. What was with him, anyway? He could plot an entire book, dream up a clever way to catch a killer, but he couldn't figure out how to get the woman he wanted.

He'd waited long enough. It was time. She must die.

Henry frowned at the screen and shut his laptop. Okay, that was plenty for today. What was Celeste doing? Probably something with the preacher. Maybe giving him a dance lesson.

Dancing, don't think about that. If he shut his eyes he could still see her face, feel that soft little bottom under his hand, could still hear her laugh when he spun her out, see the sparkle in her eyes.

What a fool he was. He'd gone and fallen in love again. With another woman who, in the end, didn't want him. Once more he didn't measure up.

* * *

"I wish you didn't have to go back to Seattle," Paul said as he and Celeste sat side by side on a log, watching the sunset turn the sky orange.

"I do have a job," she said.

"What if something else came up? Here?"

She turned to him. "Like what?"

"Like someone asking you to stay. Could you see yourself living in Moonlight Harbor?"

With Paul. "Maybe. Do you want me to stay?"

"Desperately," he said. He touched a hand to her cheek and looked into her eyes. It wasn't a look that said, "Let's get naked, babe." No, this was a look that said, "Let's take this to the next level and really get serious," and she loved him for it.

He took her face in his hands and kissed her. Now, that was the kiss she'd been waiting for. It promised passion and happily-ever-after and everything she wanted.

"I'm in love with you, Celeste," he said after he ended the kiss. "I want something lasting. I'm hoping you feel the same way."

"How could I not?" she replied and kissed him again.

"Will you stay?"

"Yes, if you want me to."

And so it was settled. He didn't come right out and propose but she knew a proposal was just around the corner. Some people would tell her she was crazy to quit her job when she didn't even have a ring on her finger, but she knew that was coming, too. She could find work in Moonlight Harbor as a substitute teacher and keep helping Jenna at the motel. Yes, everything was working out. Finally. She was smiling when they finally walked back to the house, hand in hand.

"I'm staying," she told her sister gleefully after she'd said goodbye to him. "I'm quitting my job and staying."

"Did he propose already?" Jenna asked eagerly.

"No, but he will. He said he's in love with me and asked me to stay."

Jenna hugged her. "I'm so happy for you. You've finally found the man who's right for you."

Yes, she had.

It wasn't until late that night as she lay in bed and listened to the sound of the waves hitting the beach that she realized Paul had told her he loved her, but she hadn't actually said "I love you" back to him.

Well, she would, because she did.

But if she loved Paul, what was Henry doing in her dreams all of a sudden, dancing with her at some laser-lit dance club?

"Come on over to my place," he said. "I have something special for you."

"You do?"

"Oh, yes. You're going to love it."

He led her outside the club and she realized they were in Vegas. "What are we doing here?" she asked, gazing around.

"We got married here," he informed her. "Now it's time for our wedding night."

His car looked like the Batmobile. She got in and

music started playing—"Music of the Night" from *Phantom of the Opera*. She began to feel a little creeped out.

She was even more creeped out when they arrived at their honeymoon destination. The sign said The Driftwood Inn, but it looked like The Bates Motel, complete with the looming dark Victorian behind it.

"Let's go get something to eat," she said, not wanting to go in.

"What we'll get here is better than anything you'll find in a restaurant," he said and smiled at her. Maniacally.

Wake up. Time to wake up!

He got out of the car, came around and opened her door. "Come on. You're going to love what I've got waiting for you."

"Is it chocolate?"

"Better." He took her by the hand. She tried to draw back, but he was too strong, and next thing she knew he was pulling her to their room. He unlocked the door and swung it wide. "After you."

She looked in. The room had a bed, a nightstand and a single lamp with a frayed shade. It had something else, too. A big, body-size sheet of plastic on the floor. Her eyes shot back to the bed, where a huge hunting knife lay, along with a pair of rubber gloves.

"Oh, no!" she cried.

"Oh, yes," he said. "She must die." Suddenly, he'd lost his glasses and he looked like Paul.

Aaaaack!

Celeste woke with a gurgle, her heart beating as

fast as it could. She told it to settle down. She was safe in Aunt Edie's house, her sister next to her in the bed, sound asleep. *Only a dream. You're all right.*

But she didn't feel all right. Why had Henry morphed into Paul?

Unsettled and with no desire to go back to sleep, she got out of bed. The room was still dark. She checked the time on Jenna's bedside clock. 5:00 a.m.

She went downstairs and made herself a mug of coffee. Drank it. Okay. Five-thirty. It was still ridiculously early, but she didn't want to wait any longer.

Paul's phone went straight to voice mail. Of course he was still asleep, enjoying the sleep of the righteous.

"Hi, it's me," she said. "I know you aren't up yet, but I just wanted to call and tell you I love you."

She took a deep breath and let it out again. There. She'd said it. Paul was the man for her. And now all would be well.

Chapter Nineteen

Celeste resigned from her teaching job and gave up her apartment. "We're sure going to miss you," her principal said when she came back to clean out her classroom.

She was going to miss the school, too, and all the kids. But there were kids in Moonlight Harbor and, much as she loved where she'd been, she knew she'd love where she was going even more.

So when another text from Emerson showed up on her phone, she could read it with nothing more than a shake of her head over how stupid she'd been. There was no ache, no yearning, no anger. He didn't matter anymore, not even enough to hate.

Gonna be in your town this weekend. Can we meet?

It had been a while since he'd contacted her.

Between women again? she texted. Sorry. No, wait. She wasn't remotely sorry. She erased the words and simply texted, Can't. I'm with someone now.

Someone who was a million times better than he could ever hope to be.

Is it serious?

Yup.

You sure?

Yup. Bye.

She ended the conversation and blocked him, something she should have done ages ago. *You are past history now.*

And she was all about the future.

She stored a lot of things at her mom's, but still came back with her Prius loaded with dishes, clothes and crafting supplies. This was it. New life, new beginning. Finally, everything was working out.

She got back in time to help Jenna with the final plans for Aunt Edie's birthday party. "I'd love to have surprised her," Jenna had said, "but I thought it might be too much. I don't want to give her a heart attack."

Heart attack...death... *She must die.* How was Henry's book coming along? Oh, honestly, who'd invited thoughts of him into this conversation?

"Can you order the cake?"

Cake, yes, a much better thing to think about. "Sure," said Celeste. "What are we going to give her for her birthday?"

"She says she has everything and doesn't want any presents."

"You can't have a birthday and not have presents. How about some scented soap and perfume? A woman's never too old for that."

"Good idea," said Jenna. "Want to pick some up when you're out?"

"I'll do it as soon as I finish cleaning rooms. Bet you're glad to have your maid back," she teased.

"I am. Although the rooms are probably a lot cleaner since I've been doing them." She sobered. "Seriously, I really appreciate how you've pitched in. It's saved me a bundle."

"No problem. You can thank me by giving me an expensive wedding present."

"How about a honeymoon in Hawaii?"

"Sure, and pay for the airfare, too," Celeste joked as she left to do room patrol.

"I'll get right on it," Jenna cracked.

Henry was in his room, working. She hadn't seen him since the night of the street dance and felt awkward as she entered.

He was obviously determined not to look at her, keeping his eyes fixed on his laptop screen. "The bed doesn't need changing," he said shortly.

"Fine with me." She went into the bathroom and got busy scrubbing the toilet. She straightened to find him standing in the doorway.

"Where've you been?" he asked. "Your sister just said you were away for a while."

"Packing up my stuff. I'm relocating to Moonlight Harbor."

For a moment his face lit up, then a frown descended. "I guess you're really getting serious with the preacher."

"I guess so," she said lightly.

He caught her arm. "Don't do it, Celeste. You'll be making the biggest mistake of your life."

"Are you nuts?" she said, shaking off his hand.

"No, you are. You aren't a match with this guy. He's not what you need."

"He's exactly what I need."

"Oh, yeah? How do you know?"

"I just know, so stop it, Henry. Stop trying to confuse me."

"If you were sure, you wouldn't be confused. Come on, Celeste, he's not the right man for you."

"There is no right man!" she cried. How many "right" guys had she dated over the past few years? "There are only smart choices and stupid choices, and I'm done being stupid."

"Are you kidding me? You're up to your chin in stupid. Climb out before it's too late." His voice softened. "Let me pull you out."

Before she could say anything more he pulled her, all right—up against him. He threaded his hands through her hair and kissed her, making her drop her scrub brush. Henry Gilbert sure could kiss.

No, no, no! She unlocked their lips and pushed him away. "Stop it, Henry!"

He glared at her. "You're an idiot."

She glared back. "Paul would never say something like that to me."

"That's because Paul's a wuss. And you're a fool."

She grabbed her scrub brush and pointed it at him. "And you're a jerk."

He leaned in the doorway. "Not a very creative epithet, Happy Clam Girl. You can do better than that."

She was going to ram a toilet plunger down his throat if she stayed a minute longer. "You know what? From now on you can clean your own toilet," she snapped. "And while you're at it, drown yourself."

"Not bad," he called after her as she stormed out of the room. "But you could still do better."

She *had* done better. She was so glad she'd chosen Paul.

"Your lady's gonna love this," the jeweler said to Paul as he handed over the black velvet ring box.

"I think so," Paul agreed. He could hardly wait to give it to her. He'd considered all kinds of scenarios and finally settled on having the big reveal at her great-aunt's birthday party. Celeste loved parties and they'd be with family, which would make the moment extra special. But he wanted to be creative in how he did it. At last he'd hit on a plan.

"I'll bring the marshmallows for s'mores," he told Celeste as she was finalizing details the Friday before the big day.

"Cake and s'mores. What more do we need?" she quipped.

"Oh, I might be able to think of something," he said, enjoying his own private joke.

He arrived at the party with his bag of marshmallows and his present for the guest of honor promptly at five to find that Jenna's handyman, Seth, already had a fire going. The family and several guests stood around it, wearing sweaters and windbreakers over their jeans in readiness for when the sun waned and the temperature dropped. Everyone was drinking beer, wine coolers or soda pop. Someone had placed a couple of boards between two logs, making a sort of table, and a bakery box containing Edie Patterson's birthday cake sat on it, along with packages of hot dog buns, condiments, a pot of baked beans, paper plates and plastic utensils. The cooler sitting nearby most likely held hot dogs.

Celeste was looking beautiful in a pink sweater, short-cropped jeans and flip-flops that showed off pink toenails and an ankle bracelet. She took a drink from her wine cooler and laughed at something Brody Green said to her, giving him a playful swat on the arm.

Celeste Jones was a man magnet. If Paul hadn't known that Jenna and Brody were seeing each other, he'd have been a little jealous. Pretty women attracted attention; there was no getting around it. And Celeste wasn't really flirting. She was simply being friendly. She was friendly with everyone.

But once they were married, he hoped he could convince her to get a bit less friendly with the opposite sex.

She took another drink of her wine cooler. He'd told her he didn't have a problem with her drinking, but how much *did* she drink? It was pretty early in the evening, and that bottle was already half-drained. She never ordered anything other than an occasional margarita or a glass of wine when they were out together. And lately that had been a rare occurrence. He reminded himself that it was a party, and nobody went to hell for drinking wine coolers. And if anyone from his congregation showed up and said something he'd tell them as much.

She caught sight of him and waved, and he joined her and Brody. "Looks like you're enjoying yourself," he observed, pointing to her drink. Now, why was he bringing that up?

"It's five o'clock somewhere," she quipped. "Oh, yeah, here. What can I get you, Paul? I'm sure I can't tempt you with a wine cooler, but we have Pepsi and Orange Crush."

Tempt you. Was she making fun of him? "I'll take a Pepsi," he said, and she nodded and moved to where the tub of drinks on ice was wedged into the sand.

"You are one lucky man," Brody told him.

Yeah, he was. Celeste was sweet and vivacious. Why was he being so nitpicky all of a sudden?

"Your life will never be dull with Celeste around."

She would certainly make life interesting. And he was ready for that. Somewhere along the way, his life had become routine and a little boring. He'd felt more like a spectator of life than a participant as he'd baptized babies, married people, attended birthday and anniversary parties. Of course, everyone included him in their celebrations, but he was ready for some celebrations of his own, ready to have a good woman beside him, helping him as he did his part to make the world a better place. His world would definitely be a better place with Celeste in it. He hoped he could wean her off those wine coolers.

"We're a success," Celeste said to Jenna as more of Aunt Edie's friends arrived with presents and food. Everyone had shown up bearing something, and bowls of various salads, along with sliced watermelon and enough chips to stock a convenience store, sat jammed precariously together on the makeshift food table.

"I'm glad," Jenna said. "She deserves it."

"You're a good great-niece," Celeste said.

Jenna put an arm around her shoulders. "So are you."

Paul had been visiting with their aunt, who was holding court on a log they'd fixed up for her with a large cushion and a blanket. He'd set a bag from Beach-comber, a favorite shop in town, at her feet. She gave his arm a pat and he left, returning to Celeste's side.

"What did you get her?" Celeste asked.

"Bubble bath and some lotions. My mom always said you can't go wrong giving a woman toiletries, so I thought it was a safe bet."

"There's nothing wrong with a safe bet," Celeste said. These days she was all about safe bets.

The guests began to roast their hot dogs and sample the chips, and soon people were perched on logs around the fire or sitting against them, enjoying the feast. The evening's entertainment was a tribute to Aunt Edie. Poems were read and toasts were made.

Some of the older guests reminisced about the days when Moonlight Harbor was still a newly minted town. Aunt Edie was in her element.

Celeste and Jenna hadn't allowed their great-aunt in the kitchen at all that afternoon and she almost hadn't known what to do with herself until Sabrina saved the day by doing her hair and giving her a manicure. Their mom had come down bearing presents—a new blouse and sweater—and Aunt Edie was all dolled up in them, along with some jeans Celeste had bought. *"No elastic waist, Auntie. You don't need it."* Edie was beaming as she opened her presents.

Even Pete came through with a present, giving her a gift certificate for The Drunken Sailor. "We can go out next week and keep the party going, Edie, old girl," he told her.

Celeste couldn't hold back a chuckle. Leave it to Pete, the mooch, to find a way to give a present that would benefit him, as well.

"You did a great job planning this," Paul said to Celeste as they sat side by side on a log, finishing up their hot dogs.

"That was mostly my sister," she said as she fed the last bite of hers to Nemo. "I just helped. It did turn out well, though. And I'm glad I could be here for it. I missed her birthday last year." Jenna had thrown a little party for Aunt Edie, but Celeste had been off camping with Emerson. She should've ditched him and come to the party. At least she was there now, and she hoped her aunt would have many more birthday celebrations. "Sometimes it's hard to believe Aunt Edie's eighty-four. She sure doesn't act like it. I hope I can be like her when I'm that age, all happy and full of life."

"You already are. It's one of the things I love about you."

"Aww, thanks," she said, and rewarded him with a kiss. Oh, yes, she had chosen well. She and Paul were going to be so happy together. She polished off her second wine cooler and Paul looked suddenly concerned. "What?"

He shrugged. "Just wondered how many of those you were going to drink. I'd hate to see you stumble into the water and drown," he added lightly.

She frowned. Was he monitoring how much she was drinking? "Don't worry. Three's my limit. And if I fell in the water you'd come save me, right?"

"I will always be there to save you," he said. "And I wasn't judging, really."

He could have fooled her. "You don't have to worry, Paul. I'm not an alcoholic."

"I know, but it's hard not to be concerned about people even when there's no cause to be. Occupational hazard, I guess."

"You've probably already got enough people to worry about, so there's no need to add me to the list," she said and hoped he got the message. Might as well get the man trained right from the beginning.

"You're right," he said and gave her a one-armed hug.

There. They got that settled.

"This is the best birthday I've had in years," Aunt Edie said, smiling around at everyone. "I don't know how to thank you all."

"You just keep on being you," Patricia Whiteside said and everyone murmured their agreement.

Jenna fetched the cake, and Seth broke out his guitar and led everyone in singing "Happy Birthday." Two candles, an eight and a four, sat on it, and the guests cheered when Aunt Edie succeeded in blowing them out before the wind could.

"If I have anything to say about it, you're going to make it to a hundred," Jenna said and kissed her.

"Hear, hear!" Nora cheered.

"And now it's time for s'mores," said Brody, reaching for the bag of marshmallows Paul had brought.

"Whoa, not yet," Paul said, snatching it.

"We're not having s'mores?" Brody asked, confused.

"We are," Paul replied. "But I want Celeste to make hers first." He handed her the bag and she noticed it had already been opened and resealed with a tie tab.

She untwisted the tab, opened the bag and pulled out a marshmallow.

"Not that one," Paul said, looking at it.

"O-okay." she said. Which one of them had been into the wine coolers? "Here you go, Brody. You can have the reject," she said, giving it to him."

"There's a special one in there," said Paul. "Look again."

A special one. Hmm. Maybe… She eagerly pulled out another marshmallow. Nothing special about that.

"I'll take that one, too," Brody said, and stuck it on his roasting fork.

She peered into the bag again and something glinted at her. Her pulse stopped.

"Did you find it?" Paul asked, and she could hear the excitement in his voice.

The same impatience she'd felt on Christmas morning as a child swept over her. She tipped the whole bag, sending marshmallows falling into the sand.

"Yuck," said Sabrina.

"Oh, wow!" Jenna pointed to the diamond ring poking out of one.

Everyone had stopped talking now as Celeste picked up the marshmallow and removed the ring. Next thing she knew, Paul was down on one knee in the sand, taking her hand, gazing up into her face with such love in his eyes.

He got no further than, "Celeste, will you—" before she cried, "Yes," and bent and kissed him to the cheers and applause of their family and friends.

Nemo, excited by what was going on, joined in, jumping on the couple and knocking them over, which left Celeste and their guests laughing and Paul frowning. In fact, she could've sworn she heard him say something very un-minister-like.

"Did you just say what I think you said?" she whispered, and his face flushed.

He managed to smile, though, and help her to her feet. "Even pastors mess up once in a while."

"Well, good. I'm glad to see you're human," she said as he brushed the sand off her back.

He lowered his voice. "Human enough that I can hardly wait for our wedding night."

So much for Henry's insinuations that Paul wouldn't cut it as a lover.

"I hope you don't mind me stealing the spotlight at your party," he said to Aunt Edie.

"Oh, my goodness, no," she said, tears in her eyes. "This is a wonderful birthday present. I'm so happy for you both."

Celeste wriggled the gooey ring onto her finger and accepted the congratulations of her family and the people who had all become good friends. This was a perfect moment and the beginning of a great life.

She went through the rest of the evening in a happy daze.

"I'm thrilled for you, dear," her mother said, giving her a hug before she followed Aunt Edie off to bed. "He's a wonderful man."

"Yes, he is," Celeste said.

"You finally got it right," Jenna said as the two sisters settled on the couch for their usual nighttime chat, Nemo dozing at their feet.

"Yes, I did."

"You had me worried for a while there."

She didn't have to say why. Celeste knew. She'd almost made a romantic misstep, but in the end, her brain had gone back to work and, for once in her life, she'd made a smart choice when it came to men.

She could hardly sleep that night, and when she finally drifted off, her dreams were a swirl of wedding cakes and bridal gowns and dancing the tango with Paul. Oh, yes, there would be dance lessons.

Sunday morning she practically skipped into church, thanking God with every step for how wonderfully her life was turning out. But she was too preoccupied with thinking about possible wedding dates and reception venues and where she and Paul would live to pay attention to his sermon. His little house was pleasant. It wasn't on the beach but it would do for a start. It did have a fenced yard, which would be good for Nemo. They could have company for dinner every Sunday afternoon and…

Jenna elbowed her, bringing her back to the present. "He wants you to go up front."

"Up front?" she whispered.

"Announcement time. Duh," Jenna whispered back.

Of course. Announcement time. A spike of fear burst Celeste's happy bubble, and there went her heart again. She wouldn't have minded if he told the whole city that they were engaged, took out an ad in the paper. But announcing it here, in church, in front of everyone, including the someones who didn't like her… *Oh, please, don't make me do this.*

He'd stepped away from the pulpit and was holding out a hand to her.

There was no escape. Time to put on the big-girl panties and face both friends and rivals. She made her way to the front of the sanctuary, her heart racing.

You will be a good pastor's wife, she assured herself, *and you'll love these people as much as Paul does. Even the ones who don't deserve it.*

The pep talk didn't help. Her heart was still beating like crazy and she was afraid she'd pass out.

She managed to get to where he stood without fainting, and he took her hand and drew her next to him. "I just wanted you all to know that Celeste Jones has agreed to be my wife."

This was rewarded with applause, a couple of cat calls from the younger men and plenty of sighs from the women.

Most of the women. Susan Frank looked disapproving. Hyacinth's two friends Bethany and Treeva were frowning and Hyacinth was looking pale and ready to cry.

Celeste's earlier happiness began to shrivel. Poor Hyacinth. She'd lost one man she loved and never gotten the other. It didn't seem fair. Then there was Susan who, of course, wouldn't approve of Celeste on general principles. An ache began to nibble at her temples.

Paul wanted her to stand with him after church and accept everyone's congratulations, and most people did seem truly happy for them.

Almost everyone. "You two have rushed into this awfully fast," said one of the older women.

"I know it seems that way, Mrs. Miller, but what can I say? I fell head over heels in love with Celeste, and I know you will, too," Paul told her.

"Well, of course, I hope you'll be very happy,"

the woman said. The expression on her face added, "But I doubt it."

Bethany's congratulations were stiffer than a Scotch whiskey straight up, and Treeva's wasn't much better. Hyacinth was nowhere to be seen and Celeste decided that was for the best.

"I hope we haven't made a mistake," she said later, when it was just the two of them sitting on his front porch.

"Why would you say that?"

She shrugged. "Some people seem to think we have."

"What do *you* think?" he asked softly.

"I think I hope they're wrong."

He smiled. "I know they're wrong."

Okay, she could go with that.

"I told you. You should have said something," Bethany scolded Hyacinth as she and Treeva sat with her in Books and Beans, drinking lattes.

"What could I have said? He fell for her the minute he saw her. A woman can't compete with that."

"Do you really see her as a pastor's wife?" asked Treeva.

Hyacinth shrugged. "She's nice."

"She's nice to a lot of men," sneered Bethany. "She's a ding dong."

"I don't know why we're having this conversation," Hyacinth said irritably. "It's a done deal."

"It's not a done deal until they're married," Bethany insisted.

Hyacinth shook her head. "Paul's an honorable man. Once he's committed to someone he's not going to go back on it. He won't break their engagement."

"Better a broken engagement than a broken marriage," said Treeva. "Those two will never last."

"You don't know that," Hyacinth argued, although why she was arguing for Paul to stay with Celeste Jones she had no idea.

"Okay, if you don't want him, then I guess you can stand by and watch him marry the wrong woman," Bethany said with a shake of her head. "But remember, the Lord helps those who help themselves."

"That's not even in the Bible," Hyacinth said.

"It's still true," Bethany retorted.

Hyacinth stared at her half-empty cup. The cup is half-empty… The cup is half-full. *Who cares?* There's nothing in the cup but poop.

She left her friends to talk about how poorly she'd handled the situation and how stupid she was and drove back to her little house. Once there she sat on the front porch step and watched the deer, who was grazing in the neighbor's yard, asking herself where she'd gone wrong.

The answer to that was simple enough. She hadn't been a Celeste.

Jenna took over maid patrol on Sunday so that Celeste could be with Paul. They didn't have much time alone until late in the evening, as several invitations came in from members of the congregation. Lunch, afternoon coffee, dinner—they made the rounds, and their hosts fussed over them and predicted a wonderful future.

"Every minister should have a wife," said Bootsie Edwards when they lunched with her and her husband, Kenneth. "A minister's wife does so much. A good one is worth her weight in gold."

"What does a minister's wife do?" Celeste asked.

"It varies," Bootsie said, pouring her more iced tea. "Some sing in the choir."

Celeste liked to sing, but she wasn't very good. And she couldn't envision the choir director wanting to do a version of "Girls Just Want to Have Fun."

"Some lead Bible studies."

She sure didn't know enough to do that.

"Some do home visitations."

Visiting people, she could get into that.

"Visit the sick."

Uh, no, thank you.

"Have people over. Plan events."

Now she was talking Celeste's language. "I could definitely do that," Celeste said. And she could work with the kids, plan events for them. Oh, yeah, she could see it now—fall carnivals with face-painting and bounce houses, summer day camps, crafting for the artistically inclined. She'd recently discovered the enjoyment of painting tiles. Wouldn't that be fun to do with a bunch of little kids?

"You'll find your place," Bootsie said with a firm nod.

She hoped so. She wanted to fit in, wanted to be the kind of wife Paul could be proud of.

"You will be," he assured her later when it was just the two of them, strolling along the beach, hand in hand. "Some of our people can get a little stuffy. You're exactly what we need to liven things up."

Was that why he was marrying her? To liven things up at his church? Of course not. *Don't be stupid*, she told herself. She was more than a checklist to Paul, just as he was more than a checklist to her.

Henry was in his room, writing away, when she showed up with fresh towels the next day. "So you went and did it," he said, not looking up from the screen.

"How did you find out?"

"Saw your sister earlier today and she told me. Wanted me to know you made the right choice, I guess."

She had. "Are you going to wish me well?"

"Wishing won't make it happen," he said and kept typing. *Clack, clack, clack.* "Kind of rushing into things, aren't you?"

"It's not rushing when you know it's right."

He frowned at that but said nothing.

"This *is* right," she insisted.

"If you say so. Too bad you settled."

"A pastor? That's settling?"

He stopped typing and looked at her. "It's just as bad to pick someone because you're scared of not getting it right as it is to be with someone who's wrong."

"And what would you advise me to do?" she demanded.

"To wait and be sure. There are other men out

there. Like me," he added quietly. "You never even gave us chance, Celeste."

"I told you. I'm done taking chances."

"Like I said." He went back to his typing.

There was no point in talking anymore. Nothing left to say. Except, "How's the book coming?"

"Almost done."

She nodded. Of course he didn't see her nodding because he refused to look at her. "I hope it'll be a big hit," she ventured.

He still didn't look up. "All I need is a towel. You don't have to clean. I'll be checking out tomorrow."

"You're leaving?"

"What do you care? You're engaged."

True. "It won't seem the same without you here, is all."

His hands stopped and he finally looked at her, almost hopefully. "Will you miss me, Celeste?"

"You know I will."

"Not enough, though," he said, and went back to work. "Nice knowing you, Happy Clam Girl. Have a good life."

So that was that. Their conversation was at an end. Everything was at an end. *There wasn't anything to begin with*, she told herself. Some laughs, some conversation. Some sparks. Okay, a lot of sparks.

But sparks died quickly and blew away.

She replaced his dirty towel with a clean one, then shut the door on room twelve and the man in it.

That was the end of their story. Why had he ever thought it could end differently? Celeste Jones believed she'd chosen the "perfect" man. All lesser models need not apply. He'd been stupid to hope he'd make the cut. They'd had chemistry. They'd had a connection. He'd felt it and she had to have, too. Damn it all, what was wrong with women anyway? More to the point, what was wrong with *him*?

At the moment, plenty. He was jealous and bitter and ready to relieve his anger by hurling his laptop across the room.

But he wasn't that stupid. Right now that keyboard and screen were the only comfort he had. And the only instrument of revenge. He went back to his original plot line, smiling as he typed away. Yeah, a man couldn't control what happened in the real world, but here in the world he'd created, he was God.

He poured himself two fingers of Scotch and fell onto the couch, looking out the window at the dark night. He'd caught the bastard but he couldn't save her. And that confirmed it. He was meant to be alone. And so it would be. His job would be everything and that would have to be enough. His cell phone rang. Another case.

Henry shut the laptop. The end. The end of everything.

Chapter Twenty

Life at the beach was wonderful, even more so when you were engaged. Between working at the Driftwood, doing things with Paul and helping with various children's activities at church, Celeste was busy. Now that it was official between her and Paul, she was determined to jump into her new life with both feet and she had. When she did get any spare time, she spent it pawing through the latest issue of *Bride*, and visiting every wedding website she could find.

"I always thought a summer wedding would be nice," she said dreamily as the two of them enjoyed afternoon lattes in Books and Beans. Now that September had begun, a summer wedding was no longer an option unless Paul was willing to wait.

"Do you really want to wait until next summer to get married?" he asked, reaching across the table and taking her hand.

She knew there would be no sex until they were married. Her biological clock sprang back to life and announced that she was more than ready to start her new life and a family. There was no reason to wait almost a year.

"No." Summer weddings were overrated anyway.

"How about Christmas?" she suggested. December weddings were beautiful.

"Well." He took a thoughtful sip of his drink. "We've got the Seaside with Santa festival, and people will be busy with that. Then there are all the things going on at church—food drive, Sunday School program, candlelight service. Weddings are a big deal, and I'd hate to see your special day get lost in the shuffle."

"*Our* special day," she corrected him, making him grin. "Good point, though." She let go of that idea.

"What do you think about November?" he asked. "Could you plan a wedding that fast?"

She loved all those pretty summer colors. The fall ones, not so much. But getting married was about more than the colors you chose for your wedding.

"Sure," she said. "What about getting married over Thanksgiving weekend? My mom would already be down here. Then we could go someplace warm for our honeymoon, like the Caribbean. Or Hawaii. We could book one of those cruises that goes to all the islands."

He looked a little nervous. "I don't think I can budget for something that big right off. Could we do that for our one-year anniversary?"

"Paul, I have money. I can pay for some of it." Now that she was only substitute-teaching…maybe not. It would take all her savings just to pay for the wedding.

"No way," he said. "The groom pays for the honeymoon. I've done enough weddings to know that. What do you say to staying local for our honeymoon? Like going to Seattle."

"Or Icicle Falls. They really dress that town up for the holidays, and it always starts Thanksgiving weekend." It wouldn't be warm, but they could create enough heat between the two of them that it wouldn't matter, and with all the Christmas lights and decorations, it would be almost as good as having had a Christmas wedding.

"Great idea. Icicle Falls for the honeymoon and Hawaii for our anniversary."

It was a good compromise.

Some of the other compromises—or attempted compromises—not so much. "I thought it would be fun to have Nemo be my ring bearer," she said.

"If we were doing a summer wedding and were at the beach, that would be fine. I'm not sure how well that would go over with everyone if we had a dog running around the church."

"Are you sure that's the reason you don't want him? I know you don't like my dog very much."

"I like him," Paul insisted. "But he's still not very well-trained, and we can't trust what he'd do in the middle of a wedding ceremony or who he'd jump on."

"He's getting there," she said. "He can sit and stay now."

Thanks to Henry's help. What was Henry doing these days? Where was he? Funny, in spite of all the time they'd spent together, all the conversations they'd had, she'd never asked him where he lived.

Not that it mattered. She wasn't with Henry. She didn't need to know where he lived.

Or how he was doing.

"My sister's got a little girl who's six and a boy who just turned four," Paul said. "What do you say we use them for the flower girl and ring bearer?"

"Your sister's in Africa."

"She's coming back for the wedding. So are my parents. They're all excited to meet you in person."

They'd had a couple of Skype calls together since Paul and Celeste got engaged, but that was hardly the same thing. Celeste hoped she'd measure up. What if, after spending more time with her, the new in-laws didn't approve of her?

"So what do you say?"

"Hmm?"

"About using my nephew and niece."

"I really thought it would be cute to have my dog," she said. Okay, that sounded petty and immature. "But you're right. We should use your nephew and niece."

"My mom's hoping you'll wear her wedding dress," Paul said.

"What?" Celeste had already picked out a gorgeous dress online. "But she's in Africa."

"My aunt's coming down to visit this weekend. She's bringing it."

"You talked about this without asking me?"

"Not really. My mom asked. What could I say?"

No. "Paul, a wedding gown is a very personal choice."

"I understand, but it would mean so much to her

if you'd consider wearing hers. You know, that something borrowed thing," he added with his gorgeous smile.

"I don't think—" she began.

"At least look at it," he urged.

"And if I don't like it?"

"Then you can wear whatever you want."

Big of him. She frowned.

"I'm not saying you have to. I'm just hoping you'll want to."

Very nicely put. But Celeste still felt she was being pushed into doing something she didn't want to do.

She'd already given up her summer wedding and her second choice of a Christmas wedding, not to mention having her dog as part of the wedding party. That was enough compromise.

Celeste didn't change her mind when Paul's aunt came down. They were at his house, enjoying a crab salad Celeste had made when Aunt Martha brought out the dress. The thing was a relic from the seventies, plain and uninspired.

"This dress is special," said Aunt Martha. "Oh, not because of its design," she hurried to add, "but because of the woman who wore it. My sister, Angela, is a saint."

Oh, great. Celeste's new mother-in-law was a saint. How was she going to follow that act?

"Seeing you in it will bring back such happy memories for her," Aunt Martha continued.

What about making her own memories? "I'm sure it would," said Celeste, "but it's not really my style."

Aunt Martha cocked an eyebrow. "Oh. What is your style?"

"Something a little…" *Less boring.* "More sophisticated."

"Sophisticated," Aunt Martha repeated as if Celeste had said a dirty word. "Well, of course, it's your wedding."

Yes, it was. Although she was beginning to wonder.

"You know, her daughter wore it at her wedding, too," Aunt Martha persisted.

"Then it's been well-used and well-loved," Celeste said. There. Very diplomatic. She smiled.

Aunt Martha didn't smile back.

Paul looked from one woman to the other. "Let's give her time to think about it."

"Good idea," agreed Aunt Martha.

In your dreams. Celeste managed another polite smile.

They drove Aunt Martha around to see the town, bought her ice cream at Good Times Ice Cream Parlor, and then Celeste had had enough of Aunt Martha. And she'd had enough of her fiancé, too. The wedding dress traitor.

"I'd better get home," she said as they pulled into Paul's driveway. "Nice meeting you," she said to his aunt.

"Nice to meet you, too. I can hardly wait to tell my sister all about the woman Paul's chosen."

Celeste wasn't sure if that was a compliment or some kind of veiled threat that involved tattling on her reluctance to wear Mama's wedding gown, but she murmured a thank-you and bolted for her car.

"Celeste, wait," Paul said, catching up with her. "What's wrong?"

"Wrong? Why do you think something's wrong?" Just because she'd pretty much stopped talking beyond an obligatory yes or no.

"I can tell by the way you're acting. Tell me."

"Maybe it has to do with the fact that you didn't take my side about the wedding dress. Really, Paul, whose wedding is it, mine or your mom's?"

"I thought it was ours," he said, sounding hurt.

Okay, maybe she was being unreasonable. But still… "Darn it all, a woman only gets married once." Theoretically, anyway. "I've been dreaming about my wedding day since I was a little girl. I'd really like to pick out my own wedding dress. I don't think that's asking too much."

"Of course it's not," he said. "You're right. I'll tell my mom you don't want to wear it."

She laid a hand on his arm. "Thank you. Anyway, you don't want to feel like you're marrying your mother."

He chuckled at that. "Point taken. I'll tell her about the dress when we Skype later."

But he still looked disappointed. And she drove back home not feeling quite as happy about her wedding as she had earlier.

She hoped his mother wouldn't be mad at her. In addition to visiting with his sister, she and Paul had also Skyped with his parents, and the woman had been quick to tell Celeste how happy she was that her son had found such a lovely young woman.

Now Celeste wondered if Mrs. Welch had been envisioning that lovely young woman coming down the aisle in her ancient wedding dress. Ugh. Why did women hang on to their bridal gowns anyway? That thing should have been given to Goodwill a generation ago.

"Don't do it," Jenna said, confirming Celeste's decision. Then shook her head. "I can't believe Paul didn't jump right in and tell his aunt to take a hike."

"He didn't." Celeste hoped that wasn't going to become a habit—with him wanting to please everyone but her, and she said as much to Jenna.

"I don't think so. He's been single for a long time. He needs to be educated, that's all."

"What if he's a slow learner?"

"Don't be a goof. He's crazy about you. Stop worrying. But wear the wedding gown you want."

She would. So there.

Would his mom be mad?

Angela wasn't exactly mad when they all Skyped the next Friday night, but she was disappointed. "I thought it would be a lovely tradition to continue," she said, making Celeste feel manipulated. "but if it's not to your liking…"

There was an understatement. "I'm sorry," said Celeste. And she was. She didn't want to end up being that difficult daughter-in-law who drove her mother-in-law crazy. "It just isn't me. But it was sweet of you to offer," she added, and that seemed to mollify Saint Angela.

Oh, boy, she had to stop calling the woman that. If she didn't, it would slip out at some point and then she'd really have a problem.

"Well, we want to do whatever we can to make your day special," said Saint Angela. No, *Angela*! "And we're so looking forward to spending time with you before the wedding. My son tells me there's to be a bridal shower. Julia and I are both planning to get there in time for that."

"I'm looking forward to it," Celeste lied.

"Sadly, her husband can't get away. He has too much to do."

Fine by Celeste. She'd have enough to cope with trying to make the rest of his family like her.

"You're going to love my mom," Paul told her after they'd all said goodbye. "She's the most selfless, kind-hearted woman I know."

"Except for me," Celeste teased, giving him a shoulder bump.

"You're a close second," he said and bumped her back.

Close second to a saint. That was a good thing. Wasn't it?

In addition to planning a wedding, there was campaigning to be done on her sister's behalf and a debate at City Hall looming. A new contender had entered the ring since Jenna declared her candidacy—Kiki

Strom, who owned the popular tourist shop Something Fishy.

"Well, that was rude," said an incensed Celeste when Jenna's committee met to strategize their final push.

"No, it was probably a good idea. She talked to me before she did it and told me she was worried I might not be able to carry the vote. She's probably right. I should bow out," Jenna said.

"After all the work we've done? Don't you dare," Celeste said to her.

"If I don't, we might each get enough votes to cancel each other out and let Susan win," Jenna explained.

"I doubt that'll happen," Nora said. "We all know Susan isn't that well-liked. I don't see her getting many votes."

"I'd be okay with it if Kiki won," Jenna said.

"Well, I wouldn't," said Celeste, and everyone chuckled. "You're just what this town needs."

Jenna also liked to think she was exactly what Moonlight Harbor needed—fresh blood, a younger perspective, new ideas. But really, in spite of her doorbelling and campaign promises—"I'll bring more tourists to town, which will boost our economy"—she doubted she was winning over the voters. It seemed that in every other call she made, someone brought up the Seaside with Santa festival and the joke of a parade. She was still the new kid in town, an unknown.

She barely slept the night before the candidates'

debate, and when they entered Moonlight Harbor City Hall and found the room where the city council held its public meetings packed with people, she felt sure she was going to vomit.

"You'll be great," Aunt Edie said, reading her mind.

Celeste hugged her. "Go get 'em, sissy!"

Sabrina hugged her, too. "I'm so proud of you, Mom."

How proud would she be if her mother lost the election? Now Jenna was even more nervous.

"You can do this," Brody said as he escorted her to the long table at the front of the room with three microphones sitting on it. Susan and Kiki were both already seated, Kiki smiling out at the crowd and Susan going over her notes.

She looked up as Kiki greeted Jenna. "You're almost late."

"I guess that means I'm on time," Jenna said, refusing to be intimidated.

"Political smack talk," Kiki said with a smile as Jenna sat down next to her.

Jenna couldn't do much more than nod and fumble her notes out of her folder.

Aaron Baumgarten from *The Beach Times* was going to be their moderator, and he was getting set up at a podium nearby.

Jenna's stomach did a nervous flip. What was she doing here?

Making a difference, she told herself and made an effort to sit up straight and look unafraid.

The whole unafraid thing lasted for all of five minutes. Aaron began to introduce the candidates and the fear came back, bigger than ever. Especially when she heard the other two candidates' credentials mentioned. Both women had, at one point, served on council. Both had owned businesses in town for years.

"And we have Jenna Jones, who runs the Driftwood Inn," Aaron concluded.

That was it. No previous experience in city government. Not even a longtime resident. She forced herself to remain upright but inwardly she was slumping, wishing she could slink away.

"The first question for our candidates," said Aaron, "is what do you offer to the community and what can you bring to the office of councilperson? We'll start with Jenna Jones."

I don't want to go first! Jenna cleared her throat. *Remember your talking points.* "I bring new ideas and a fresh perspective." There. Succinct and to the point, just like she and Brody had discussed.

"Thank you," Aaron said. "And next, we'll hear from Susan Frank."

Susan didn't bother to clear her throat. She launched right in. "I bring experience and common sense. New ideas, of course, are always welcome."

Oh, yeah, I've seen how welcoming you are, Jenna sneered inwardly.

"But they have to be balanced with common sense. Not all new ideas are practical and Moonlight Harbor needs people in leadership who understand the difference."

Boy, if that wasn't a slam on Jenna's Seaside with Santa disaster, she didn't know what was. She ground her teeth.

"And Kiki Strom, what do you bring?" Aaron asked.

"I think I bring both new ideas and common sense," Kiki said easily. "I'm sure you've all been inside a certain big fish here in town," she continued, getting some chuckles and smiles from the audience, "so you know I'm an idea person. But I have some experience under my belt and I can also be practical."

Well said. Why hadn't Jenna thought to mention that she, too, could be practical?

"All right," Aaron said. "Here's our next question. What changes would you like to see taking place in Moonlight Harbor and how would you implement them? Kiki?"

"I would like to see more tourist dollars come to town. To that end, I'll work to make sure word gets out about us up and down the I-5 corridor. We have so much to offer. We simply need to market ourselves better."

Jenna's thoughts exactly. Too bad she hadn't been able to go first on that question.

"And Susan?" Aaron asked.

"Of course, Kiki's right. We also have to get control of our deer population. We need to pass an ordinance prohibiting people from feeding them apples, which is, by the way, not good for them."

The town was divided on what to do about the exploding deer population. All the gardeners would have loved nothing better than to see them all magically vanish, while the animal lovers adored watching them stroll across their lawns. The tourists loved them, too, and often stopped their cars in the middle of the road for a picture. Taking a stand on whittling down the population would be popular with some but not with others. *Bold move, Susan.*

"And Jenna," said Aaron.

"I agree that we need to attract more visitors to Moonlight Harbor. This is a charming town, and more tourist dollars can only boost our economy."

"And do you have an idea for how to make that happen?" Aaron prompted.

Oh, yeah, that. "Uh, yes. I think we should seriously consider building a convention hall in town."

"That will raise taxes," Susan argued.

"Yes, but it will benefit us in the long run," Jenna argued back.

"This is a good example of the type of ideas that come from someone with no experience and no understanding of what's practical," Susan said.

"A convention hall would be very practical," Jenna insisted. What kind of debate was this anyway? They were supposed to be taking turns, not interrupting each other.

"That's an example of what'll happen if you elect her, people," Susan informed the crowd. "Convention halls cost money and we all know who will get the bill."

"And who will prosper in the end," Jenna said hotly. "All of us."

"Okay, ladies, we're going to move on," Aaron said, finally getting a word in.

The debate continued, but Jenna struggled for the rest of it, feeling she'd lost her edge.

It came time for the final question, and Aaron asked each candidate to share why she'd decided to run for the position on city council. "We'll start with Jenna Jones."

Because nobody wanted Susan and I was an idiot. Jenna cleared her throat again. "I've been coming to Moonlight Harbor ever since I was a child. Many of you know my aunt, Edie Patterson, who was one of the first business owners here." Jenna Jones, endorsed by Edie Patterson. "I decided to run because, like all of you, I'm invested in this town and its future, and I want what's best for it." *There. Top that, Susan Frank.*

"I, too, love Moonlight Harbor," Susan professed. "I want what's best for this town and I think I'm the logical choice. We need rational heads at the helm and I can provide that."

Rational heads. More like hardheads. Still, it was a good sound bite. Why hadn't Jenna thought to say something like it?

Kiki was last to speak. "I love Moonlight Harbor, also. How can you not? And I love its people. We have a great history and I believe we have a great future. I think I bring a rational mind to the table, as well as experience. Vote for me. I won't let you down."

There it was, the perfect combination, wisdom and heart. With that one closing remark Kiki had just won the debate, hands down.

Kiki was well-liked and hardworking. Jenna had become enamored with the idea of getting on city council, rolling up her sleeves and making things happen. But Kiki could also do a lot of good. At this point, if Jenna stayed in she'd only take votes away from her friend and Susan could win by default.

That would not be good for Moonlight Harbor. Two days later Jenna did what she knew she should have done the minute Kiki announced that she was standing for election. She withdrew from the competition.

"I can't believe you're doing this," her sister protested.

"I think it's best for the town," Jenna said simply. And wanting what was best for the town—wasn't that why she'd decided to run in the first place? "Kiki will be great." And boy, did Jenna hope she won.

Come election night, she and her team, minus Sabrina, who'd lost all interest after her mother pulled out of the running, sat in Aunt Edie's living room, monitoring the results on the local TV station. It looked like Kiki was, indeed, going to win.

"Well, that's something," Aunt Edie said and headed off to bed.

"It all worked out the way it was supposed to," Jenna told the others when the winner was finally announced.

"Consider this a temporary reprieve," Brody told her. "We've still got some turkeys on council who need to go. You can run again."

"Oh, no. Once was enough. Besides, it wouldn't be fair to make everyone give up so much time and money again," Jenna said. She pointed to Brody. "Next time *you* run for city council and I'll door-bell for you."

"Oh, no," he said, shaking his head. "Nice try, but you don't get off the hook that easily. All in favor of making Jenna run in the next city council election, say aye."

"Aye," everyone chorused.

"I need the deductions," Ellis added.

"There you have it," Brody said.

"We'll see," she said. "Meanwhile, let's call the winner and congratulate her. When she answers, everyone yell 'congratulations.'" She dialed Kiki's number and put the phone on speaker.

Kiki answered on the second ring and everyone did as instructed, Jenna shouting the loudest.

"That's so sweet of you all," Kiki gushed. "Jenna, I hope you're really okay with how things turned out."

"I absolutely am. I stand by what I told you. You're going to do a wonderful job of watching out for us all."

"You know, if I hadn't had people fretting that *someone else* would win, I'd never have stepped in."

"I get it," Jenna said. "I'm a newcomer and I realize a lot of people felt I wasn't that well-known."

"You got out a lot and stumped, though," Kiki said. "There'll be a slot opening for the next election. You run and join me on the council and we'll do great things together."

Brody leaned over Jenna's shoulder and said into the phone, "She will," and Jenna smiled and shook her head at him.

* * *

"Just between you and me, are you disappointed?" Celeste asked after the party had broken up and they were getting ready for bed. Her sister had worked so hard and all for nothing.

Jenna shrugged. "Maybe a little. I do have ideas about what we could do for this town."

"Then you should run again."

"I have to admit, I'd like to get out there and do something important."

That was Jenna. Never thinking she was doing enough.

"Are you kidding me? You're raising a great daughter, running your massage business, looking out for Aunt Edie and keeping the Driftwood going," Celeste said, ticking off the list of accomplishments. "You're my superhero. If I can make half the success of my life that you're making of yours I'll be happy."

"You will," Jenna said and hugged her. "You're well on your way."

Yes, she was.

Celeste had tried to talk Paul into taking dance lessons with her but failed, even after reminding him that they'd be doing the traditional bride and groom dance at the reception. "I'm not that into dancing," he'd admitted. She gave up. Most guys weren't into dancing. There were plenty of other fun things to do in life.

They'd nailed down the local Elks hall, which was available for parties, for the reception. Not the elegant reception hall she'd always envisioned, but her mom and Jenna had promised they'd make it look spectacular. Sabrina, who had been mooning around since Tristan left, was commissioned to search for decorating ideas online and she'd been happily researching fall themes.

"It's going to be great," Jenna said for the hundredth time as they drove to The Drunken Sailor, the only place where Celeste was getting to do any dancing. "And we'll all look great in those chocolate-brown dresses. A good color pick."

Chocolate-brown and rust, a color combination Celeste had decided she could live with.

"Yeah, it is," Celeste said, and tried to inject some enthusiasm into her voice.

"How about a little excitement here."

"I am excited. I love my dress, the cake will be gorgeous and I'm happy we're doing a cookie bar, too. I just wish we weren't having the party at the Elks." *And that I was getting married at the beach and that I liked my mother-in-law's gown. And that...* She didn't go any further. She was afraid to.

"It'll be fine," Jenna assured her. "You've got prewedding jitters is all."

Yes, that was it. Which was stupid, really, considering whom she was marrying.

The minute they were in the door, she ordered a wine cooler. Then kept Brody company at the bar, drinking it and then a second one, as well.

"Hey, go easy," he cautioned. "You're gonna fall on your ass when you try to dance."

"Maybe I won't dance," she muttered. "What's

the point? Paul doesn't like dancing. I'll never dance again after I'm married."

"Sure you will," he said.

"Can you see him here?"

"Well, no. But that doesn't mean you can't come. Sister time and all that."

"True," she said, and took a long draw on her wine cooler. "But you're supposed to do stuff with your husband when you're married."

"Don't you guys already do stuff together?"

"Of course we do." They took walks on the beach, went out to eat, played games with her family, watched baseball on TV. She'd get into baseball. Eventually. There would be church events to plan, family to hang out with and then kids to raise. They were going to have a wonderful life.

"Then don't worry if there are some things you don't do together," Brody advised. "You're still a person in your own right after you get married, Celeste."

Maybe that was what had been bothering her. Maybe, deep down, she was wondering if she would be.

But Brody was right. She knew that.

"How come you're not out there dancing?" Victor King asked her when the dancers took a break and came to the bar for drinks.

She shrugged. "I don't feel like it."

He looked surprised. "Since when?"

Since I got engaged.

Celeste ordered another wine cooler, and later that night, after she and Jenna got home, she ate half a bag of Dove chocolates.

* * *

Cold feet, that was all it had been. Not even that, just nippy toes, a condition brought on by the wedding gown affair. Now that things were all resolved and Celeste had her wedding gown and the date was growing near, she was excited about becoming Mrs. Paul Welch. Their November wedding date was fast approaching and, as far as she was concerned, it couldn't come soon enough.

Julia had finally given her the sizes for her flower girl and ring bearer, and her bridesmaids, Vanita and Sabrina, and Jenna, her matron of honor, had their dresses and shoes. All that was missing from the wedding picture was the groom's family.

They flew in the week before the big event, in time to offer hugs and congratulations and to sample Celeste's cooking, which her father-in-law-to-be praised highly. "Those cookies were really good," he told her, then said to his wife, "You should get the recipe."

They had rum in them. Would Saint Angela approve? *Stop it! You have to stop calling her that.* Celeste doubted it. Angela had already told her she and her husband didn't drink and that she hoped Celeste and Paul wouldn't be serving alcohol at the wedding.

"We'll have a nonalcoholic punch," Celeste had said. "And just champagne for the toast." And if Saint… Angela didn't like that, she could toast the happy couple with punch.

"I see," Angela had said in a tone that implied she'd rather not know.

"Don't worry about it," Paul told Celeste. "No

one's going to be bothered if we have champagne
for a wedding toast. If my mom gives you any more
grief, remind her that Jesus's first miracle was turning water into wine at a wedding."

At least there was no alcohol served at the bridal
shower, which took place on the Sunday afternoon before the wedding. The same woman who'd hosted the
Fourth of July party opened her home for the shower,
and even her big house had trouble accommodating
all the guests. Everyone loved Pastor Paul and had
turned out to support his bride-to-be.

Celeste was nearly overwhelmed at the turnout
and had to dab her teary eyes. Even Hyacinth, who
had to be a masochist, was there and trying to smile.

"Thank you all so much for coming," she said. "It
means a lot." And it did. These people were going to
be an integral part of her life soon. She'd wanted to
belong and seeing so many smiling faces encouraged
her to believe that she could, indeed, fit in. It also
went a long way toward warming up her nippy toes.

"Of course," said her hostess. "We all love Paul."

And we love you. That was implied—wasn't it?

In addition to the church women, Paul and Celeste's families were present and so was Vanita, who
had come down specially for the occasion. It took an
hour to open all the gifts, which ranged from Crock-
Pots to gardening tools and paper products.

Her mother gave her a selection of spices along
with a cookbook and a Safeway gift card, and Aunt
Edie had put together a recipe box filled with all her

specialties. "Now you'll be able to make all kinds of tasty dishes for your husband," Aunt Edie told her.

"She needs all the help she can get in that department," Jenna teased.

Her future mother-in-law and Julia, her future sister-in-law, gave her a gift card and a framed picture of Paul. "Every woman should have a picture of her husband on her nightstand," Angela told her.

"Here are some other things every woman should have," Vanita said with a wink as she handed over a giant gift bag.

The bag was filled with thongs and lacy bras in Celeste's size and a filmy black nightgown that brought some jealous *oohs* from the younger women. It also had some sex toys that Celeste decided not to put on display.

"You'll have fun with those," Vanita said in an undertone.

Meanwhile, Angela was talking with their hostess. "You know, I'd hoped she'd wear my wedding dress, but she didn't want to. But that's our culture these days, isn't it? No one seems to care about tradition."

Really? Was her mother-in-law going to hold this over her for the rest of her life?

As if *she'd* cared about tradition when she picked out that dress? Why hadn't she worn her own mother's wedding gown?

"And was the dress you wore your mother's?" asked the other woman.

"No," Angela said sadly. "My mother's dress was lost in the fire when her house burned down."

Yikes! So Angela had experienced her share of troubles. Maybe she'd hoped to wear her mother's wedding gown. Maybe that gown had been her grandmother's. Suddenly, Celeste wasn't having fun.

"I think that's a nice tradition," said Hyacinth, who'd seated herself next to Angela and was picking a cookie crumb off the coffee table. What a suck-up.

"Never mind her," Vanita whispered.

"Which her?" Celeste whispered back.

"Both of them. One can't keep him to herself anymore and the other can't have him, so neither one matters."

Except when you married a man you married his family, too. Celeste had heard the saying often enough to believe it. In Paul's case she was marrying into two families, his bio family and his church family, and already three members of the church family had snatched away the welcome mat. Darn it all, maybe she *should* wear Angela's dress.

She so loved the one she'd already bought. But she decided she loved Paul more. It would make him so happy if she wore his mother's gown. It would mean a lot to Angela, too. Weddings were about more than what the bride wore. They were also about what the bride did, and this bride knew what she had to do.

As the party was breaking up she drew Angela aside. "I'm wondering if the offer of your wedding dress is still good?"

Angela looked like a woman who'd won the daughter-in-law lottery. "Of course it is," she said, and hugged Celeste. "You've made me so happy."

And that would make Paul happy.

"What about making yourself happy?" Jenna argued when Celeste told her of her decision.

"I am. I think it was the right thing to do."

Jenna frowned. "Don't turn yourself inside out trying to be what you think everyone wants you to be. Paul's marrying you because he loves you the way you are."

"I know. And right now the way I am is wanting to do something noble."

Hard to argue with nobility. Her sister shut her mouth.

Celeste didn't regret her decision. Well, maybe for a moment when Paul brought the wedding dress over later that afternoon and she saw it again. But seeing how thrilled he was, she knew she'd made the right decision.

"That's quite a haul," he said, taking in all the shower presents she'd received. They took up half of her great-aunt's tiny living room. "Can you say that?" he asked Jolly Roger, who was watching from his cage. "Quite a haul, quite a haul."

"Quite a haul," Roger repeated, sounding like a mini-Paul.

"It takes a lot to set up housekeeping," said Aunt Edie.

"Well, let's see what we've got," he said.

He was properly interested in everything. She felt suddenly self-conscious about showing him Vanita's gifts. If Nemo hadn't stuck his doggy nose in the bag, intrigued by the scent of the edible body lotion, tipping the whole thing over, she would have conveniently ignored it.

"What's this?" Paul righted the bag and looked inside.

"Just a few things," Celeste said and went to grab the bag. She wasn't fast enough.

"Eye candy," said Jenna.

"I like eye candy." He brought out a red thong and grinned. "This is nice." He approved of the nightgown, too. "You'll look beautiful in it," he said. "And what...?" He'd obviously found the other goodies. "I don't think we'll need some of this. Do you?" he said softly.

Of course not. Who needed anything extra when your man was a good lover?

She was sure Paul would be.

Unbidden, the love scene from Henry Gilbert's book sneaked into her thoughts.

She sent it packing and assured herself that sex with Paul would be just fine.

Anyway, there was more to life than sex.

Really.

Chapter Twenty-One

The wedding invitation had been sitting on Hyacinth's kitchen counter for two weeks, mocking her. Okay, enough already. She grabbed it, tore it to pieces and tossed it in the garbage.

Not that she needed it anyway since the time and date of the wedding was burned into her brain like an image from a scary movie.

It was in three days, slated for the Saturday of Thanksgiving weekend. Every member of the congregation would be there. Except her. The bridal shower had been bad enough. She was through with torturing herself.

She called her mother. "I thought maybe I'd stay for the whole weekend."

"That would be lovely," said her mother. "But don't you have to be in the shop on Black Friday?"

"No, I've hired some help for the weekends. I think I can get away."

"We'll be so happy to have you, dear. It's been a while."

Yes, it had. She'd pretty much run away from

home after losing her fiancé, run to Moonlight Harbor where she'd found a whole new life. Sadly, she'd also found more heartbreak. Maybe she was meant to be alone. Maybe that was what God had in mind for her.

The Lord helps those who help themselves.

She frowned. What did Bethany know? She wasn't exactly a spiritual giant. Anyway, it was too late now for Hyacinth to help herself. Or Paul.

She told her mother she was looking forward to seeing her and ended the call to go to work. She only hoped no one from church would come in and start gushing about the happy couple. If that happened, Hyacinth knew she'd lose it and whack the woman with a bolt of fabric.

Amazingly, she didn't lose it when Mrs. Morris, one of the church widows, came in to purchase fabric for her latest quilting project. "My granddaughter's getting married in the spring and I want to give her a quilt for a wedding present."

"I think that's a lovely idea, Mrs. Morris," Hyacinth said. "Why don't I hold on to these and you can come back in and purchase them on Black Friday. We'll be having a sale, thirty percent off."

"I don't mind paying full price," Mrs. Morris said. "But I may have to come back and buy more. I want to do my part to keep you in business. It's so nice to have a fabric store right here in town. All of us quilters are delighted you moved here."

Hyacinth had been delighted to be in Moonlight Harbor, too. Until recently.

"What are you doing for Thanksgiving?" Mrs. Morris asked as Hyacinth began cutting fabric. "Do you have a place to go?"

So kind. All the older women at church watched out for her.

"Thanks for asking. I do. I'm going home to spend the weekend with my parents."

"Not the whole weekend, I hope. Pastor's wedding is on Saturday."

As if she needed reminding. She gritted her teeth and gave the scissors a vicious run down the fabric.

"I'm sure it's going to be a beautiful wedding," Mrs. Morris rhapsodized. "She's such a lovely girl."

Hyacinth was a lovely girl, too. *Keep it together. Don't hit Mrs. Morris with this bolt of quilter's weight cotton.*

"This will be the biggest wedding we've seen in Moonlight Harbor in years," Mrs. Morris continued as if it was a royal wedding.

Hyacinth didn't need to see it. She forced her features into pleasant lines. "So tell me what you're doing for Thanksgiving."

That distracted the older woman and she rattled on about her son and daughter coming down and bringing her sister, what she was making for dinner and what they were bringing. It was enough to keep them away from the dreaded subject.

Until Mrs. Morris had paid for her fabric and was getting ready to leave. "I do hope we'll see you Saturday night. It's important to support our pastor, don't you think?"

No, it wasn't. Not when he was making the mistake of a lifetime. "Have a nice Thanksgiving, Mrs. Morris," Hyacinth said, dodging the question.

Mrs. Morris left and Hyacinth locked up shop and flipped the sign on the door to Closed.

In the past, when she thought of her bachelorette party, Celeste had always seen herself and her girlfriends wearing boas and riding in a limo to some hot dance club or casino. Of course her friends would hire a male stripper to embarrass her, and there'd be lots of yummy cocktails and laughter.

Well, she was a different person now, so no casino. Definitely no male stripper.

One thing she did have, and that was the laughter. How could you not when you were with Vanita and Courtney and the fun-loving Tyrella? They didn't go to the casino. Instead, Jenna threw her a chocolate-overdose party at the house, and even provided the boas. They played charades and drank champagne and ate copious amounts of chocolate, along with cookies Aunt Edie had made. Jenna had also baked mini lava cakes and they ate those, too, along with ice cream provided by Nora.

Surprisingly, Jenna even made sure Celeste got her male stripper, who turned out to be Brody, dressed in a cop uniform he'd probably borrowed from Victor King. He didn't fill the shirt out quite as well as Victor, but he still looked pretty darned sexy. She couldn't help but feel relieved that Jenna and Courtney had left her future mother and sister-in-law off the guest list.

As it was, her mother had frowned disapprovingly until Brody started to dance. That was more comic than erotic, his performance a caricature of a male dancer. He accidentally knocked Courtney in the head when he tossed a shoe over his shoulder and he nearly fell over trying to pull off his pants. When he finally succeeded, he revealed some ancient purple shorts that looked like they'd escaped from a Richard Simmons workout tape.

"Oh, my gosh, you are the funniest male stripper ever," Vanita told him. "Can I hire you?"

"Who else is getting married?" Celeste asked her.

"Nobody. I just want to see the show again," Vanita joked.

"That was a one-time performance, ladies," Brody said as he climbed back into his pants.

"Oh, yeah?" teased Nora, holding up her phone. "I recorded it for posterity. What do you say, girls? Should we put it up on the Moonlight Harbor Facebook page?"

"Don't even think about it," Brody told her. "I've got handcuffs," he said, holding them up.

"Be still, my heart," said Vanita, pressing both hands to her chest.

"You'd better get out of here before Vanita gets any more worked up," Jenna said to him, and walked him to the door as the women called out their thanks.

"Would you really have put that up on the Facebook page?" Tyrella asked Nora.

"No. We want the poor man to stay in business."

"Anyway, I'm not sure you'd want Pastor Paul seeing that," Tyrella told her. "He might not approve."

He probably wouldn't. Celeste, the future minister's wife, bit her lip.

"Yeah, because Brody was an embarrassment to the entire male sex," Courtney said in an attempt to lighten the moment.

"I didn't stop to think that through," said Jenna, who'd come back into the room. "I just thought it would be funny. Bad judgment on my part. You can blame me," she said to Celeste.

A guilty silence fell over the group.

"Hey, whatever happens at a bachelorette party stays at the bachelorette party," Courtney said.

"Who's for more ice cream?" asked Aunt Edie.

"Yes, ice cream," said Tyrella. "No one can disapprove of that."

Hopefully not. The fun and games resumed, and by the time the party was over Celeste was smiling again. Maybe Paul would think Brody's appearance was funny.

But she wasn't going to take a chance and tell him about it. Keeping secrets from her husband already...

"This has been a great party, you guys," she said. "Thank you so much."

"We're happy we could celebrate with you," Nora told her. "You're getting a wonderful husband."

Who probably wouldn't have laughed at Brody's performance.

He texted her the next day.

How was your party?

Fun. We played games and ate a ton of chocolate.

Nope, he didn't need to know about Brody.

How was yours?

I bowled a 200.

Was that good? She had no idea.

What else?

Ate pizza. Talked about you and what a lucky man I am.

She smiled.

You sure are. LOL

Gotta go. Pick you up later.

Yes, later was the wedding rehearsal and the rehearsal dinner, which was to be at his house. His mother was preparing Paul's favorite dish—lasagna. She hadn't asked Celeste what she liked. Not that it mattered. She liked lasagna just fine.

Everyone showed up at the church for rehearsal at six, Sabrina excited about her first outing as a bridesmaid, Vanita jaded. "I've been an effing bridesmaid too many damn times," she said, her language making Angela Welch frown.

"I'll make sure you catch the bouquet," Celeste promised her.

"What about me?" Sabrina protested.

"You've got years to go. Wait your turn," Vanita cracked.

The good-natured joking went on—with everyone laughing and Vanita checking the ring hand of the groomsman who was going to escort her down the aisle. "Married. It figures," she said in disgust.

Then it was time for Celeste to practice her walk, her mother by her side. For a fleeting moment she wished she had a daddy to give her away, but then reminded herself that her mother was her best friend and there was no one better for the job.

And no one better to be given to. She smiled at Paul as he held out his elbow so she could slip her hand through his arm. "You already look beautiful. I can't even imagine what you'll look like tomorrow," he said to her.

What a lovely thing to say. Celeste smiled in response.

"Now I'll ask the congregation to be seated and I'll talk about the sanctity of marriage," said Paul's father. "It's a big step and a big commitment and I like to remind the bride and groom and their families and friends of that."

A big commitment. Was he trying to scare them or something?

Paul's dad continued going through the order of

the service—the music, which was being handled by the church musicians, and the lighting of the unity candle. Celeste had thought it would be meaningful to pour sand into a vase since they were at the beach, but Paul's parents had talked her into using the candle instead.

"Then it will be time to kiss your bride," said Mr. Welch.

"Better practice that," goaded one of Paul's groomsmen.

"Good idea," Paul said and kissed her.

It was such a sweet kiss, her heart turned over.

But her engine didn't start. Oh, well. There'd be plenty of time for that on their wedding night.

With the practice over, they all went to Paul's house where Celeste's new sister and mother laid out the spread. Lasagna, garlic bread, a big tossed salad and lemon bars, Mrs. Welch's specialty, for dessert. Aunt Edie had offered to bake cookies and been told there was no need.

"These aren't nearly as good as my lemon bars," she whispered to Celeste.

"I know," Celeste whispered back and hugged her.

Aunt Edie wasn't officially part of the wedding party, but Celeste had invited her anyway, and that had been fine with Paul. "Of course. She's family," he'd said. Oh, yes, Celeste was marrying a truly good man.

Paul's house wasn't that big, so part of the group settled around his little dining room table, while the rest found seats in the living room.

As was only right, Celeste wound up seated with

her new in-laws. "We're so happy Paul's met a woman to share his work with him," his mother told her.

"Thank you," Celeste murmured.

"It's not easy being a pastor's wife," Angela continued, which made Celeste gulp.

"But I'm sure you're up to it," she added.

Celeste hoped so.

"You'll have to come to Burkina Faso and see the work we're doing there," put in his sister. "We can always use help."

"Um." Africa still wasn't at the top of her list of places she wanted to see. Not on her list at all, in fact.

"Yeah, we will," said Paul, who was seated next to her. Wait a minute. What happened to there being plenty of people who needed help here in the US?

"Make sure she gets her malaria shot," his mother added.

Malaria.

"I thought we were staying here," she said to Paul later when it was just the two of them sitting on his porch, watching the stars.

"We are."

"Then what was with all that talk about Africa?"

"Just to visit and help out. You wouldn't mind that, would you?"

Well. She chewed on her lip and inspected her fingernails, which were in need of a mani before the wedding. "I don't think I'm cut out for Africa." And definitely lacking in the nobility department.

"You're cut out for more than you think you are," he said, and put an arm around her.

She'd rather he'd said, "We won't go if you don't want to."

But maybe she'd like Africa. Giraffes and all that. She'd heard that many of the people there were very friendly. And it would be good to start doing important things, like Jenna and her new sister-in-law.

"But no Africa until after we have our anniversary in Hawaii," she insisted. Yep, noble to the core.

"Absolutely," he promised. She was just relaxing into a smile when he said, "We can do Africa the next year."

That night she dreamed she was inner tubing down the Amazon with Paul, alligators—or was it crocodiles? Something creepy, anyway—swimming alongside them. "Isn't this great?" he enthused. "We should come here every year," just as a giant snake fell from a tree and landed on her.

She woke up before it bit her, but it was a long time before she got back to sleep. Pre-wedding jitters. That was all.

She finally drifted off again. She was in her mother-in-law's wedding gown, ready to walk down the aisle. Hundreds of candles cast a soft glow on the people, all smiling at her. And she was standing next to a man she knew was her father.

"I've waited for this day for a long time," he said. "I'm sorry I had to leave you. I hated dying before I even got to know you. But I'm glad to be able to see you marry a man who will really appreciate you for the wonderful woman you are."

"Oh, Daddy," she cried, and went to hug him.

But he was gone.

She couldn't decide if that last dream had been comforting or upsetting, a blessing or some kind of veiled message. Whatever it was didn't matter. She had a big day ahead of her, a lot of responsibilities to concentrate on.

And in case she'd forgotten, her aunt said the same thing. "This is a big day."

"Big day," muttered Jolly Roger from his kitchen perch.

Pete was already in the kitchen, downing French toast. "Another one bites the dust," he cracked.

"Ha-ha," Celeste said sourly. No wonder Jenna didn't like the old guy. She helped herself to coffee but refused the offer of French toast. Something hadn't sat well with her the night before, probably the lasagna, and her stomach was feeling queasy.

Her mom and Jenna came in from a beach walk, cheeks rosy, smiling faces. They looked so happy and carefree. Celeste was feeling anything but. Darned lasagna.

"Lunch at The Porthole, then manis and pedis at Waves and hair at Courtney's," Jenna reminded her. Everyone went to the local salon to get their nails done, but when it came to hair, only the older women frequented Waves.

Once they got beautiful, Nora was hosting the bridal party for appetizers. Then it would be time to go to the church and get ready. The wedding was at six to accommodate any friends coming home from Thanksgiving celebrations out of town, and the church was going to be packed. Nearly everyone on their guest list had responded to the invitation with an enthusiastic *yes*.

In a few hours she'd be married.

The darned lasagna took another bite out of her stomach lining and she went in search of antacid.

Finally, her tummy settled and she got down some tea and a piece of toast. All the women went out to lunch, but she just picked at her crab salad.

"Too nervous to eat," Aunt Edie observed. "I was nervous on my wedding day, too. The wedding night, you know." She patted Celeste's hand. "Don't worry, dear. You'll be fine."

Yes, she would. Everything would be fine.

The rest of the day passed in fast motion—hair and nails, makeup, a final girl party at Nora's where Celeste had two glasses of champagne to settle her stomach. Then it was off to church, to change into her wedding gown.

There in the designated changing room, surrounded by her family, she let her mother slip her borrowed wedding gown over her head and then clasp the vintage pearl necklace that Aunt Edie had given Celeste around her neck.

Her mother stood next to her, smiling at their reflections in the long antique mirror the church kept on hand for such occasions. "You look beautiful."

"You're just saying that because we're related," Celeste joked.

"No, I'm saying that because it's true. You're as lovely on the inside as you are on the outside."

Paul had said much the same thing, and yet, sometimes Celeste wasn't so sure. She hoped she'd be lovely enough on the inside for Paul.

The church wedding planner poked her head in the door. "Okay, ladies, it's showtime."

Showtime… Put on a show… The show must go on. Celeste wished she'd taken another antacid.

They moved into the foyer, and through the open doors to the sanctuary she could catch a glimpse of all the wedding guests. The church was filled with deep-red and white roses and baby's breath. The candles glowed softly. One of the musicians was playing Pachelbel's Canon.

It was time.

She felt like someone having an out-of-body experience as she watched the ring bearer and flower girl go down the aisle. Murmurs of approval drifted back to her. Yes, the kids had been a better choice than Nemo. But she wished her dog was there with her.

Next went Sabrina, followed by Vanita and Jenna. Then it was time for her and her mother to do their walk. Suddenly, it seemed a long way down to the altar. *The Green Mile*.

Emerson had persuaded her to watch that depressing movie once. Why was it invading her thoughts now, of all times?

"Are you ready?" her mother whispered.

No! She nodded and they started their stately walk. What was she doing?

Going to Paul. There he stood, looking so handsome in his tux. Her future. He smiled at her, his face glowing with love.

Everyone else was smiling, too, and it made her think of marathon runs where people stood on the sidelines and cheered the runner on. *You can do it!*

Yes, she could. She wanted to.

She walked past Tyrella and Nora and her husband, all sitting together, beaming at her. And there was Patricia Whiteside, and Courtney, who gave her a thumbs-up.

So many faces. She knew Hyacinth and her friends had to be somewhere, but she didn't search the crowd for them. No point spoiling this perfect moment.

Next thing she knew, she was standing beside Paul. He offered her his arm and they made the few steps to stand in front of his father. This was it. The big moment. Her mouth went dry.

Mr. Welch asked the traditional, "Who gives this woman?"

Celeste turned to see her mother smiling with tears in her eyes. "I do. Happily."

The congregation was seated, and Mr. Welch reminded Celeste and Paul of the seriousness of what they were about to do. Then he threw out the time-honored statement. "If anyone knows a reason why this man and this woman should not be united in holy matrimony, let him speak now or forever hold his peace."

"I do," said a timid voice.

Chapter Twenty-Two

Paul's father blinked in astonishment. "Excuse me?"

Hyacinth could feel the flush of embarrassment from her chest clear up to the roots of her hair. Everyone was staring at her, probably wondering if she'd suddenly gone insane. Maybe she had, because this was not a Hyacinth sort of thing to do. But she needed to say her piece.

"I know a reason why they shouldn't get married." Perspiration was forming on her brow, gathering between her breasts. "They're not...right for each other."

"Hyacinth," Paul chided, shocked.

"It's true," she said. "I know you're in love with her, I get that. I mean, what man wouldn't be? She's gorgeous and fun. But that doesn't make her a good fit for you. You haven't stopped to...to think seriously about this."

Susan Frank, sitting next to her, pulled on her skirt in an effort to get her to sit down. "That's enough, Hyacinth."

She could see one of the church leaders approaching from the corner of her eye. He was going to drag her out of the church as if she was a crazy woman.

Maybe she was…

She should've stayed at her parents' the whole weekend like she'd planned. Then she wouldn't be here now, making a fool of herself.

Instead, Paul would have made the mistake of his life with no one to save him. She'd had to come. And she had to keep talking.

She rushed on. "You want a love that will last a lifetime. In the end, she'll drive you nuts and you'll bore her. Not that you're boring," Hyacinth hurried to add. Oh, boy, she was getting this all wrong. She should have kept her mouth shut. No one was believing her anyway.

"That's enough, young woman," Paul's father said sternly. "Sit down."

"In the end you won't be happy, at least not as happy as you could have been with the right woman," Hyacinth finished and fell back onto her seat, her face on fire. What was everyone going to think of her now? Of course they'd hate her for trying to ruin Paul's wedding, not to mention his life. She'd have to leave the church, leave town.

But she couldn't regret saying what she'd said. Maybe she wasn't the woman for Paul, either. Although she loved him with all her heart, if she couldn't have him she at least wanted him to be happy.

He sure didn't look happy now. Ugh.

"She's right," Celeste said and the entire crowd gasped.

* * *

Hyacinth *was* right. She and Paul weren't a fit, not really. She was more in love with what he represented than the man himself.

"I'm sorry," she said to him. Sorry that she'd waited until the last minute to do what, deep down, she'd known all along she should have done. "I wanted so badly to pick the perfect man, and I did. You are. You're just not the perfect man for me. And I'm not the right woman for you. You'll make a great friend—if we can ever get past this. But you won't make a great husband, not for me. And I sure won't make a great wife for you." She took off the engagement ring. It was a bit of a struggle. It had always been a little tight.

Paul usually had the appropriate words for every occasion. Not this time. He stood there, staring at her, his face a study in hurt and disbelief. She took his hand and placed the ring in it. "You need to find the girl this fits," she said. Then she turned and raced down the aisle, her bridesmaids hurrying after her. She'd barely cleared the sanctuary before the stunned silence became a babble of confused voices.

In the foyer Jenna grabbed her by the arm. "What are you *doing*?"

Celeste spread the wedding gown wide. "I can't go through with this."

"He's the best thing that ever happened to you. You've said it yourself. Oh, sis, are you sure?"

"I'm sure," Celeste said, tears in her eyes. What a mess she'd made of everything. If only she could have been sure before they'd set a date for the wedding. Before she'd even accepted the ring. It had all seemed right at the time. Now, she'd made a fool of Paul and wasted her savings on a non-wedding.

Their mother arrived on the scene. "That was a perfect example of love and unselfishness."

Yeah, that was her. Loving and unselfish, leaving her groom at the altar. She burst into tears on her mom's shoulder.

"Celeste."

Great. Now here was Paul. "I'm sorry," she wailed. "I'll pay you back for all the honeymoon reservations, I promise."

"Like I care about that? This is my fault. I rushed you into this. I rushed us both into it. We should've taken more time."

"Then at least we would have broken up before… this," she said on a sob.

"Maybe we wouldn't have. Maybe we'd have worked out our differences, whatever you think they are."

"It's not that we have differences. It's that we *are* different. Paul, I meant what I said. I hope someday we can be friends. I'm just so sorry I embarrassed you." *And myself.*

"It's okay," he assured her, but he looked like he was going to cry any minute. He gave her a kiss on the cheek and then walked out of the church, probably to go bleed out in private.

She put her fist to her mouth to keep from screaming, and the tears continued to rain down her cheeks.

"Come on," her mother said gently. "Let's get you out of this dress."

She nodded. "Yes, then let's get me out of here." People were starting to leave the sanctuary, still talking. About her. She fled to the dressing room.

Once she was freed of her dress, which her mom promised to return to Angela, she left her family to clean up her mess at the church and went home to her dog. "Here's a good boy," she cooed as he met her at the door. "Are you glad to see me?"

"Rooraroor," he said, tail wagging.

She knelt down and buried her face in his fur and he tried to kiss away her tears with his tongue. "It's just you and me now," she said. With no job and no future and, once again, no man in her life. Had she blown it when she walked out on her own wedding? She needed to go to the beach.

She changed into jeans and a sweatshirt and jacket, trying not to think about the fact that only half an hour ago she'd been wearing a wedding dress. The church, all the flowers, the people—the whole scene replayed itself in her mind like some stupid rom-com. Why, oh, why, had she given up her job and her apartment? Now she was stuck here in Moonlight Harbor as the town fool.

She and Nemo got to the beach to find that the sun had taken a bow and been replaced by the moon in all its luminescent glory, and it was making a glittering path across the water. A fairy path, Aunt Edie used to call it, and when she was a girl Celeste could almost see a troop of fairies pirouetting on the water.

A beautiful night. It should have been a beautiful night for her and Paul, but she'd ruined it. She shivered, and her dog whimpered, sensing her sadness.

"It's okay, boy," she said. Not really, but oh, well. She'd brought along matches and started gathering wood for a fire. She couldn't bring herself to go back into the house. Couldn't bring herself to go anywhere.

She had a pile of wood and was laying down kindling when Seth found her. "Want help with that?" he asked. Then, before she could answer, he added the newspapers he'd brought to the kindling she'd started to stack. "You know, it's okay to change your mind," he said as he lit the fire.

"Kind of waited till the last minute to do it," she said, and her lower lip trembled.

"Better the last minute than too late."

She sighed heavily and plopped onto the sand. "I feel terrible. I feel bad for Paul. Sorry for myself, too," she added with a rueful chuckle. "But I also feel... I don't know. It's hard to explain. Not really relieved, but just, somehow, settled. Like I followed an instinct I'd been ignoring. Does that make sense?"

"Absolutely." He sat next to her and let Nemo crawl into his lap. "It's a big step. You don't want to step wrong and go off a cliff."

"He's such a great man."

"Yeah, he's cool."

"And so kind and thoughtful. Am I losing it? *Did* I do the right thing?"

"You know you did. Otherwise you'd be at the Elks lodge now, cutting cake."

"The reception!" She'd run off and left the caterers dangling.

"Don't worry. Jenna's on it. She told people to go on over and enjoy the food."

"That should be some party," Celeste said miserably. "They'll be able to entertain themselves talking about the bride who walked the wrong way down the aisle."

"It looked more like running to me."

"You're so not funny," she told him, but couldn't help smiling a little.

"There, that's better," he said, chucking her under the chin.

Jenna was the next to show up, bearing their favorite old beach blanket and a couple of wine coolers. "I thought I'd find you here," she said, handing Celeste one.

"Sorry I left you to clean up my mess," Celeste apologized.

"Not much mess to clean up," Jenna said as she spread out the blanket for them to sit on. The caterers will take care of that. I told people to take their presents home."

Celeste groaned. "I have all those shower presents to return, too."

"I'll help you," Jenna promised.

Celeste let out a shaky sigh and moved to the blanket to sit shoulder to shoulder with her big sister. "I guess I blew it, huh?" She was sure Jenna thought so.

"No, you didn't. No woman in her right mind walks out on her wedding if she's really in love."

"Maybe I'm not in my right mind," Celeste said and took a draw on her wine cooler.

"It's a possibility," Seth teased.

Jenna frowned at him, then turned her attention back to her sister. "I'm sorry I kept pushing you to be with him. I guess I didn't want you to end up married to a loser like I did."

Celeste nodded. "I get it."

Brody and Tyrella arrived next, along with Aunt Edie and Pete, Aunt Edie bundled up in a heavy down coat and a hat and gloves. "Is this where the real party is?" Brody joked and tossed Celeste a bag of Cheetos, her favorite snack.

"Yep," Jenna answered for her. "Pull up a log, guys."

Nora and Courtney arrived soon after, bringing chicken wings and coconut prawns from the reception. "Figured since you already paid for it, you should eat some of it," Courtney said.

All that money. Well, at least the guests at the reception were enjoying it. "Is everyone talking about me?"

"Oh, yeah. Not necessarily in a bad way, though. Most people just think you guys got engaged too quickly."

Most people. That meant some people didn't have anything nice to say about her and she had a pretty good idea who they were. She ripped open the bag of Cheetos.

Pete produced a couple of bottles of champagne. "Thought we might as well drink some of this."

"Our champagne for the wedding toast," Celeste said sadly. "There's nothing to toast now."

"Sure there is," Pete said, sinking down on a log. "To the next time."

If there ever was a next time.

"That's an excellent toast, Pete," said Aunt Edie, who'd brought along a bag filled with plastic cups.

"Well said," Brody agreed. "Fill 'em up."

They all toasted to the non-bride's future and sat around the fire, sharing tales of romantic misadventures.

"You should've seen the old bat I almost married before I came here," Pete said, shaking his head. "She was a real harridan. Lucky escape."

"For which one of you?" Jenna murmured.

Celeste wasn't up for giggling but it did make her smile.

"In the end, things have a way of working out just as they should," said her mother. "Don't worry, darling. Your story's not over yet."

Story… Henry. What was Henry doing tonight? Probably typing away, murdering someone.

And Paul. He'd been so kind and understanding. What was he doing?

Paul sat in his house, staring out the living room window at the night sky. By now he and Celeste would have been on their way to Seattle to spend the night in the pricey hotel he'd reserved. A wedding night in Seattle, followed by a stay in Icicle Falls;

they'd both been excited about it. At least he thought they had.

James, his music director and best man, had canceled the reservations for him and taken away his tux, promising to return it to the formal-wear shop in nearby Quinault first thing in the morning. No wedding night, no honeymoon, no wife, no future, all thanks to Hyacinth Brown.

Don't let the sun go down on your anger. He'd preached on that Bible verse before. It sure was easier to preach about than to do. He was still angry with Hyacinth. He was entertaining very un-pastor-like thoughts of bopping her on the head with one of her flower vases. Where did she get off telling people they shouldn't get married? Since when had she become a marriage counselor? What did she know about him or Celeste?

More to the point, why did she do it?

Someone knocked on the door. He didn't get up to answer it. *Go away.*

But he hadn't locked the door and the person came in. James, his best man. "Thought I'd see how you're doing," he said.

"I feel like I've been sucker punched but I'll live."

James took a seat on the couch. "Sucks to have this happen."

Thank God he didn't quote any Bible verses or try to cheer Paul up by reminding him that everything worked together for good. Paul would have had a psychotic break and decked him.

"Why did she do it?" he asked his friend.

"Which *she* are you talking about?"

Paul gave a grunt. Good question. "I meant Hyacinth."

"That's a no-brainer. She's crazy about you. Don't tell me you've never noticed the way she looks at you."

"Uh, no." Hyacinth was the woman who helped out around church, decorating, doing flowers, volunteering at the food bank and with food booths during town celebrations. She was nice enough, quiet, not bad-looking, but not the kind of woman you noticed when she walked into a room. Not like Celeste.

Celeste. The very thought of her made his chest ache.

"Well, she is," James said. "Not that she did what she did 'cause she was jealous or anything. I think she really felt like she was saving you from making a mistake."

"She saved me, all right," Paul said bitterly.

"I'd say something like 'it could be worse,' but I'm not sure how. I bet you're gonna get a great sermon out of this, though."

"Oh, well, then, it was all worth it," Paul said with a sarcastic shrug. Maybe he'd convert to Catholicism and become a priest. No women, no marriages and no being left at the altar.

Celeste was plagued with dreams on her non-wedding night. In one, Paul came after her with a gun in one hand and a copy of Henry's book in the other. He took a shot at her, but missed, and she dreamed on to find herself walking on the beach in the moonlight. There was Henry in the distance. She called to him and waved. He turned to look at her, then walked away and vanished in the mist. Oh, yeah, happy dreams. At least he hadn't tried to cut her up with a hunting knife. She still didn't know where that dream had come from.

"Come on, get dressed," Jenna said when Celeste finally staggered down to the kitchen in her bathrobe in search of morning coffee. "Let's clean some rooms and then take Mom out to lunch before she goes home."

"Here?" Go out in public the day after her wedding disaster?

"We can drive over to Westhaven."

"Good idea."

Spending the day with her mother and sister and her niece, who all made sure to say nothing whatsoever about the previous night, went a long way toward making her feel like maybe her life would go on.

"I love you, Aunt Celeste," Sabrina said, threading her arms through Celeste's as they walked along the waterfront. "I hope you find the right man."

She'd have better luck finding a unicorn eating a four-leaf clover.

Chapter Twenty-Three

Life went on. Celeste bit the bullet and showed up at church the next week.

Jenna had convinced her that nobody was going to be judging her and that the person being hardest on her was herself. "Come and get it over with," she'd urged.

Get it over with. Her sister had made it sound like they were talking about a trip to the dentist or getting a mammogram. Celeste had known she had to face Paul sooner or later but she hadn't been excited about the prospect of doing it in a church filled with people. Of course, she hadn't been excited about seeing him anywhere. But she was still in Moonlight Harbor and so was he, and they needed to get past their wedding disaster. So although she would've preferred later, she'd sucked it up, thrown on some clothes and let her sister drag her off to church. Resolution was good for the soul. No, wait, that was confession. Well, resolution was good, too.

She walked in bracing for surreptitious and scornful looks. Instead, she received hugs and words of encouragement.

Even Susan Frank, the town's resident pill, offered her consolation. "Better safe than sorry," she said.

Safe. Was that what you called it? Safe sure felt crappy.

She was standing with Jenna and Tyrella when she saw Hyacinth edging toward her. Celeste felt in sudden need of antacid. The woman hadn't said a word to her yet and Celeste was already embarrassed. And she didn't know which one of them she was more embarrassed for.

Hyacinth was dressed for kicking off the holiday season, wearing a red wool coat and a patterned red scarf over her black sweater and slacks. She'd put on a red wool beret and actually looked almost glamorous. Except for the fact that her cheeks were the color of her scarf.

"Um, Celeste, could I talk to you for a minute?" she asked timidly.

She had no idea what to say to this woman. *Thanks for that little speech last Saturday night.* Or *Looks like you were right all along.* Or *You bitch.* She clamped her lips shut as they stepped away from the others and waited for Hyacinth to take responsibility for the first words.

"I'm really sorry," Hyacinth said, tears rising in her eyes. "I…" She stopped and bit her lip.

Embarrassed us all? Ruined my life?

But she hadn't. Ruined Celeste's wedding, yes, but no one had forced her to end things and flee back down the aisle. She'd done that all on her own. She was alone now because of the choice she'd made, pure and simple. But it had been the best choice for both of them. She was sure of it. Hyacinth had acted as a catalyst, nothing more. It wasn't fair to blame her for what had happened.

She could have forced Hyacinth to sweat it out, trying to come up with the words she was desperately searching for, could have paid her back for the scene she'd made by making her grovel. But that wouldn't have been fair, either, especially considering the fact that the woman had actually saved her and Paul from taking a giant misstep.

"You know what. It's okay."

Hyacinth looked at Celeste as if she'd just grown a halo. "Really?"

"Really. I meant what I said that night. You were right. I just couldn't admit it. I thought I was sure, but if I'd been really sure, I'd have gone over and bitch-slapped you and then gone on with the ceremony."

Hyacinth looked momentarily shocked, then she smiled. "You really aren't right for him."

Celeste smiled, too. "No, I'm not. He's all yours."

The red invaded Hyacinth's cheeks again. "That's not what I meant…"

Celeste patted her arm. "It's okay. I hope it eventually works out for you guys."

Still blushing furiously, Hyacinth nodded and scuttled away.

"You handled that well," Jenna said.

"You were listening?"

"Of course. You didn't notice me scooting closer? Come on, let's go in."

The service started and Celeste found herself suddenly feeling antsy. Maybe she should have stayed home. Maybe it would have been better to run into Paul in the grocery store. Or not at all. Perhaps it would be best, after all, if she left town.

Except she'd been enjoying substituting at the local grade school and middle school. She liked the kids. And she was happy being with her sister. Moonlight Harbor was feeling more and more like home. Maybe it wasn't too late for her and Victor King, who really was a nice man.

Oh, yeah, bring out the checklist and rush into another relationship with a man who's not The One. And piss off Courtney, while you're at it.

She frowned and tried to concentrate on the music.

It ended all too soon and there stood Paul in front of everyone, looking great in his jeans and dress shirt—untucked, of course, the current style for all hip, young pastors. Celeste's heart became restless, pacing around in her rib cage. She squirmed in her seat.

"Hello, everyone. It's good to see you all here this morning." He smiled, letting his gaze roam the congregation. Then he saw Celeste and the smile faltered. He cleared his throat. "Now that Advent is here, it's time to turn our thoughts to the reason we celebrate Christmas. And today I want to talk about those shepherds on the hill, who heard the angels proclaiming, 'Peace on earth, goodwill toward men.' That was

God's message to us. He wanted us to experience true peace of mind. Sometimes, that can be hard to achieve. I bet some of you were wondering about my peace of mind last week."

This produced some nervous titters and a few glances in Celeste's direction. She felt like a big old chestnut roasting on an open fire. Oh, yeah. Good idea to come to church.

She slumped down in her seat, wishing she was invisible, and shot a look to where Hyacinth was sitting. Once more, Hyacinth's face matched her red scarf.

Two embarrassed women for the price of one. *Not cool, Paul.*

"But I want to tell you all that the message of hope hasn't changed. It's still there. It's always there. God always wants the best for us, and we need to want the best for each other, as well." Then he looked directly at Celeste and smiled. "I want the best for everyone here."

She managed to smile back, even though her face was still burning. She *did* want the best for him. And maybe she and Hyacinth together had freed him to find it.

It was hard to remain after the service but she forced herself to, Jenna and Tyrella both standing next to her for moral support. But when Paul finally approached they moved a respectful distance away.

"I do want the best for you, you know," Celeste said to him.

"I know."

"And I think Hyacinth does, too." *May as well put*

in a good word for the other woman. Christmas was just around the corner, after all, and it was never too soon to show that Christmas spirit.

He nodded and took her hand. "I wish you'd change your mind."

"It's probably a good thing all our wishes don't come true." She sighed. "Oh, Paul, you are the most incredible man."

He made a face. "Said the woman who left me at the altar."

"For your own good. For mine, as well."

He nodded again, taking that in. "Was it the other guy?"

She didn't pretend not to know who he was talking about. "Probably. Although it's too late for that."

"Part of me hopes that's true," he said with a smile. "But that's not the noble part. I do hope you find what you're looking for, Celeste."

So did she, but she had her doubts.

Okay, he'd survived talking with Celeste. Barely. His gut hurt and he didn't want to talk to any more of his congregation. He wanted to go home and watch football on TV, stay inside his house for the rest of his week. The rest of the year. The rest of his life.

You'll get past this, he reassured himself. His dad had told him as much before he and Mom left town. His parents had been high school sweethearts. Dad wasn't exactly an expert on rebounding from rejection.

At the rate he was going, Paul would be. And oh,

no. Here came Hyacinth. The smile he was faking refused to stick around.

"Hyacinth," he greeted her curtly. *Yeah, very pastoral.* He reminded himself to remember what he'd just preached.

"Pastor, I..." She stumbled to a halt.

So many things he wanted to say to her. *What were you thinking? Isn't there some other church you could go to? Some other man's life you'd like to ruin?* He corralled the words, determined not to let anything he'd regret escape.

She blinked, cleared her throat and tried again. "I know you're really mad at me."

No. Now, why would I be mad at you?

"But I..." Suddenly, her eyes flashed, showing him a Hyacinth he'd never seen before. "I'm sorry. If you think I liked standing up and making a fool of myself in front of everyone, you're crazy."

People were beginning to look their way. He frowned, took her arm and led her to a corner of the foyer. "No one made you stand up. No one forced you to say what you did."

"No one but me. I had to do it. And not just because...because I care for you but because, well, I care for you and I don't want you to be miserable."

"I was pretty happy before you saved me from being miserable," he said.

"Of course you were. Your big crush hadn't worn off yet. You were stupid in love." Her eyes popped open wide, registering the same shock he was feeling. "Oh, I'm messing this up. I just wanted to tell you I'm sorry, that I didn't do what I did to make you miscrable."

Well, you did.

"Except I'd rather see you miserable now than even more miserable later."

"Hyacinth, you had no way of knowing I'd be miserable later."

Her chin shot up. "Oh? I think I did."

"Yeah? How?"

"Because she didn't go through with it. If I was wrong, she wouldn't have listened to a word I said. She'd have bit—slapped me. She'd have told me I was all wrong and to mind my own business and that there was no other man on the planet she wanted to be with more than you."

Ow. That hurt. But there it was in a nutshell. He'd been sure beyond the shadow of a doubt that Celeste was the woman for him. She'd proved him wrong when she rejected him.

He took a deep breath and let it out. Then he nodded. "Maybe you're right."

"Can you forgive me?" Hyacinth asked in a small voice.

"I'm working on it." And maybe, after this conversation, he needed to work a little harder. "Give me time, okay?"

"I'll give you all the time you want," she said softly, then hurried away, ducking out the door without talking to anyone else.

He watched her go. He had to admit that what she'd done had taken real guts.

* * *

Everyone survived the misery and awkwardness of the big breakup. Jenna was as good as her word and helped Celeste return everyone's shower presents, leaving them free to turn their attention to the upcoming holiday celebrations. Unlike the year before, the Seaside with Santa festival, which was held on the second weekend in December, was blessed with good weather. Some of the Driftwood Inn's visitors from the previous year returned, including Darrell Wilson and his wife, Kat. She was in scarves again, an obvious sign that the cancer was back.

"We're not giving up," Darrell told Celeste and Jenna, and Celeste hoped their determination would be rewarded.

Their favorite crazy sisters, Karen and Lisa, were back, too, and everyone gathered in Aunt Edie's living room for a reunion. Taylor Marsh was there, as well, with her husband and little girl, excited to announce that she'd sold her third house since moving to Moonlight Harbor.

"Brody's a great mentor," she said.

"I'm great at a lot of things," said Brody, who'd invited himself to the party. He waggled his eyebrows at Jenna, who simply smiled and shook her head, and Celeste knew that before the evening was over he'd be catching her under the mistletoe Aunt Edie had hung in the entryway. Heaven only knew where Seth would catch her, but it was a sure bet he'd get in a kiss, too, before the New Year began.

Celeste rode on the Driftwood Inn float in the festival parade, this time in a nice warm coat and mittens. So much easier to wave at the crowd when your arm wasn't frozen stiff.

Christmas came, and the family gathered to exchange presents. Celeste told herself she was content to simply be with her family.

But even surrounded by people she loved, she felt empty. What was that myth about Zeus feeling humans were too powerful and cutting them in half? The two halves then had to spend their lifetimes searching for their other half. She felt that was what she'd been doing her whole adult life. Paul had been a great guy, but he hadn't been her other half. Was Henry? If so, she'd sure done a good job of losing him forever.

She searched for him on Facebook and couldn't find him. Couldn't find a website for him, either. *Where are you, Henry Gilbert?*

On New Year's Eve, Jenna hosted a beach fire party again. All their friends, both new and old, came. But shockingly, Aunt Edie opted to stay in the house. "It's getting too cold for these old bones," she said. "And I'm feeling tired."

Aunt Edie was never tired. "Should we be worried?" Celeste asked Jenna. Too late to ask. She already was.

"I don't think so," Jenna said, but she didn't say it with much confidence. "She's eighty-four now, so we really shouldn't be surprised if she's slowing down."

"I'm okay with her slowing down, but I don't want her to stop completely."

"Me, neither. Don't even go there. She's just tired, and it is pretty cold out here. I'll take her a s'more later."

"Pete's in there with her. You'd better holler really loud before you enter so you don't walk in on something," Celeste joked, making her sister frown. The moochy old guy would never make Jenna's list of favorite people.

Brody still hadn't arrived, and Celeste noticed that Seth took advantage of his absence, seating himself on her sister's other side and asking if she wanted a hot dog.

If Paul was there, he'd have roasted Celeste a hot dog. She felt suddenly very sorry for herself.

Well, she could roast her own hot dog. With a frown she put one on a fork and stuck it in the flame, setting it on fire. She'd never had the patience to roast the things slowly. She seemed to lack patience in a lot of areas of her life.

More guests arrived, and soon afterward, Seth pulled out his guitar and started taking requests. Celeste left before anyone could ask her to sing. They would, of course, want a reprise of "Girls Just Want to Have Fun" and she was in no mood to sing about that. People began setting off fireworks and she could hear the pop and whine as the fiery patterns lit the sky.

It felt like everyone but she was having fun. New Year, new beginning, she told herself.

To that end, she decided to get back to her children's book about the happy dog the next afternoon when Jenna and Sabrina were both out and Aunt Edie was napping.

*Hank the happy dog...*she began.

No, not Hank. *Horace the happy dog...was in a rotten mood. His life sucked. "I think I'll bite somebody," he growled.* Good grief, that wouldn't cut it. *Hank...* Not Hank! *Horace the happy dog wasn't happy these days. He missed the man he'd met on the beach.*

Celeste scowled at what she'd scribbled and crumpled the piece of paper. Writing was overrated. So were writers.

How had Henry rung in the New Year?

"I know," she said to Nemo, who was stretched out at her feet, "Not every mess-up can be fixed. I need to move on."

Celeste's life soon fell into a pattern. She was substitute-teaching a lot and helping out at the motel when she could, as well as contributing to the household expenses. She went to church with her sister, though not quite as regularly as she'd gone when she and Paul were an item. And she still helped out in the Sunday School nursery. At the rate she was going, it would be as close as she'd ever get to a baby of her own. She painted tiles with Aunt Edie and helped her in the kitchen, and went line dancing Sunday evenings with Jenna and tried to have fun.

Even though no one had partners on the dance floor, a lot of people seemed to be partnering up off it, having dinner together before the dancing started, then leaving together.

Victor King still didn't have anyone, but he'd given up on Celeste and she didn't do anything to encourage him. He was handsome and sweet, certainly no Emerson, but the chemistry wasn't there, and Courtney still had hopes of making him fall for her. Besides, even if Celeste tried to start something with Victor she'd only repeat the mistake she'd made with Paul. At least she could manage a conversation with Paul once in a while when she saw him at church or ran into him in town.

As for Hyacinth, he seemed to be avoiding her. Celeste had seen the woman looking longingly at him and actually felt sorry for her. Love hurt.

It really hurt on Valentine's Day. Her sister got a dozen stemmed roses and Godiva chocolates from Brody and a single white rose from Seth. Pete got Aunt Edie a fancy bar of lavender soap, and Tristan sent a humble but pretty flower arrangement to Sabrina. Celeste bought herself a box of chocolates at the grocery store and ate half of it sitting in her car in the parking lot.

The Sunday before she'd come to line dancing alone—alone, so pitiful—had imbibed one too many drinks and made a scene explaining to Seth, who'd been minding his own business trying to play pool, just how much it sucked to be alone. All alone. With—hic!—no one.

Victor King had taken away her keys, and Seth

had brought her home and told her to get over herself. And she'd thought he was so understanding. Ha!

Sabrina celebrated her sixteenth birthday in March, and Jenna threw her a party at the funplex. Tristan made the trip down from college, bringing her some earrings set with her birthstone. She passed her driving test and Jenna experienced a moment of my-baby's-growing-up sadness.

At least she had a baby to watch grow up. Celeste told her biological clock to unwind. There was no point in bothering to tick.

Then, one day in April, she stopped at the rack of books in the grocery store, checking out the new romance novels—and saw it. The book cover had a dark background. In the foreground a red stiletto lay on its side, abandoned on a cobblestone street. The title, *She Must Die*, was in red. Heart racing, she grabbed the book from the rack. *A brilliant debut for a promising writer*, read the blurb over the title.

That promising young writer was someone named Dirk Slade. Dirk Slade? She flipped to the back of the book and there was Henry's picture and a short bio.

Dirk Slade lives on a houseboat in Seattle, Washington. He's currently working on his second book.

She pulled out her phone and did a quick internet search. She found his author page on Facebook. And there was his website. She went to the page that listed his appearances and saw he was reading the next weekend at a small bookstore in Seattle.

Wasn't it time to go spend a weekend with her mom?

* * *

Henry had a respectable turnout at his book signing, about thirty people, mostly family and friends seated in the rows of folding chairs, but he saw a couple of new faces, too. That was gratifying.

In fact, the whole first-book experience was gratifying. His mom had bought copies for all her friends, and his brother had bragged about him at his racquet club. His dad had said, "I always knew you'd do it, son." This from the man who'd cautioned him not to go crazy with this writing thing and quit his job.

Oh, yeah, life was good.

As good as life could be when you didn't have a woman. One woman in particular. Off and on he'd searched the internet for some write-up about her wedding, but had never found anything. Just as well. He was having enough trouble with his second book as it was. He didn't need to be distracted, thinking about Celeste all happily married, settled into some snug beach shack with Mr. Perfect, having company over for dinner and then, after they left, hopping in the sack with him.

He told himself a lot that he hoped she was happy. He lied a lot.

"Henry, we'd all like you to read an excerpt for us," said the bookstore owner.

Yes, the required reading by the author. Henry opened to the page he'd marked and began to read. "'He'd planned it all so carefully, and now it was time. He could feel his heart rate climbing as she approached. It was exhilarating, a reminder that he was still alive and that soon she wouldn't be. She deserved this. She had it coming. Maybe someone more poetic would have said it was written in the stars. All he knew was she must die.'"

Henry read on for a few more pages, stopping right where the killer grabbed his victim, a real cliffhanger, then shut the book and looked up at his audience. People clapped and he saw smiles and nods.

And there, hovering at the back of the group, half hiding behind a bookcase, he saw Celeste Jones.

Chapter Twenty-Four

Henry blinked. He had to be hallucinating. No, the woman was real. Well, then his glasses were dirty and he wasn't seeing clearly. That was it. She looked like Celeste but it wasn't her. Couldn't be.

Still. It could…

In his dreams. That was the only place he ever saw her.

He had to meet that woman, whoever she was. Whoever she turned out to be.

"Dirk would be happy to sign copies of his book for you all," the bookstore owner announced, and the customers left their seats and began to form a line by the table next to him, which was stacked with books.

All Henry wanted to do was race past everyone and meet the woman lurking behind the bookshelf. But a middle-aged woman was standing in front of him.

"My son wants to be a writer," she said. "Would you sign this for him?"

That was what he was there for. "Sure," he said. He signed his name in her book and added a brief message, wishing the young man luck.

More people were waiting. He seated himself at the table and began to sign books and prayed that the Celeste lookalike wouldn't leave.

"This is so cool," said Geoff, one of the guys in his writing group.

"You're next, dude," Henry told him, and scrawled *Don't let your dreams die* inside Geoff's copy. Kind of what he'd done when it came to love, but you couldn't have everything.

The line of people kept edging past him, his mother snapping pictures the whole time. And then, the last person in line handed him a book.

His breath caught. There she was, standing in front of him. Maybe she was a hallucination. She had to be. If he started talking to her, would people think he was crazy?

The hallucination spoke. "Hi, Henry. Will you sign my book?"

He could hardly believe it, could hardly breathe. *Stay calm.* "You don't like gory stuff. Remember?"

"I didn't say I was going to read it."

There it was, the smile he remembered. She slipped the book in front of him with her right hand. He couldn't see her left hand, which was just as well. He had no desire to see that band of gold on it.

He wrote *For Happy Clam Girl*. Then he signed his name under it and handed it back. "How's your book coming?"

"Stalled out. No inspiration."

"You're married now. I guess you've got other things to think about."

"I'm not married."

Of course. They were probably going to have a big, kick-ass affair. "Still planning the wedding, huh?"

"Been there, done that." She raised her left hand. Her ring finger was bare.

He blinked in surprise. He had to be hallucinating again. "What happened?"

She sighed. "I could write a book."

That made him smile. "Yeah?"

"I got as far as walking down the aisle."

She wasn't married. They weren't together. He could feel a bubble of hope swelling in his chest.

Oh, no. Don't go there. You don't need your heart stomped on a third time. And twice by one woman. Yeah, there's the definition of insanity.

Still, he couldn't resist asking, "So what stopped you from saying *I do*?"

"I realized I was making a mistake."

"I could've told you that. In fact, I *did* tell you."

"You're still a jerk," she snapped. "Did you know that?"

Back to their normal repartee. He smiled at her. "Yep. I am."

"And how about you? Did your old girlfriend come back now that you're famous?"

"Nope. Wouldn't have taken her back if she did."

"I suppose you've found someone, though, some literary groupie."

"I'm still looking. Want to apply?"

Just then his mom came up. "Henry, we're going on over to the restaurant."

"Okay. I'll see you there," he told her.

She turned to Celeste, assessing her in the way only a mother could, but since he didn't make any introductions, she simply smiled politely and left.

"Not ready to introduce me to the family yet?"

The stupid in him was more than ready. "So spill. What really happened with the preacher? Did you guys have a big fight?" *Did you think about me at all after I left?*

"I realized I wasn't in love with him. You were right all along. I was afraid to get it wrong and I almost did. Darn it all, Henry, I'm so tired of messing up. All I wanted was to get on with my life and be happy. And Paul was...*is* a great guy. He seemed like the right man."

"What made you realize he wasn't?" Henry asked and held his breath.

"You. I couldn't stop thinking about you, Henry. You're cranky and sarcastic and insulting."

He frowned. "Gee, how could you resist?"

"See what I mean? But you're also easy to talk to, smart and kindhearted. And you like dogs," she added with a smile.

"I like yours."

"He likes you, too, and so do I. And I like your love scenes," she said, her cheeks taking on a rosy hue.

"Yeah? They're fiction, you know."

"You'll have to tell me where you get your ideas," she said with a teasing smile.

"I might." She didn't say anything to that and for a moment he sat regarding her. How he'd wanted to see her again. What was he doing just sitting there like a doof, for crying out loud? "A bunch of us are grabbing something to eat. Want to join us?"

"Yes," she said without hesitation.

He stood. "Okay, let's go."

"I want to take things slow," she said as he walked her to the register. "Messing up one wedding was enough to last me a lifetime."

He slipped an arm around her. "We can take it as slow as you want. You wouldn't believe how good I am at taking it slow."

He'd waited for this for a long time. It was going to be so perfect. Yes, there she came, her hair glinting in the sunlight. She had no clue as to what lay ahead. But then, neither did he. All he knew was that, whatever was in store for them, it was going to be good.

Henry smiled at his laptop screen. Oh, yeah. Good stuff. Not written by Dirk Slade. He had another pen name for the romance novel he was writing on spec— Hope Brimwell. Murder and mayhem were great, but once in a while a happy ending was, too.

He shut down the laptop and left room number twelve. No more time to write today. He had a wedding to attend.

Wedding number two.

The last weekend in August brought beautiful weather, perfect for a beach wedding. The bride wore a strapless, ivory satin dress she'd purchased some time ago—it hadn't been worn by anyone's mother— and pink high-heeled sandals, along with the diamond pendant necklace her groom had given her and the tiny diamond earrings her mother had lent her so she'd have something borrowed. Her bridesmaids all wore sundresses in beachy colors of coral, pink and turquoise. The flower girl was the groom's niece. The ring bearer was the bride's dog and he was very well-behaved.

Pastor Paul Welch officiated. During the rehearsal he'd made a quip about something feeling familiar, and Henry had been about to deck him, pastor or not, when he said to the bride, "But this feels right." Pastor Paul was still single and looking for his perfect someone, and Hyacinth still had hopes he'd look in her direction.

She was present, too. She'd done the flowers for the wedding—her gift to the happy couple.

The bride and groom wrote their own vows, and of course, the groom had to work in his nickname for his bride—Happy Clam Girl.

She was, indeed, happy. This time Celeste Jones had finally gotten it right and found her prince.

* * * * *

If You're New To Town

Welcome to Moonlight Harbor! We have so many wonderful people in this town it can be hard to keep them all straight. Of course you know **Jenna Jones** and her family, including her great-aunt, **Edie**, her daughter, **Sabrina**, and her sister, **Celeste**. Then there are the two men in her life, **Brody Green** and **Seth Waters**, and her two good friends **Nora Singleton**, who owns Good Times Ice Cream Parlor and the funplex, and **Tyrella Lamb**, owner of Beach Lumber and Hardware. But let's get you better acquainted with some of the town's other residents. You might have met them earlier and I'm sure you'll encounter them again as you spend more time with all of us.

Annie Albright is a sweet, quiet woman. She's one of the regulars who hang out at Aunt Edie's house every Friday night for girlfriend gatherings. She has a small daughter and is currently working as a waitress. She dreams of someday having a food truck and doing catering, but hobbled to an alcoholic husband, she finds it hard to move forward with her dreams.

Austin and Roy Banks are transplants from Texas. Austin is into makeup, big hair and Western attire. She teaches line dancing on Sunday evenings at The Drunken Sailor and her husband, Roy, runs sound for her. "Come on out and try it," says Austin. "You'll love it."

Alex and Natalie Bell—You haven't seen much of them, but you may have eaten at one of their establishments. They own two: Beachside Burgers and Doggy's Hot Dogs. Their two businesses and their three boys keep them hopping. Hope you can see more of them soon!

Aaron Baumgarten, Mr. Millennial, is a reporter for *The Beach Times*. As you've seen, he likes to stay involved in town matters.

Luna Edwards has lived in Moonlight Harbor for twenty years. She was married when she first hit town and opened Waves Salon. We'll have to take you there and let you get better acquainted soon. She no longer has the husband but she still has her salon and both of them are going strong.

Susan Frank owns Beach Babes apparel. She's pushing sixty and her shop caters to… Let's just say that you won't see the fashions she carries in any women's magazine. What else can we say about Susan? Well, every town needs a sourpuss, right? Enough said.

Jonas Greer is really new to town. He's a firefighter—
be still our hearts!—and he's single. How many hearts
he sets on fire before he finds his one true love is any-
body's guess.

Whit Gruber is in his sixties and is Aunt Edie's ac-
countant. His life is so much easier now that Jenna has
turned things around financially for the Driftwood Inn.

Victor King often works as Frank's partner. He definitely qualifies as one of Moonlight Harbor's finest.
Buff and good-looking, he's hard on crime but soft
on women.

Rian LaShell owns Sandy Claws, the town's pet
supplies shop. She's still in her thirties, slender and
exotic-looking with her taupe-colored hair and cat's
eye-style eyeliner. Rian is single and before Jenna
came to town, she dated Brody Green. Is she dating
anyone now? Not yet.

KJ and Elizabeth MacDowell are fairly new to
town. The sisters started a craft shop in town called
Crafty Just Cuz. If you're the artsy type and you enjoy
crafting, you'll find all the supplies you could ever
wish for at their establishment, as well as Saturday
workshops on everything from painting tiles to decorating cakes.

Cindy Redmond is much loved. With her reddish
hair, round face and busty figure she looks a little like

a walking Tootsie Pop. Or maybe people just think that because she's so sweet. She and her husband, Bruce, own Cindy's Candies, the best candy shop on the Washington coast.

Rita Rutledge is close to Jenna in age. She owns Books and Beans. She's divorced and there's currently no one in her life. Any applicant for her heart had better appreciate a good cup of coffee and a good book.

Sherwood Stern is the president of Harbor First National Bank and master of the regretful smile. He wasn't much help to Jenna when she was trying to revive the Driftwood. But hey, if you need a loan maybe he'll be nicer to you.

Frank Stubbs. What can we say about Frank? He's a good cop but a bit of a doofus. Short and squat, he lives up to his name. He's always after Jenna to go out with him but deep down, knows that's a hopeless cause. Maybe someday Frank will find someone who appreciates him. Let's not hold our breath on that one.

Kiki Strom is a mover and shaker. Her shop, Something Fishy, shaped like a giant shark, is one of the town's most popular attractions. People looking for souvenirs enter the shop through the shark's giant mouth. Kiki is in her early seventies and still going strong. She wears her gray hair in spikes and is always stylishly dressed. She doesn't shop at Beach Babes.

Patricia Whiteside is one of the town's treasures. Like Jenna's aunt Edie, she's lived in Moonlight Harbor for years and, like Aunt Edie, was a pioneer in the town's hospitality industry. She owns the Oyster Inn, a charming upscale B & B that always does well. Happily for Jenna's pal, **Courtney Moore**, she recently added a small boutique to the place's amenities and you can find many of Courtney's fashion creations for sale there.

Pastor Paul Welch—you've certainly gotten to know him. Who knows what his future holds? You can be sure of one thing: in the future he's going to be a lot more cautious when it comes to love.

So those are most of the key people in town. Hang around. You're bound to meet more. Hope you'll enjoy your time here at the beach as our stories continue to unfold.

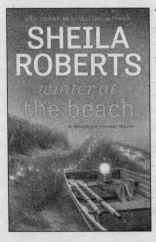

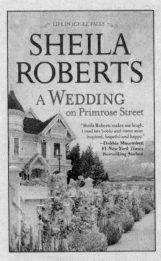